The Stubborn Suitor

Emily Stanwood was everything Charlotte was not, yet Charlotte loved her younger sister dearly. When Emily made her London debut and was instantly hailed as the Regency's ideal of feminine beauty, Charlotte was overjoyed at Emily's triumph.

Unfortunately, the most noble Duke of Imbrie did not join all the world in falling under Emily's spell. He perversely persisted in wooing Charlotte.

The Duke and Emily were clearly the perfect match—and Charlotte was determined to bring them together, even if it tore her own heart in two. . . .

SECOND SEASON

Elsie Lee

A DELL BOOK

Published by
Dell Publishing Co., Inc.
1 Dag Hammarskjold Plaza
New York, New York 10017

ISBN: 0-440-17977-7

Printed in the United States of America

Previous Dell Edition #7977
New Dell Edition
First Dell printing—May 1979

for

Anne McCaffrey

& Mister Ed

CHAPTER I

AS THE DOWAGER had put it: "The Stanwoods may look as high as they choose for their marriage contracts," but in 1811, Lady Eleanor Stanwood would have been glad to look no farther than beneath the next chair and take whatever she found for her eldest daughter.

Dearly as her family loved her—and they did, for a variety of mundane reasons—there was no denying that Charlotte Stanwood was All Wrong for presentation to the marriage mart.

At the outset, she looked wrong. Aged eighteen and a bit, she was unduly thin, energetic and wiry, with a wealth of waving hair to equal her father's prized team of chestnuts, and grey-green colored eyes—which is to say she was insipid in a pink gown, bearable in blue, and stunning in deep green. Unfortunately, the prevailing fashion was for ethereal blondes with delicate white skin, and Miss Stanwood was pronounced a shade too tall, although she never lacked dance partners because a number of the beaux discovered this was her only accomplishment. Faced with a hostess determined to present him to quite the dullest wallflower in the room, any Pink of the *Ton* would bolt across to Miss Stanwood. "At least she follows creditably, and she don't say anything until it's over."

That lack of conversation was Lady Stanwood's despair, and her cup of humiliation overflowed when the odious Mrs. Drummond Burrell graciously bestowed upon Charlotte the patroness's permission to waltz at Almack's. "Unless," she smiled thinly at Lady Stanwood, "her shyness makes the dance unacceptable to Miss Stanwood?"

"Shy?" Lord Stanwood choked incredulously when his lady reported the incident. "No, no, milady—you can't have heard right, or the woman's got the wrong girl. There never was anyone with more to say for herself than our Sharlie."

"So I'd have said," his wife agreed dolefully, "but why must she sit mumchance upon all occasions?"

Charlotte herself merely sighed apologetically. "I'm sorry, mama, but I can never think of anything to say. I don't seem to have learned the right words for London."

Lady Stanwood could not repress a snort. "This," she stated, "is what comes of education for females. I warned your father, but he *would* allow you to join your brother when Mr. Appleby was preparing him for Oxford . . . and now we see! French is unexceptionable, and Italian, but *German* . . . and no elegant young female should ever have heard of Latin or Greek. In fact, I don't know why any man needs to know them, either."

"Neither do I," Charlotte admitted, "but Oxford doesn't agree, and you know very well, ma'am, that Geoffrey would never have completed his preparation but for not wishing me to get ahead of him. He'd have been playing truant every fine day."

"Exactly—and he still played truant and took you with him, miss! Romping about the countryside, when you should have been learning a semblance of gentility."

Charlotte sighed again, "I did try, but I wasn't born with the knack of it."

It was sadly true. Dearly as she loved Charlotte—and Lady Stanwood privately admitted a partiality for this one among her six children, while striving not to show it—no governess or special master had ever been able to turn Sharlie into a drawing room ornament. She was staggeringly non-musical, unable to manage even the simplest sonata or carry a tune, although she could whistle as melodiously as a blackbird. Of genteel accomplishments she had none, being afflicted (apparently) with three left thumbs. Her knitted scarves and netted purses contained mysterious holes in odd places. Her embroidery had always to be laundered as soon as she'd set the final stitch, so one could see what her design was . . . not that it mattered, and much of the time Lady Stanwood felt she would rather *not* see it. A series of drawing masters failed to train Sharlie's eye for any sort of perspective, while paint was abandoned at an early age. She got it all over everything, including her baby brother.

She did have accomplishments, of course. Unfortunately, they were unsuited to a pretty-behaved young female. Charlotte was far and away the best horsewoman in the county, could manage the estate and stables competently whenever her father went to a race meeting or hunt. She could set a rabbit snare as well as any poacher, cast for a trout or handle a gun to equal her brother. She knew every inch of Stanwood, exactly where the badgers lived and when the gamekeeper should concentrate on eliminating an intrusive kestrel. Every tenant automatically went to Miss Sharlie, if his Lordship were unavailable, and if Lady Stanwood wanted a specialty from the succession houses, she told Sharlie to ask MacLean for it. Sharlie was the only person in the world the head gardener would obey.

It had long been obvious to Lady Stanwood that her darling hobbledehoy was a country woman from toes to topknot, that Geoffrey would succeed his father and manage Stanwood in exactly the same careful-casual manner, while Emily would appear once at Almack's, be hailed as an Incomparable and take her pick among the dozen most eligible men in England. Emily was everything Charlotte was not, including stupid, but Lady Stanwood had no fear of settling her handsomely within the first Season. In fact, between Emily's guinea-gold natural curls, melting sapphire eyes and alabaster skin, the problem was how to keep her free until she could be got to London. Every lad in the neighborhood —and to Lady Stanwood's mind there were far too many of them—had been dangling after Emily for the past two years, which made it the more imperative to establish Charlotte before her younger sister burst upon the *haut ton.*

To this praiseworthy plan, Charlotte objected hotly. "I've *been* to London, and you know very well I did not Take. The *ton* thought me a bumpkin, and I found them a dead bore. It will be the same this year. Worse!" she foretold gloomily. "I'll be called an antidote."

"But I cannot feel you have had your full chance."

"I couldn't *help* falling ill of the mumps."

"No, but it did cut short all possibilities," Lady Stanwood pointed out, and changed the subject while Sharlie was muttering, "*What* possibilities?"

Not only had Miss Stanwood failed to create a ripple in London, she had acquired an odious childhood complaint midway, and just as Lady Stanwood had every expectation of an offer from Sir Ruthven Crevelly . . . not that he was more than acceptable, but it was maddening that Charlotte should fall ill before a definite declaration. Sir Ruthven was the nearest thing to a prospect Sharlie had achieved, but when she retired to Stanwood Hall, he transferred his interest to Miss Farnsworth, and long before convalescence, the banns were up, the marriage heralded at St. George's.

Lady Stanwood was philosophical in the connubial chamber. "After all, he was a thought too old, and I understand some of the estates are encumbered."

"He's a prosy bore," Lord Stanwood stated, "and if Sharlie took him, she'd have to be desperate, which you know she isn't, milady. She's her grandmother's money in trust until she's thirty unless I consent to her marriage, which I'll tell you now I'd not have given for Crevelly. Plus there's her portion from me that's been safely funded since her birth. If she don't choose to marry anyone, she needn't."

Lady Stanwood fixed him with an awesome eye. "Do I understand you right, milord: you would see your eldest daughter UNWED?"

"Why not, if she don't find someone she fancies?" her spouse inquired bluffly. "But she will. You'll see, milady! Aye, she's not just in the common style of your milk-and-water misses, but there's many a man'd prefer Charlotte's blurting out what she thinks to the simpering 'Oh, la, sir, I vow you're a rogue'!" Lord Stanwood did a broad caricature that drew a reluctant smile from his wife, at which he roared with glee. "Come, Nelly—we married for love as well as suitability, and I've never regretted it . . ."

"Nor I," she admitted with a naughty chuckle.

"Why should our Sharlie have less, eh?" Lord Stanwood set a strong arm about her plump form and hugged her. "Leave the lass alone. Take her to London for a second try, if you insist, but she's not to be pressed, pushed, made to feel it's her duty to be well-established, you understand?" His face was serious. "Let her find what she wants in her own way—and if there's nothing she wants, let her come home to Stanwood and be happy in her own way."

Lady Stanwood felt all the sense of her lord's dictum, but still . . . there might be someone new on the Town this year, the fashion standards might have altered to bring Sharlie more in the mode. She'd at least got her feet wet last year. Surely she'd know better how to go on, might show a little more confidence. She steeled her heart to protests. "Your father agrees it is only right you shall make your curtsey once more. It is by no means impossible you will encounter someone for whom you feel a decided partiality—and let me tell you, my dear, it is infinitely more comfortable to be a married lady than the wealthiest of spinsters. Come, my love," cajolingly, "your father declares you are not to be pressed in any way, merely that you are to see if there is one who will suit you."

"I won't find him in London," Charlotte muttered mutinously, but her mother disagreed.

"On the contrary, it is the only place you will find him," she said firmly. "Do not be thinking you will tumble over an eligible husband in a hedgerow, nor even in a hunting houseparty, for I assure you it is no such thing. The gentleman of suitable birth and property may admire your horsemanship, but he will wish also to see how you conduct yourself in the society you will grace as his wife, and *that* can only be determined during the Season."

"Exactly," Sharlie countered, "which puts you at Point Non Plus before you begin, ma'am. You know full well I *have* no grace. We learned that last year."

"Nonsense, you never lacked partners at Almack's,"

Lady Stanwood said feebly, but Charlotte swept it aside.

"Yes, but when it is not a dancing party—can you imagine how I feel to sit beside you, with no more than a few civil words from your friends?" Sharlie's grey-green eyes darkened unhappily. "Always to go out to supper with a gallant friend of papa's, or to pretend happy gossip with the other wallflowers? No, mama, don't ask it of me! Can't you take Emily instead? Truly, I'd rather stay at Stanwood, and you know Emily is fated to be the Incomparable of the year."

"Yes—which is exactly why I want you married before her presentation," Lady Stanwood murmured involuntarily.

"If you mean no one would look twice at me after Emily, you're right. It seems a stupid waste of time and money to spend another Season trying to get rid of me. I warrant you I'll never attach anyone suitable," Charlotte pleaded earnestly. *"Please,* mama?"

Lady Stanwood took refuge in the universal wifely bolthole. "I will speak to your father," but she had nearly abandoned the project when Algernon Whipsnade was observed kissing Emily in the conservatory.

"Oh, yes, milady. MacLean saw it quite clear," Miss Tinsdale reported sweetly, while dressing her mistress's hair before dinner. "Please not to jerk your head so sharply, milady. It makes the curls all uneven."

"Never mind the curls! What did MacLean do—aside from running to tell the first person he saw?"

"He cleared his throat, milady, and Mr. Whipsnade sprang away."

"Are you telling me that Miss Emily—MY daughter—was participating in an embrace?" Lady Stanwood's fulminating eye fixed her dresser in the mirror, causing immediate retreat.

"Oh, no, *indeed,* milady!" Miss Tinsdale sounded shocked. "It seemed to MacLean as if she'd been taken by surprise and was protesting, but being as Mr. Whipsnade is well-grown for his years—like the Squire," she simpered genteelly, "I dessay as Miss Emily were overborne-like."

Recalling the ham-like arms of the Whipsnades, Lady Stanwood could well believe it. "I see," she made her voice indifferent. "That will do, Tinsdale. Hand me the Norwich shawl, and you may go," but when the dresser had left the room, Lady Stanwood lost no time in hastening to the young ladies' sitting parlor. She found, much as expected, Charlotte absorbed in the Farming Gazette, while Emily pored over the Ladies' Monthly Museum. She looked up with a happy smile, "Did you want me, mama?"

"Tinsdale told me Algy Whipsnade had called this afternoon. I said she must be mistaken, I would have been informed." Lady Stanwood's heart sank at Emily's involuntary blush and lowered eyes.

"Not precisely *called,* mama."

"He didn't call at all, mama," Sharlie stated. "He rode over to get the spermacetti ointment papa promised, and unluckily Emily was just come in from a ride. Algy walked beside her to the house."

"What was she doing in the conservatory, then?"

"You wanted a fruit for dinner, ma'am. I told MacLean to have it ready, and asked Emily to take it to cook, because I was making a bran poultice."

Emily hung her head, "The fruit was in a basket, I only stepped in to get it, and . . . well, Algy was trying to be gallant, and he reached behind me to take the basket."

"And squeezed her hand under his, and breathed 'Miss Emily!' worshipfully," Sharlie added impatiently. "MacLean was there all the time, mama, though Algy didn't see him at first—and I wish you will not allow Tinsdale to upset you with her exaggerations."

"I am not upset. I merely wish to know whether Algernon Whipsnade attempted to kiss Emily."

"Of course not, mama! He wouldn't dare," Emily flushed with indignation.

"Not now, but he's working up rapidly," Charlotte chuckled.

Emily's usually soft eyes flashed. "You *KNOW* I don't encourage him," she cried. "He's just a boy we've always known. Please, mama . . ."

"Yes, my love. Charlotte, stop teasing!" Lady Stanwood said severely, but Sharlie was bubbling with mirth.

"How can I resist, mama? I know Emily never encourages improper advances—but she has only to sit still. That's sufficient to *encourage* every male in the room!"

Lady Stanwood bit her lip to suppress a smile, and applied herself to soothing Emily's agitation. This was easily done, her naturally sweet disposition could not long contain anger, and a hearty hug from Charlotte restored serenity. "Pea-goose!" Sharlie said affectionately. "You must accustom yourself to your effect on susceptible gentlemen . . . and I wish I may be present to observe your first entrance at Almack's.

"Now, *there* will be a moment, will it not, mama? All conversation will cease while the assembly feasts its eyes upon you, Emily. Dukes and earls will rush forward, elbowing each other aside and pleading for introductions. Your card will be filled in a trice, and Mrs. Burrell will have a spasm—after refusing permission to waltz." Sharlie's eyes danced. "How snifty she'll be, won't she, mama? You must know, Emily, she abominates feminine beauty, having none herself. She loathes all the Incomparables, her tongue is forked like a snake, she will shake her head sadly that anyone should have given you admission . . ."

"And blame Sally Jersey!" Lady Stanwood's composure broke down before Sharlie's dramatic description.

"More likely Lady Sefton because you're close friends," Sharlie swept on, "and all the time Princess Esterhazy will be giving Emily permission to waltz with the most eligible man in the room. Oh, mama, do say I may be there? It would compensate for being at my last prayers, if only I can see Mrs. Drummond Burrell's face upon glimpsing Emily!"

Privately, Lady Stanwood concurred: it would be good to confound Mrs. Drummond Burrell, who held herself altogether too high. A short interview with Lord Stanwood confirmed the situation. "It won't do, Nelly," he said firmly. "For one thing, I'll warrant Whipsnade don't want his heir marrying aught but good County blood. Emily wouldn't suit him at all, pleased as he is for friendly notice by the Hall. There's no help for it, you'll have to remove her before Algy fixes his mind."

"But what am I to do with her, Robert? If I present her, it's death to any chance for Sharlie—and if I keep her in the schoolroom, she'll be moped to death with no friends."

"Phoo, she'd make plenty among the other younger sisters—not but what Sharlie mightn't do better with Emily beside her," his lordship observed. "She'd be easier, more herself in company. You'd have all the beaux flocking after Emily, they'll see Sharlie at her best. She'll catch a few eyes. Among them she may find something suitable."

"Shall I take Emily into society, then—or merely to small home gatherings?"

"Lud, ma'am, how should I know?" Lord Stanwood said impatiently, tugging on riding gloves and reaching for his crop. "Send her to one of her aunts, if you like, but she can't stay here with no more than a housekeeper and governess. I'll be off to Leicestershire shortly, and I'll not interrupt easy relations with Whipsnade by forbidding his son my house. Emily must *go,* until you are in residence again. That's all. As for where, that's up to you, Nelly. It's agreed I'll not interfere with what you think best for the girls."

"Yes," she remarked drily, "which is only to say I'm all to blame if I don't settle 'em to your liking, Robert."

His lordship grinned impenitently. "You will," he prophesied. "You've never failed me yet, Nelly."

Warmed as she was by his approval, Lady Stanwood was still considerably unsettled in mind, but Sharlie's involuntary cry of pleasure when her mother suggested that Emily might come with them decided everything.

"Truly, mama? Oh, it would make all the difference—to have someone to talk with, to watch the faces . . ."

"I hadn't meant a formal presentation," Lady Stanwood said weakly. "A few small gatherings, but not Almack's or any of the major *ton* parties."

Sharlie laughed. "Do, do be sensible, ma'am! You cannot keep her in the schoolroom. She must go to church, or walk in the park, or have the occasional treat of a play or Vauxhall, and you know that one glimpse will suffice to set every male in London on our doorstep." She sobered slightly at Lady Stanwood's troubled expression. "Oh, are you thinking she will take precedence over me? Well, of course she will, mama. That's the fun of it. I expect a few crumbs will fall my way, the beaux who cannot escort Emily will escort me in order to be near her."

"Wouldn't you *mind?"*

"Not in the least! I've no taste for society, mama, but as Emily's sister I could see all the things I missed last time, and let the beaux see her. Oh, please ask papa's permission?"

"It was he who suggested it."

Sharlie raised her eyebrows. "He wants Emily away before Algy Whipsnade makes a cake of himself—but why not, mama? I can tell Emily how to go on, we can companion each other in public, which will leave you more free to renew your acquaintances. Do admit you'd enjoy presenting an Incomparable only a year after a Tragedy!"

"You are *not* a Tragedy," Lady Stanwood protested, but Sharlie laughed mischievously.

"No, I wasn't even that," she agreed. "I was just—nothing. I doubt anyone would recall my name, but you'll see they will if I'm Emily's sister. It'll be the greatest fun, and," her expression was thoughtful, "if Emily comes, perhaps papa will send our riding horses. We would need them, you know, for a party to Richmond and—and normal exercise in the park."

Lady Stanwood suppressed a chuckle. Charlotte was not quite so full of self-abnegation as it sounded. On a horse, she easily outshone Emily. "Very well, my love, it is settled: Emily comes with us."

Thus, in the last days of January, a fourgon containing such household furnishings of chairs, linen, silver and chests as Lady Stanwood found indispensable to her comfort rumbled ponderously away to the London road. Early in February a secondary coach went forth, bearing Lady Stanwood's dresser (Tinsdale), her ladyship's butler (Beamish), and a superficially meek Young Person (Maria) who was deemed worthy of being abigail to the Misses Stanwood—and if Tinsdale and Beamish had known her private thoughts, they would have left her at the first milestone. "A pair of twitty old barstards as don't know a goose from a hen," but since Miss Maria did know a goose from a hen, by the time London was reached, Beamish was murmuring "An excellent choice, Miss Tinsdale. A very pretty-behaved young female—wants more countenance, but you'll be all she needs."

To which Tinsdale inclined her head with dignity. "I'm happy you approve, Mr. Beamish. I fancy I know how to select good material."

Five hours later, Lady Stanwood was being gallantly handed into her travelling chariot by her lord. The fact that his prized hunter waited impatiently with a groom at its head melted her heart with affection. That Lord Stanwood should stay from the hunt in order to hug and kiss her heartily—if only Charlotte and Emily could do as well in their husbands!

"Come, girls, into your places," she commanded briskly. "Robert, enjoy your stay at Blandford. Send me word when to expect you, and take care not to break your neck. I should miss you." One foot on the coach step, Lady Stanwood looked back at her husband and murmured, "My very dear . . ."

A blue gleam lit Lord Stanwood's eyes, and he bent over her hand with a most unhusbandly pressure that made him look a bit roguish, although he said only, "Your servant, ma'am." Clapping his hat over brown curls, he strode away to swing into the saddle and was gone with a final wave.

Lady Stanwood disposed herself comfortably in the middle of the coach seat, a daughter on either side. The hot bricks were tucked beneath their feet, a fur travelling rug laid tenderly over their laps, the steps were put up, and the door was closed. The postillions blew their horns lustily, the coachman cracked his whip, and the carriage started forward with a slight jerk while the footmen sprang agilely to their step at the rear.

Faster and faster turned the wheels as they swept down the gentle gradient of the drive, past the modest gate-house and into the road for the London turnpike. The day was crisp but fair, superb hunting weather, in fact, although only Charlotte sighed. The coach was well-sprung, drawn by Lord Stanwood's prized "fourteen mile an hour tits," who hit their stride on the Turnpike. Traffic was not great in mid-week; Jem-coachman was expert. The ladies bowled along with only the slightest sway, preceded by the postillions to blow up for the toll-gates. If all went well, they would rest an hour at Melsham for a nuncheon, and could hope to reach Park Street by six—a wearisome journey, but Lady Stanwood had the greatest dislike of sleeping in even the finest public inns.

"One never knows who one may encounter, to say nothing of *what* may have been left behind by a previous lodger," she stated oracularly, "and one has no wish to afford transportation to London for bugs."

Accordingly, when Lady Stanwood journeyed to town, it was understood she would go straight through the seventy miles and sleep in her own home if it killed everybody. Charlotte's wiry energy could match her mother; Emily proved more susceptible. Hitherto, she had travelled in the nursery carriage at a pace suited to Georgie, Edmond and Louisa. There were frequent stops for rest and refreshment, an overnight stay with one or another family relative. It was altogether comfortable, playing games or telling stories to amuse the youngsters. Nothing had prepared Emily for the bruising pace set by Lady Stanwood. She grew, first, monosyllabic—then white-faced, clinging desperately to the strap and braced rigidly against the tilt of the coach. Long before Melsham, she was pressing a handkerchief to her mouth, interspersed with deep sniffs of her vinaigrette, and Lady Stanwood had ordered the horses slowed to a sedate walk.

"I'm so *sorry,* mama," Emily apologized faintly.

"Never mind, my love," Lady Stanwood patted her hand. "I should have recalled you are afflicted by motion. Sharlie, let down the window. Perhaps a little fresh air will revive her. Try to be calm, dear; very soon we'll reach the inn, and you'll feel better."

"She'd be better sooner if she were dog-sick," Charlotte said, loosening the window strap. "I told you not to have jam on your muffin, Emily. Mama, if you could move away, and let me come next to her? Lean forward and breathe deeply, Emily."

With a moan, Emily thrust her nose to the coach window while Charlotte braced her—and precisely at that moment a curricle swept past, grazing the coach wheels. Lady Stanwood uttered a faint scream. The coachman shouted hoarsely and struggled to control the plunging horses. The footmen leaped to the road, racing forward to calm the beasts, and Emily gave up the ghost. "Uh, open *door!*" she wailed. Sharlie managed it just in time, and for a few minutes all was confusion, complicated by the more sedate passage of several other vehicles. At last Emily could be withdrawn to sit limply in her corner.

Lady Stanwood's strictures on the driver of the curricle were matched by the anathema floating back dimly from Jem-coachman, while the carriage slowly started forward. "Young jackanapes! I've no patience with these whipsters and their wagers—endangering lives, frightening the horses, thinking it a lark to smash themselves to pieces and calling it 'bang up to the knocker, driving to an inch'!"

"I know, mama, but they all do it," Charlotte said

resignedly. "Even Geoffrey, although I'm bound to admit he *did* do it, and for all papa gave him a severe scold, he was boasting insufferably that his son not only grazed the wheels of seven carriages—which was the wager—but managed an eighth for good measure." She looked from the carriage window and added, "Melsham! Nearly there, Emily. You'll soon feel better."

"I don't think I'll ever feel anything again except sick," Emily murmured tearfully, as they drew into the inn yard.

Lady Stanwood descended. "Do stay with her, Sharlie, while I send for the landlady. Move slowly, Emily, and come into our private parlor when you can. Ah, good day, landlord—we are slightly delayed, Miss Emily became unwell with the motion. Is your good woman about? I should like a place for my daughter to lie down. Is there a sofa in our parlor? And hot water, if you please, with tea as quickly as may be . . ."

"Yes, milady . . . a pleasure to see your ladyship again . . . Mr. Beamish left your instructions when he passed through earlier, and all's prepared. Please to step this way. Sukey, send for Mrs. Belknap . . . bring hot water . . . bring tea . . ." In a spate of deep bows the landlord bustled away, followed by Lady Stanwood.

Assisting Emily to the ground, Sharlie could see a curricle drawn into the stable yard. "Is that . . . ?"

"Ar, that's the cove," Jem-coachman nodded grimly. "A crest on the panel, and old enough to know better than to be going that gait on a public highway. I'll have a word to say to that groom, strutting about, giving orders to ostler. A foreigner he is, by the sound of him."

"Well, for heaven's sake don't get into a brawl," Charlotte warned. "It's not the groom's fault, and we're behind time already."

"Yes, miss," Jem sighed. "Of course, there is nothing he can do against his master—but what sort of master can't be satisfied with a good English groom? We'm main against these Frenchies and such."

"Never mind your opinions, it's your job to get us to London today. No brangling, you understand? Come along, Emily."

"I feel sick again."

"You won't be, darling. There's nothing left but queasiness, you'll be better directly you sit down," but one glance at the long dark hall leading to Lady Stanwood's parlor was too much for Emily.

"I have to sit down *now!*"

"All right, darling." Hastily Charlotte opened the nearest door to reveal a second parlor, and supported Emily to a chair. "There you are!" She applied herself to removing her sister's bonnet and stroking her forehead gently.

Behind her a deep voice said harshly, "This is a private room, madam. Be good enough to leave at once."

Startled, Charlotte looked over her shoulder to face a dark-visaged man lounging in the farther chair by the fire. His long legs were encased in dusty boots and propped on the hearth guard. A many-caped driving coat was thrown carelessly on the settle with a shallow-crowned beaver atop. In one hand he held a balloon glass of brandy, in the other was a cigarillo with a curl of smoke rising up, and his black eyes were hard as obsidian.

Charlotte suppressed herself. "I beg your pardon for the intrusion, sir. I did not know the room was occupied."

"Well, now you do. I've just told you. Pray remove yourselves, I've no taste for female companionship at the moment."

"Nor we for that of men," Charlotte flashed, "even

were they gentlemen . . . and if, as I collect, you are the whipster driving that curricle, allow me to tell you that *you* are entirely to blame that my sister is completely overset."

He set aside glass and cigarillo, hauling himself to his feet with eyes blazing. "By God, madam, allow me to tell *you* that no whipster could have got around your dawdling coach without a catastrophe! The London Turnpike is not meant for 'taking the air' at two miles an hour," he thundered. "If you've a wish to sniff the countryside, enjoy a view, take the side roads. A turnpike is intended for business traveling with fast horses. Even the mail and baggage coaches do better than ten miles an hour . . . and for you to be twiddling along, half-stopped on a blind curve, is courting far more danger than a mere wheel graze!"

"Oh, please, Sharlie!" Emily whispered, agonized.

"Yes, darling. Can you stand and lean on me?" Charlotte supported her sister's trembling form, turned silently for the door, but Emily was mindful of her manners.

With an effort, but very pretty dignity, she said, "I do beg your pardon, sir. It was only momentary weakness. We will withdraw to our own parlor."

The black eyes widened incredulously as Emily's lovely face came into view. She gave him one glance of tear-drenched gentian blue eyes, one timid half-smile, and stepped resolutely to the hall. "Oh, I say," he'd come out of his bemusement and strode forward, "it's I who should beg your pardon for my filthy temper, ma'am. Pray, allow me to assist you—or should you not sit down again, and I will remove myself until you feel more the thing?"

"Indeed, we will not trouble you longer, sir," Charlotte said demurely, bubbling inside at Emily's effect on him. Lady Stanwood was coming along the hall with the landlady behind her. Charlotte delivered Emily's tottering figure to them, and looked back at her involuntary host. "I bid you good day, sir—and if you are for London, I trust you will leave before us?" Gently, she shut the door and followed her mother.

Behind her the parlor door opened again—violently. "I say . . ." With infinite relish, Sharlie ignored him. Without a backward glance, she proceeded along the hall and entered the rear parlor. One quick sideways peek she had: he was standing, stricken, gazing after them. Then she quietly closed their door.

CHAPTER II

FORTIFIED BY TEA and plain rusks, Emily declared herself perfectly able to continue. "Are you quite *sure?*" her mother asked. "Once the decision is made, it cannot be changed—but nothing is simpler than to send the postillion to Cousin Emma and break our journey overnight at Stevenage."

"No, no, I shall be quite all right, mama. I am certain I have got my 'coach legs,'" Emily said gaily, "like the sailors who talk of 'sea legs.' Do let us go straight on and sleep in our own home."

It did seem she was restored by the hour's rest. So were the horses. In February, London was devoid of company. Lady Stanwood's coach threaded easily through sparse traffic to reach Park Street only an hour behind time. Lingering while her mother and sister ascended the entrance steps, Charlotte asked the footman, "Who was driving that curricle?"

"His Grace, the Duke of Imbrie, Miss Stanwood. Coachman had a word with the groom—not even a Frenchie *he* was, but from some outlandish country you never hear'd of—but pleasant-spoken, I *will* say. There weren't no brangling. Coachman said as how groom explained the Duke had no choice, wot with London mail coach on t'other side of road and him poled up with his bays that hadn't had a run in a week.

He had to chance it, Miss Stanwood, and for all it was startling to her Ladyship and Miss Emily, coachman says he's never seen sweeter handling of the ribbons! Four-Horse Club his Grace is, and the curricle built to his own design."

"Ah? Thank you, Thomas." She gave him the pleasant smile that made every Stanwood servant her friend, and went up to the front hall, where she found her mother seated regally on a chair hastily brought from the salon. Lined up before her were all the house servants, in states ranging from alert attention (the housekeeper), to calm self-confidence (the chef), to abject terror (a very small tweeny). It was her ladyship's custom always to inspect the staff upon arrival, inquiring the name of any newly hired person. Park Street was never entirely closed, but out of season it was thought unnecessary to maintain more than housekeeper, chef, three maids and two footmen. Thus there were always new faces when Lady Stanwood came for the Season.

She would conduct this one interview, issue a number of commands, convince newcomers she was a tartar—and subsequently leave all to the housekeeper. Exactly this scene had occurred last year, but today Sharlie interpreted differently. She saw that within thirty minutes, her mother had re-established the staff hierarchy by approval of the permanent members, and gained willing service from augmentees by a show of interest. Nor would Lady Stanwood forget any name or face for so long as a person remained. She chose the key positions carefully, made them responsible for smooth functioning, and interfered only when absolutely necessary. Very thoughtfully, Charlotte followed her mother up the stairs. She had not hitherto paid much attention to domestic management, but judging by Lady Stanwood's method, it was far simpler than she'd thought.

In her bedchamber she found Maria, bright-eyed with pride in her post of abigail. "Miss Emily is laid down on her bed. Her Ladyship says as how she's to have a tray tonight. 'Tis a pity the journey made her ill."

"I told her not to eat so much breakfast, but she would do it," Sharlie returned. "At least it's a good lesson, she'll not do it again. How was your trip, Maria?"

"Very long, but in course it was all new to me, miss. Mr. Beamish told me not to gawk, but how could I help? I'd not want to miss anything. Eh, what a deal I'll have to tell when I get home!" She smiled shyly at Charlotte, "I'm that proud to be chosen, I'm not sure if I'm on my head or my heels. You'll forgive my chattering, miss?"

"Of course. I was just as excited on my first visit—but you must write all down before you forget, Maria. I'll give you the materials, and we'll send it by one of the grooms to Stanbury."

The maid's eyes sparkled. "Eh, that'd be main special, miss!"

"Not really. We've always grooms going back and forth—why shouldn't they carry a letter?"

"No reason, I suppose, miss—except I'm only a servant."

"You're also a person, and your mother will want to know you are well and—I hope—happy."

"Oh, Miss Stanwood—happy! Anyone's happy to work for the Stanwoods!" Maria stammered pinkly, and Sharlie smiled at her—but had she known it, she had just acquired a slave! Maria's sixteen-year-old heart was bursting with loving devotion to be called a *person* whose mother would worry. She was filled with a fierce determination to obey Miss Stanwood's lightest wish, as she produced an evening frock. "Miss Tinsdale would have me press this for tonight, but seeing you were so delayed, I made bold to press another as well."

Sharlie eyed the dresser's choice of insipid pink muslin with disfavor. "Which did you choose, Maria?" When the girl held up a green dress, her thralldom was completed at Miss Stanwood's nod. "I'll wear that. You've a good eye for the color to suit me, Maria."

"Yes, miss." Carefully she brushed out Charlotte's thick hair, until Sharlie chuckled and took the brush away.

"You're too gentle, Maria! I've a scalp of iron beneath this horse's mane." Ruthlessly, she raked her hair until it lay in shining waves. In a few quick tosses, she'd pinned it into a roughly Grecian style with the ends floating free. Observing the maid's concentration, she laughed merrily. "Don't try to learn this! Tomorrow the coiffeur will change me completely to the modality, whatever it is this year." Charlotte got up from the dressing table, carelessly draped a shawl about her shoulders. "I'll peep in at Miss Emily, and you needn't wait for me tonight, I'll put myself to bed. You must have a good rest in preparation for tomorrow. Good night."

A single glance showed Emily was fast asleep. Sharlie closed the door softly and descended to the salon where her mother was frowning over a letter. "Listen to this," she said, bewildered. " 'His Grace, the Duke of Imbrie, respectfully apologizes for the inconvenience caused Lady Stanwood's coach near Melsham this afternoon.' What d'you make of that, Sharlie?"

"Why, that he wishes to be on terms with us," Sharlie chuckled. "I thought he would! You must know, mama, that he was quite odiously uncivil when I took

Emily into the parlor to rest. I'd no idea it was occupied and she was feeling faint, but he ordered us out! I'm sorry, mama, but he didn't even look the gentleman: lounging in a chair with brandy and a cigarillo. I'm afraid I gave him the rough side of my tongue, and *then* he got a sight of Emily." Charlotte laughed aloud, describing the scene. "I had not the opportunity to tell you before, ma'am, nor did I know the name until we reached Park Street, when Thomas told me. Of course Jem-coachman spoke to the groom. And so his Grace has apologized for grazing the wheels of your coach! Famous! Who is he, mama? Do you know him?"

"More by repute than in person," Lady Stanwood frowned with an effort for memory. "He is one of the premier dukes, but averse to Society—a widower—or am I thinking of Fanscot?"

"No, no, you must be right, mama, for he would never apologize had he not wished for a second look at Emily, which must be inadmissible were he married. I told you how it would be, ma'am. I wish we may get Emily to Almack's once before she is bespoke!"

"I fear you are right," her mother murmured distractedly, "but *Imbrie* . . . was he not the one? No, that was Tolliver—at least I am nearly sure it was Tolliver—but perhaps I am confusing him with Marley. Oh, lud, I wish your father were here to tell me how to go on."

"Why, there's naught so difficult, ma'am. You've only to send a civil reply, accepting his apology, and there's an end to it. Shall I write for you?"

"Yes, I suppose so. One does not wish to be impolite, although from your description . . . Still, the direction is Grosvenor Square, so I must have been thinking of Tolliver, for he was sold up, you know. Beamish could easily ascertain . . . but one cannot inquire of servants, it gives rise to gossip.

While her mother rambled on uncertainly, Charlotte was writing: *Lady Stanwood is most appreciative of his Grace's note, but feels no apology is needed. She wishes, rather, to commend his Grace on his expert avoidance of accident, due to the necessary slowing of her coach.* "There—that should suffice, I think. If you approve, ma'am, I will send it at once."

Lady Stanwood came out of her abstraction and scanned the note. "Suffice for *what?*" she inquired with faint suspicion.

"For easy relations should we meet," Charlotte said innocently. "You know papa does not like any unnecessary difficulties with neighbors, and Grosvenor Square—it is practically next door. We may see the duke at St. George's, or riding in the Row, and no doubt he and papa belong to the same clubs."

"No doubt," Lady Stanwood agreed drily, "but I question our meeting at church, and until the horses arrive, you'll not be riding. Furthermore, an apology for grazing my coach wheels does not constitute an introduction, Charlotte."

"No, ma'am. Shall I not send the note, then?"

Her mother read it again. "Oh—you may as well," she said finally, "and write another to Lady Inverclyde, asking her to call tomorrow morning, or as soon as may be. Flora will know about Imbrie . . . Flora always knows everything . . ."

At No. 10 Park Street, Lady Stanwood and her daughter dined lightly on oyster fritters, stewed neck of veal, a Davenport fowl and buttered salsify, removed with a green salad dressed in the French manner and ended with a pupton of pears accompanied by *Crème à l'Anglaise.*

At No. 10 Grosvenor Square, the Duke of Imbrie dined more heartily on two thick slices from a baron of beef, preceded by turtle soup and succeeded by boiled lamb with spinach, baked fish and roast pigeon. This was removed with an omelet, some white collops, an apple pie and a Savoy cake, accompanied by several dishes of preserved fruits and a large bowl of roasted chestnuts. His Grace was sitting over the Port, peeling a chestnut and staring moodily at the great branched candelabra, when the dining room door crashed open and a medium tenor voice said, "Devil take it, Robsey—no need to announce *me* to m'cousin. Bring another glass, someone. Julian, how are you? What do you in London?"

"I am mending my temper," the duke grimaced, but his expression lightened as his visitor threw himself carelessly into a chair, and indeed Lord Arthur Voss was good to look upon. The family resemblance was strong, yet softer in Lord Arthur. His curls were more brown than black, his eyebrows curved correctly above twinkling sherry-colored eyes instead of the duke's heavy slashing line of black that nearly met at the center and was satanically upthrust toward his temples. Both men possessed the handsome classic-modelled Voss nose and deep chin dimple, but Lord Arthur's lips were slightly fuller. He seemed always to be on the verge of smiling. In fact, his was a happy nature, rated a prince of good fellows by his enormous circle of friends and described as more Corinthian than Pink of the *Ton,* although no fault could be found with his evening dress.

Conversely, the duke's coat of wine red velvet heavily braided and slashed to permit a fall of finest Mechlin at wrists and throat was clearly of Continental design despite its excellent fit. An immense ruby nestled in the jabot; another, set in gold and carved into his personal seal, adored the duke's right index finger. Otherwise, he wore no dangling fobs, no tassels to his knee garters, nor bows to his evening slippers, yet the austerity of his clothing served only to emphasize the air of command that was subtly combined with a reckless cynicism.

In short, the duke looked what he was: the Most Noble Julian Giles Herestone Voss, seventh Duke of Imbrie, Marquis of Herestone, Earl of Imbrie, Baron Voss of Bascombe, *and* of Keighly, *and* of Rickaby, all of which consequence had been his from the age of seven.

Lord Arthur grinned at his cousin's morose expression. "Aunt Laura been hectoring you again?"

"When does she not? If ever a woman enjoyed ill-health with that damned long-faced parson hovering over her—and tough as an ox for whatever she *wants* to do! Not content with filling Calydon Towers with my relatives, most of whom I don't remember and all of whom I would prefer to forget," said the duke wrathfully, "she'd arranged a series of visits to introduce suitable females to my notice! And with this devilish weather, nothing but storms and black frosts since October, I've had no more than five days of hunting—I'm trapped, Arthur. I can't even escape to my neighbors. I find there's at least five girls who used to be in the schoolroom, and all of a sudden *they're* being hustled forth in sprig muslin, playing the *harp!*"

"It's your own fault for being such a desirable *parti* shrouded in all the mystery of foreign travel. If you'd stay home for a few seasons, the *ton* would soon tire of you, Julian," his cousin chuckled.

"But not of my bank account," the duke retorted. "Have you any idea what it's like? If I dance twice with the same young lady, or linger in conversation for ten minutes . . . escort a girl to the supper room on two successive evenings . . . it is instantly seen as a distinguishing mark of attention giving rise to *expectations*. The alternative is to spread my favors evenly between a number of young ladies, but i'faith, there's not enough to make one tolerable brain among 'em. They seem more insipid every time I go into company. Is it the fashion of today, or do I grow old, Arthur?"

"Neither! Had you stayed in England after Isabella's death, I fancy you'd have remarried in a year. Then you could have found a wife near your age and grown up together. Now, after ten years of wandering, you are more critical. The marriage mart presents schoolgirls. You'd do better to inquire for the spinsters, Julian. The girls left on the shelf often flower handsomely in five or six years," Lord Arthur observed wisely. "That's if you were wanting a wife?"

"I don't! Why should I? I have my heir, I've reliable stewards with you to oversee them, and Uncle Biddulph to supervise my Funds. I don't say I wouldn't like to spend rather more time in England now. Between Boney and this new kick-up in America, travel grows hazardous. I'd as soon stay here until all's settled. I had it in mind to remain a year, but not if I'm to be chivvied," Julian said restlessly, "and so I told my mother. I don't know what bee she's got that causes this sudden determination to see me leg-shackled again. She will have it that the care of my twins is too great for her advanced age, and she's not long for this world. Did you ever hear the like?"

Arthur suppressed a smile. "What did you say?"

"That Giles will go to Eton in winter term. Your mother has found a suitable governess for Lucinda. They'll either stay at Calydon, or remove to Bascombe if mother wishes to occupy her own house in Bath."

"And yourself?"

"Damned if I know," Julian scowled. "I flung out of

the place in a temper, meaning to take the first ship leaving to anywhere, but it won't do. I came home to settle the children's future. Since I'm here, I should make a tour. I'm promised to Beaufort for a week, I'll go on to Melton, renew my acquaintance. After that it depends on the weather. If propitious, I'll cross to Keighly, although Ireland depresses me. Otherwise, a week or two at Rickaby—the same at Bascombe, and as much of London as I'm allowed to enjoy. At least they don't permit women in the clubs!" The duke tossed off his wine at a gulp. "Sorry, Arthur—I'm blue-devilled tonight. Yes, Robsey?" as the butler entered with a small salver.

"A note for your Grace."

"Already?" Julian raised his eyebrows sarcastically, but smoothed when he'd read the sheet. "Do we know any Stanwoods?" he tossed it to his cousin.

"I think we do," Arthur said cautiously. "More mother's generation than ours, although I fancy there was a Miss Stanwood last year. What is this apology?"

"There is still a Miss Stanwood, with a devilish sharp tongue!" Julian remarked, refilling his wine glass. "Oh, I was in a temper . . . letting the horses out, y'know. I came around a curve—there's the mail coach coming at me and this hellish old traveling chariot blocking my road. I could have hauled in, I think but I chose to go past and grazed the chariot wheels. No harm done, just a bit of jolting, so I went on to draw up in Melsham . . . and damned if two girls didn't invade my parlor! I was in no mood for it, I can tell you.

"To say the truth," Julian smiled the sudden impish grin that captivated his intimates, "I thought it was a put-on: two females who'd seen the carriage crest, y'know, and were casting themselves innocently in my way. You've no idea what they'll do to catch my eye!

Anyway, I ordered them out, and one of 'em gave me a roundabout—called me a whipster who'd upset her sister, and by God, it was true—not that I knew it then, but when she moved aside and the other one rose, she was a sick little schoolgirl. I felt cheap as a clipped farthing.

"And to make all worse, Stepan gives me the stable gossip. It's a Lady Eleanor Stanwood and her daughters. The coach was slowed because the young'un felt queasy. She cast up her accounts at the wheel graze, and to round it off, they're bound for Park Street. Damned if I ever heard their name, but Park Street—you know they're part of the *ton.* So I wrote a civil apology for the inconvenience, and here is a civil acknowledgement. That's all."

"What a dull little story," Lord Arthur remarked, getting to his feet. "I'm for White's and a few hands of piquet. Come with me, Julian, and chase the blue-devils?"

"You chase 'em better than piquet," the duke rose with a smile, "but I'll go along to see who's in town . . ."

His Grace remained a week in Grosvenor Square, by which time he had received twenty-seven carefully-casual invitations from such company as was to be found in the unfashionable months, bidding him to "a small informal evening," or a "few friends for dinner." Among them all one name was missing: Lady Stanwood. Julian was obscurely pleased by this. He might have been even more pleased had he known that the Stanwood ladies had dismissed him from their minds.

They were, in fact, completely concentrated on clothes. Daily the coach took them to Bond Street where they pored over the latest fashion plates and fabrics at Madame Elvire's . . . or ordered slippers from

Dashwood, purchased gloves, embroidered silk stockings, knots of ribbon or feathers for the hair, gauze scarves and reticules, and bonnets from Fanchette. It all took an immense deal of time, and Lady Stanwood thanked heaven she had arrived early enough to be certain all would be completed in time. In the few hours left of each day, Emily was informally introduced to tea parties and instructed in the finer points of social behavior—not that it was necessary.

Emily took to London like a flea to a dog's back, although Lady Stanwood reproved Sharlie for the simile. "I wish you would come out of the stables!" But Charlotte was irrepressible, and her mother saw—with astonishment—that Lord Stanwood had been right: with Emily beside her, Charlotte was her normal amusing self, unafraid to join a conversation or offer a quick comment. If it passed over the heads of the party, Emily's appreciative laughter advised them that Charlotte had been *comic,* and caused a ripple of titters. They made, in fact, an excellent team, and as the weeks passed, Lady Stanwood felt more and more confident of success for both her daughters when at last the Season could fairly be said to have begun.

There were few beaux in town. The *haut ton* was chasing foxes and hinds in Leicestershire; the middle *ton* was occupied in similar sports in lesser counties, and a handful of all-sorts was on repairing leases awaiting next quarter's allowance. The non-sportsmen mincing along St. James Street from club to club were all that London had to offer, but it was not long before they had seen Emily at this or that "informal evening." Long before the Corinthians, the Tulips, the Pinks of the *Ton* and Tops of the Trees were trickling back to town, Emily Stanwood was hailed as The Incomparable of Incomparables.

With her appearance at Lady Sefton's ball, Emily was established. Clad with the utmost simplicity in pure white satin with an overdress of palest pink gauze fastened with pearl clasps and a single strand of pearls about her lovely throat . . . with her thick gold curls dressed into a style invented for the occasion by an enraptured hairdresser whose English deserted him from emotion at such luxuriance to play with . . . a beaded reticule and lace fan dangling from her wrist, and carrying a tiny nosegay of sweetheart roses, Miss Emily Stanwood's blue eyes glowed, her pink lips gently parted in excitement, she looked upon the world with delight as she curtseyed gracefully to her hostess.

"Lud, Nelly, where got you this one?" Maria Sefton demanded robustly. "Your hair was never so gold, Robert's eyes were never so blue. Well, I can see at a glance that this Season may hold a bit of excitement!"

Shepherding her daughters into the ballroom, Lady Stanwood was fully confirmed in her lord's opinion. Gentlemen from every part of the room unobtrusively hastened forward for presentation—but those who could not get a dance with Emily, turned politely to Charlotte. Emily was subtly assisting: Charlotte must be in her set for a gavotte, Charlotte must be at her table for supper, Charlotte must be included in any engagement to drive or stroll in the park, but by evening's end, Lady Stanwood observed signs of quickening interest for the older daughter alone.

Within twenty-four hours, Lady Stanwood found herself in the enjoyable position of being bitterly envied by at least ten other mothers. Several *wondered* (very delicately) that she would present two daughters in one Season. Several more were *amazed* at how Charlotte "has come on! Dear Lady Stanwood, when one thinks of last year—so shy, poor child, with never a word to say for herself."

"She was sickening for the mumps," Lady Stanwood riposted suavely. "*Now* you are seeing Charlotte for the first time, and as for presenting two at once, there is sometimes strength in numbers, is there not?" But she would have been less than human not to savor a Triumph, and even more than Sharlie, she was anticipating the opening of Almack's. In a burst of generosity, she wrote a long description of success to Lord Stanwood, ascribing all to *his* wisdom in bidding her take Emily to reinforce Charlotte, "for all goes on as you thought, my love! I could wish you might be with us for the first Assembly, to observe for yourself. Pray send me word if we may expect you."

"Damne, if I won't!" said his lordship, much touched by his wife's praise and quite ready to believe all was entirely his idea.

Accordingly, when the hunt party dispersed from Blandford Park, Lord Stanwood stopped at the Hall long enough to supervise the return of his hunters, confer with his bailiff, and dispatch riding horses to London before poling up his curricle. If the truth be known, just as Lady Stanwood secretly preferred Charlotte, her husband's partiality was Emily: she hadn't any more brains than he. Lord Stanwood was a fond father; he was proud and satisfied with his heir, he appreciated Sharlie and depended upon her for help with the estate, but Emily of the golden curls and blue eyes was his favorite. It occurred to him as enjoyable to go early to London in order to witness her capture of Society, and be on hand for the numerous offers he was sure to receive.

Meanwhile, Charlotte had her own ideas. These were based on the information Lady Stanwood gained from Flora, Lady Inverclyde. "Imbrie?" said that lady, raising her eyebrows. "Lord, is he in England? Oh, quite unexceptionable, Nelly—and I wish I may live to see the woman who'll catch him in parson's mouse-trap! No, no, 'twas Fanscot was sold up. Tolliver killed his man and fled the country. Marley married one of the Bettison girls and retired into Norfolk. Imbrie's *entirely* different."

Eyes downcast, Charlotte listened carefully to the old lady's pungent sketch. "Rich as Croesus, but not one of your rackety gamesters—always ready to go, but keeps himself in hand. He married Isabella Darlington, she died in childbirth—none of the Darlingtons ever had any stamina," Lady Inverclyde sniffed contemptuously. "It must be ten or twelve years past. He's been traveling the world ever since . . . comes home occasionally, appears at a few Assemblies and balls, and off he goes again. The *on dit* is that his heart's buried with Isabella, but I don't credit it. In *my* opinion she cured him of marriage: one of your wispy die-away misses with a simper. Julian's an engaging scamp who can charm a bird from the tree if he wants, but he needs a woman of wit and brains. Well, well, so he's back? I must ask him to dinner, he'll come to me," Lady Inverclyde chuckled maliciously. "*I* don't have any marriageable daughters!"

In succeeding weeks, Sharlie forgot the duke in the press of engagements, the excitement of Emily's success. There was papa to anticipate, the boxes arriving daily from the modistes, the fun of receiving a few bouquets for herself (even if only sent by beaux anxious to please Emily), the silly girl-gossip over breakfast trays. It was all delightful. Park Street hummed with harmony, from Lady Stanwood holding her head high for her charming daughters, down to the staff who were quite aware that *their* young ladies were taking the town by storm.

It was Sharlie who insisted on a daily walk. "The

time must be found for a half hour in the park," she decreed. "Emily and I are accustomed to outdoor exercise at Stanwood. I am sure it will not be good for our health if it is omitted. When—if—papa sends our horses, we may make arrangements to ride, but for the present we should take a walk, or Emily may grow city-pale. She must be in looks for the Assembly!"

"You speak as though I were a horse being brought to block," Emily protested.

"No, no, my love," Lady Stanwood interposed swiftly, "but this will be your *official* presentation to Society. Naturally, you must look your best, and Sharlie as well. By all means, a daily walk."

Thus, each afternoon the sisters donned walking boots and heavy coats, proceeded up to Brook Street, across Park Lane to the park and thence down to Hyde Park Corner, where they turned and came home. Three days before the Assembly, they were approaching the turn when a man strode toward them from Knightsbridge. Charlotte's country-keen eyes recognized him in no more than a few paces: the Duke of Imbrie. A few paces more, and as he faced the girls, his expression grew uncertain. He made a half-gesture to remove his hat, and checked. "I beg your pardon—I thought that I knew you . . ."

"No, your Grace," Charlotte said regretfully. "Mama says that a near accident on the turnpike does *not* constitute an introduction."

The duke recoiled slightly, narrowing his eyes to study the pair, and suddenly the charming smile spread over his face. "Miss Stanwood, is it not? But I have lately been hunting with your father—I'm Imbrie, you know—and I feel sure he will not object to my escorting you wherever you and your little sister are bound."

"We are merely going home. Emily and I take a walk every day."

"Half an hour," Emily confided softly. "Sharlie thinks we should exercise, and it is exactly fifteen minutes from here to Park Street, so that once down and back is thirty minutes, which is half an hour, is it not?"

The duke was staring at her in fascination. "Yes," he recollected himself with a start, "Yes, I believe it is. May I accompany you?"

Emily looked uncertainly at Charlotte, who said, "I feel sure it is not at all the thing and mama will give us a scold, but if you are known to papa—he will be here tomorrow to present you, unless," worriedly, "it should prove he does not wish for the acquaintance—but however, I think we may chance it, Emily."

The duke extended an arm to each young lady and eyed Charlotte anxiously. "Have you reason to think your papa may object to me?"

"Oh, none whatever," Charlotte assured him sunnily. "He is thought to be an excellent judge of character, and if you have been hunting together—at Blandford Park, I collect?—but you do understand," earnestly, "that young females cannot be too careful?"

"Indeed, I do," the duke agreed cordially. "Why, I might be no more than a groom, yet still entitled to say I have been lately hunting with your father."

Emily trilled with laughter. "Oh, how nonsensical, your Grace! Grooms do not hunt, they stay in the stables."

"Why, so they do, although I can't believe you know much of them, Miss Emily."

"Oh, no, it is Charlotte who understands all of that. She can make poultices and hot fomentations. Papa absolutely *relies* on her," Emily said, wide-eyed, "but we shall have our own horses and grooms as soon as he arrives."

"And then you will ride for your exercise rather than walk?"

"Yes," Emily nodded, "although the Row looks to be very crowded. I think it will not be at all like riding in the country."

"No, I'm afraid it is not . . . and are you enjoying London, Miss Emily?"

"Oh, very much! Everyone is so kind, there are so many invitations, so much to do, it is quite delightful."

In such modest conversation, the trio arrived at Park Street, where his Grace bared his head and bowed politely. "Miss Stanwood, you have been remarkably silent. Are you enjoying London?"

"Yes, indeed! Do you go to the opening Assembly, Duke?"

"If you will promise me a dance," he said promptly.

"Whichever you please, but you will need to be beforetimes to get one with my sister," Charlotte chuckled. "Have you anything left, Emily?"

"Only numbers three and seven. The others are waltzes, and I'm not approved as yet."

"May I have number three, then?" He bowed gracefully over Emily's hand, smiled at her blushing agreement, and turned to Charlotte as Emily tripped up the steps to the opened front door. "But you are allowed to waltz, Miss Stanwood? I shall claim them all, and the supper dance as well!"

"With pleasure—but wouldn't you prefer to sit with Emily during the waltzes?"

"Already I suspect this would be hazardous. I should be crushed to death," he said dramatically. "No, I hold to it, Miss Stanwood: all the waltzes, and the supper dance."

"How absurd you are," Sharlie chuckled, "but as you please—unless," demurely, "papa does not wish for your acquaintance."

The duke looked alarmed. "Is he such a high-stickler, then? I had not thought it from the way he was clearing his fences at Melton, but perhaps he is different in London. I shall wait upon him instantly to ascertain his sentiments, Miss Stanwood."

"Please do," she breathed fervently, "for if the answer should be 'no'—what shall I do with those waltzes?"

"The real question is what *I* shall do with them, Miss Stanwood. You, I am persuaded, will have no difficulty in disposing of them, while I," he sighed, "will be standing in a corner—desolate."

"Oh, no, you will not," she prophesied mischievously. "One of the patronesses will present you to a suitable partner."

The duke laughed, and bent over her hand. "Your servant, Miss Stanwood."

In high fettle, Charlotte ascended the steps into the house, where Lady Stanwood was standing in the drawing room doorway. "What is this that Emily tells me? You have been escorted by Imbrie?"

"Yes, it was *famous,* mama. Don't give me a scold! You know Lady Inverclyde said he was unexceptionable, and he has just been hunting with papa at Blandford Park." Sharlie's eyes sparkled. "We encountered him as we were about to turn back and he recognized Emily at once. The instant he knew she'd be at the Assembly he begged for a dance, and said he would wait upon papa for a correct introduction. I *told* you he was catched by her, and would want a second glimpse."

"So you did," Lady Stanwood murmured, "but I cannot like this, Charlotte. Indeed, you should not! What will Imbrie think? It was altogether too bold, too free."

"He'll think that he met the daughters of an unexceptionable Baron known to the Duke of Beaufort," Sharlie returned confidently. "He's no poker-backed societarian, mama. His manners were perfectly easy, conversing with Emily on her impressions of London. What did she say?"

"Oh, that he was very distinguished, all that was kind and gracious," Lady Stanwood shrugged, "and she had promised him a dance. It remains to see whether he will claim it. I wish she may not refine too much upon the possibility."

"Not she! If he is not there well in advance to set his name on her card, Emily will have a dozen substitutes," but going up to her chamber to put off bonnet and coat, Sharlie was inwardly chortling with glee.

The climax to the perfect set-down for the odious Mrs. Drummond Burrell would be the sight of Miss Emily Stanwood going down the dance with his Grace, the Duke of Imbrie!

CHAPTER III

THE RIDING HORSES had reached London. Maria brought the news with the morning chocolate, and had much ado to prevent Miss Stanwood from throwing a coat over her nightdress to make an instant inspection. "Indeed you must not visit the stables unclad, miss! Her ladyship would dismiss me. Besides, you'll want to be into the saddle as soon as you see your mare, and *that* you can't do without proper clothing. Please, miss," artfully, "and I'll read the news from home."

Thus coaxed, Sharlie returned to bed and drank her chocolate, while Maria stumbled laboriously through the letter. Emily was only half-listening, but every detail was absorbing to Charlotte, who commented, discussed, chatted with her maid in a friendly way Lady Stanwood would have deplored.

Had *her* employers so far forgotten themselves, Miss Tinsdale would instantly have given notice! She was already uneasy in the servants' hall, but Maria still knew a goose from a hen and was as reticent as possible. It was no part of her plan to be dismissed by the twitty old cat; she meant to enjoy every bit of Miss Stanwood's social success, and make herself so indispensable that Miss Stanwood would retain her upon marriage . . . for Maria had no doubt that her mistress would achieve a brilliant match! Miss Emily was beautiful, it was more fun than work to dress her for a *ton* party, but Maria's heart was given to Charlotte, who knew Stanbury and cared about its people.

In fact, it was more satisfying to attire her than Emily. "It's a challenge-like," Maria said to herself. "Miss Emily's beautiful no matter what, but Miss Stanwood pays for dressing. She needs special colors and styles, to show her off." Nightly as the sisters descended to the salon, Maria's proud eye was for Charlotte. Despite downcast eyes of modesty, her bosom swelled when Beamish approved Miss Stanwood's appearance.

"Complete to a shade, Maria! Exactly the presentation WE expect for OUR ladies, do you not agree, Miss Tinsdale?"

"I've not Miss Tinsdale's knack with the curling stick," Maria disclaimed sadly, but the dresser was in a good mood.

"No, but it will come in time," she stated regally, "and I agree with Mr. Beamish tonight. Miss Stanwood looked just as she should."

"Oh, thank you, ma'am," Maria murmured reverently —and drew a suspicious glance for her excessive meekness.

So it was essential that Maria restrain her mistress until she was garbed for riding. She breathed a deep sigh of relief when she'd got Miss Stanwood into habit and boots—not that she would suit Beamish. "Give me the old brown habit, Maria; it's good enough for the stables," said Sharlie, thrusting her hair any-whichway under a hat and stamping into unpolished boots. "Cancel your tea parties, Emily—we'll ride this afternoon."

"Oh, dear," Emily murmured unhappily.

At eleven o'clock, Sharlie stood apologetically at the door to the breakfast parlor. "Mama, shall I delay you by changing, or will you forgive me in all my dirt?"

Lady Stanwood looked at her daughter severely. "I should have known you'd be in the stables. This once I will overlook your appearance, Charlotte, but it is not to occur again."

"Yes, mama," Sharlie smiled coaxingly, "but how could I resist? I had to shake the fidgets out of Moonshine, and the Park was deserted at this hour—only grooms exercising the mounts. We had a magnificent gallop. John rode Firefly, so she'll be ready for you later, Emily."

"Thank you, Sharlie," Emily said bravely, "but I don't know . . . I believe we're promised to Lady Penderby, are we not, mama?"

Lady Stanwood caught Sharlie's disappointment. "Yes, but it is only an old lady's tea party, you were asked out of courtesy . . . I'm persuaded you'd be moped to tears. I'll make your excuses," she said smoothly. "A ride in the Park will put roses into your cheeks, and you know papa comes in time to dine."

"Yes, mama," Emily murmured, "not but what I always enjoy . . . but of course you are right that the party will go on better without young females."

"Lud, I should think so!" Sharlie helped herself to a generous slab of ham, added a pan-fried scup, an omelet, and pulled the jam jar closer. "May I have the muffins, please, Jenny?"

"If you eat all of that," Lady Stanwood observed, "we shall need a seamstress to let out your dresses before you ever wear them."

"Oh, I beg your pardon, ma'am," Sharlie grinned with her mouth full, "but I can't lose country ways all in a trice, and the air was particularly fresh this morning. Moonshine was full of frisk, you know."

"I'm sure she was, but remember," warningly, "you cannot ride in London as in the country, or you'll be rated a wild hoyden."

"Emily will only shine the more! No, I'm funning, mama—I will be good, I promise."

It was a promise to be broken unavoidably that very afternoon, although Lady Stanwood had no fault to find in her daughters' deportment when they set forth. Emily's habit of azure blue cloth and snowy white boots, the close hat with its seductive plumes curling at one side, was a vision of loveliness atop her roan mare, but Charlotte was even more breath-taking to her mother's fond eyes. Her habit was the green of pine needles, her boots were gleaming black, and in the sunlight her hair was burnished alluringly beneath an audacious bonnet that was only permissible (or so Lady Stanwood had persuaded herself) for a second season. She was even more dubious as to its wisdom now that she saw it on Sharlie's head, but it was undeniably *right*. It was also the height of dash, without a plume and severely designed to sweep up to the left, down to the right, and buckled beneath the ear.

Sedately, the sisters started forward with the groom behind them. Lady Stanwood was half-minded to order her coach to follow for a turn of observation, but once into the Park, she might be caught in a press of carriages and unable to fulfill her engagement to Lady Penderby. She would go another day—*any* day, for now the horses were here, Sharlie would be on them every afternoon, no matter what Emily chose to do.

Lady Stanwood smiled to herself in her carriage. Sharlie was enjoying herself through Emily's success. She wanted to display Emily on a horse as part of the overall effect; it had not occurred to Charlotte that she herself would be displayed and might create more interest than Emily. In retrospect, last year had been a disaster partly of mismanagement. Sharlie should have had Moonshine and a groom; Lord Stanwood thought it unnecessary, "She'll be driving or going out to tea—no point to a horse eating its head off in the stable."

How could they have been so stupid? It was a family joke that Sharlie preferred horses to people. If she were wanted, one had only to look in the stables. Had she had Moonshine last year, much might have been different, "but she would still have succumbed to the mumps," Lady Stanwood reminded herself. "This year will be a success."

Could she have seen her daughters pacing along the Row, she would have been confirmed in her optimism. The sisters drew all eyes. Ladies rapidly assessed their riding habits and reacted variously to the wicked severity of Charlotte's bonnet. Men spared envious glances for the horses. Lady Stanwood had been right that the Park would be slow going. It was not yet the height of the Promenade, but already carriage drive and bridle path were becoming crowded, while sauntering beaux and parasol-shaded misses strolled the walks.

Charlotte found it irksome to be held to no more than a genteel trot, but Emily was much relieved at the leisurely gait. If this was London riding, she could certainly manage it. Few of the other riders today were known to the Misses Stanwood, but Charlotte felt (with an inner chuckle) it would not be long before they got themselves presented.

One of them managed it very cleverly at once: the Duke of Imbrie.

Charlotte was keeping a sharp eye out for any of Lady Stanwood's friends on the carriage drive, making sure that Emily was noticed, when a waving hand drew her to the side rail for Lady Inverclyde. Superbly indifferent to snarling traffic, the old lady smiled approvingly at Sharlie. "Very dashing bonnet, my dear—becomes you mightily!" she cackled naughtily. "Nelly'll have a deal to explain how she came to permit it—and how is she?"

"Very well, ma'am, and gone to Lady Penderby. Papa joins us tonight for dinner."

"Does he so? Come to sort through the offers for Emily, eh? How many's she had?"

"None, of course." Charlotte looked shocked. "I expect papa will be able to give you the tally in a few days, ma'am."

Lady Inverclyde laughed, "He'll have a few for you, too," she prophesied, peering beyond Sharlie. "Oh—Imbrie. Back in town, eh?"

"As you see, ma'am." Mounted on a superb black stallion, his grace smiled imperturbably as Sharlie turned, startled. "May I solicit a presentation to your fair friend, milady?"

"Phoo, nonsense, Imbrie—playing off your foreign tricks, eh?" she snorted. "Miss Stanwood—make you acquainted with the Duke of Imbrie, but pay no attention to him. He's a graceless scamp."

"I fear she is right, Miss Stanwood," the duke sighed sadly. "Your servant, ma'am . . . unless you do not wish for the acquaintance?"

"And if I did not, how could I say so," Charlotte asked innocently, "when her ladyship has presented you?"

"With a *caveat!*" Lady Inverclyde reminded her, and poked the coachman with her cane, "Drive on, Thompson. My compliments to your mother, Charlotte. Imbrie, come to tea tomorrow." With a final cackle, she was gone, leaving Charlotte struggling to keep a straight face.

His grace laughed infectiously. "Remarkable woman: says just what she thinks and damn the consequences. Very refreshing!" he smiled at Sharlie, "But do you ride alone? I had thought I saw your sister with you."

"She went forward to speak with friends," Sharlie

looked about vaguely. John-groom was conversing with another groom. Emily was some way along the bridle path, leaning to talk shyly with two Tulips while Firefly fidgeted. Suddenly all heads turned to a fracas on the drive, where a perch phaeton had tangled with a curricle, resulting in loud voices, neighing animals, and splintering wood. Cutting across the sounds was a feminine scream: Firefly had bolted.

While the duke was staring about for the cause, Charlotte said *"Gehe, Mondschein, gehe!"* and before his incredulous eyes, had set her horse for the one railing spot that was empty . . . leapt it as one entity with the beast, and was tearing across the sward on a diagonal to intercept her sister's terrified horse.

She'd been not a second too soon, as Imbrie realized when he sought to follow. The railing was now crowded with horrified spectators who were too addled to clear a way until he rose in the stirrups and roared, "MOVE aside—give me room!" Then he was over with the Stanwood groom behind him, but knowing that even with a head start, Charlotte would never reach her sister in time to prevent possible tragedy. The girl was no horsewoman, she'd dropped the reins and was clinging to the saddle . . . she was bound to be thrown.

And from the farther side of the Park, another horse was racing to the rescue.

With her eyes on Emily's swaying form, Charlotte was doubly petrified by the would-be saviour. All too likely his horse would cause Firefly to rear, or change course with a buck that would dislodge Emily.

He didn't.

He circled his horse expertly, came up on the offside, and plucked Emily from her saddle as easily as a dandelion! Once free of weight, Firefly became uncertain—shortly stood sweating and shivering until John-groom fastened a leading rein. Meanwhile, Sharlie was facing Emily's rescuer with heart-felt gratitude. "How can I thank you, sir!"

"My pleasure to serve you, ma'am," he returned cheerfully. "Sure, 'twas touch and go who'd reach her first: you or myself. 'Tis magnificent ye are! Did we have a few men could handle a horse like you, Boney'd be *rompu* by now."

Despite anxiety, Charlotte could not refrain from smiling at him, and he'd have been worth a smile without his gallantry. By his accent, he was Irish; by his words and uniform, he was a Peninsular. Mostly he was incredibly handsome. Red-gold curls *à la Brutus,* eyes as brightly blue as Emily's, a jolly baritone voice and an infectious grin—Charlotte's natural friendliness was incapable of dignity at this moment. "You're a better horseman than I, sir. Masterly, the way you circled to save my sister before Firefly bucked." She leaned over to pat Emily's hand, "Darling, it's all over. You're quite safe, don't cry, shhhh."

Emily couldn't *shhhh.* She lay limp and trembling in the young man's arms, her breath catching in tiny sobs and tears streaming down her pallid cheeks. She was entirely lost to propriety, she'd have clung to anyone, but the major problem was how on earth to get her back to Park Street. It was swiftly settled by the duke, reining in abruptly on the other side with a keen glance for the rescuer. "Servant, sir," he said tersely. "I am the Duke of Imbrie."

"Captain Sir Eustace Gayle, 2nd Brigade of the Light Bobs—your servant, sir."

"Hah! One of Vandeleur's lads, eh?" The duke's heavy eyebrows rose slightly. "Very neat capture—congratulate you!—never seen a prettier circle, but expectable from a Light Bob, and what do you in London?"

"Oh, I was in the way of a bullet at Ciudad Rodrigo," Sir Eustace shrugged casually. "Invalided home to Gayle, but *Ireland*—I'm always surprised it hasn't sunk from water-log between visits! So I'm billeted on my aunt, bothering the War Office to return me."

"Missed Badajoz, then? And a good thing, from what I hear."

"Faith, and it was, I suppose—not but what I'd have liked a swipe at Johnny Crapaud."

Charlotte found her voice, ringing with indignation. "John, assist Miss Emily to transfer to me. Come, darling, and we'll take you home while these gentlemen continue their conversation."

His grace's lips twitched, but Sir Eustace protested, "Oh, 'tis no trouble at all, ma'am—beg you'll allow me. No need to disarrange Miss Emily, she's most securely fixed, a mere featherweight."

"But I think we must not incommode you farther, sir. John!" commandingly.

"Yes, Miss Stanwood," but when the groom reached up for Emily, she shuddered and cowered, and was understood to wail, "No, please . . . oh, Sharlie, I can't!"

Sir Eustace looked down—Emily looked up pleadingly. "Sure, and ye needn't, then," he murmured softly, kicking his horse into a turn to pace sedately toward the railings, leaving the others to follow.

By now a growing group of pleasurably excited people were swarming forward to see the 'orrid accident. Charlotte bit her lips with a stormy glance for the Duke, but she had no choice but to turn Moonshine to accompany Sir Eustace. John-groom silently brought up the rear, leading Firefly. Looking neither to right nor left, Charlotte was aware of his grace's black stallion politely pacing alongside. She was further aware of his suppressed amusement, although what he found laughable escaped her.

"Ow, miss, is the young lady dead, then? Coo, it does make me come over queer-like!" an onlooker sighed avidly. "Wot 'appened? I missed it."

"What a pity," said Sharlie coldly, continuing on her way while the questioner drew back protesting aggrievedly, "I was only *arskin'.*"

"And you have had an answer," his grace's voice said courteously. "I would suggest you retire, madam. The horses are fidgety. We should not like a *real* accident, should we?"

"Oh, h'I should think not! Come away, Maggie, do! H'I don't like the look of them beasts—great murderin' animules, if you arsk me."

Charlotte firmed her lips again, but a deep chuckle from the duke betrayed her into a silent quiver of laughter. "Ah, that's better, Miss Stanwood," he approved. "A few smiles will convince the populace there is nothing worthy of gossip. Now, where is the young idiot heading? Gayle," he raised his voice irritably, "you'll not get out that way." His grace spurred forward, closely followed by Charlotte. She could see his expression change, nor—when she drew up beside the Captain—could she wonder, for Emily was entirely restored. *Most* reprehensibly, she was smiling, blushing faintly, chatting with shy animation in the arms of a complete stranger!

"We'll not trouble you farther, Sir Eustace. I'll relieve you," said the duke impersonally. "Come, Miss Emily."

"Oh, I say," the Captain began, but Imbrie merely raised his eyebrows and repeated, *"Come,* Miss Emily."

Emily had no choice. His grace reinforced words with action, and calmly picked her from Sir Eustace's lap in one smooth motion. "Your servant, sir," and the duke trotted off without a backward glance, leaving the

Captain almost open-mouthed. While Charlotte applauded his grace's quick thinking to protect Emily's reputation, it was more of a set-down than was deserved. Sir Eustace had saved Emily, after all. "Allow me to thank you once more, sir," she said cordially. "I am persuaded my father, Lord Stanwood, will wish to do so in person when he arrives this evening."

The Captain's face cleared magically. "Faith, and I'm glad ye think so, Miss Stanwood. I'll make bold to step around tomorrow to inquire for Miss Emily," he grinned mischievously, "with my credentials. I fancy my aunt, Mrs. Ixton, has the pleasure of Lady Stanwood's acquaintance—or perhaps 'tis her husband knows your father—but I'll find someone for a proper presentation, never doubt it. I'm not minded to lose my chance for such riding company as yourself, Miss Stanwood."

Sharlie could feel herself coloring beneath his admiring blue eyes, but the mention of Mrs. Ixton had relieved her mind. She was indeed known to Lady Stanwood, Charlotte distinctly recalled meeting her last year. "I feel sure your ingenuity will not be gravely tested, sir," she murmured demurely. "Bid you good day, Captain."

Cantering swiftly across the sward, she came up to the others as they reached the railings, to find the duke efficiently transferring Emily to John-groom, then dismounting to assist her into Lady Inverclyde's carriage. "Eh, what's all this? What's amiss?" the old lady demanded. "Come up, come up, child. No, the dog will *not* bite you, Emily. Push him out of the way—well, *sit* on him, then. He'll move fast enough, I warrant you —get *down*, Cupidon! Now, what's happened? Was she thrown?"

"No—merely, her horse bolted, but she was rescued by another rider."

"Captain Sir Eustace Gayle, who is nephew to Mrs. Ixton," Charlotte inserted blandly. "Most gracious of your ladyship to take up my sister. I pray it does not too greatly inconvenience you."

"No, no," Lady Inverclyde said absently. "Ixton? One of the Stidhams, or was she a Guthrie? Tchk, there's no keeping up with the Irish, but I fancy I know the woman."

"Very possibly, ma'am—she is known to mama and I have met her, too."

"Ah? That's all right then." She eyed Emily severely, "Not goin' to faint, are you? Can't abide fainting misses! Look all right to me, color's normal . . . straighten your bonnet, Emily, and sit *up.* We'll take another turn, let 'em see you're all right," poking the coachman with her cane. "Go on, Thompson—around again, and don't swear at Lady Parks' coachman this time. Send your groom home, Sharlie, and finish your ride. Imbrie can escort you. On a horse, he's safe enough!" Cackling gleefully, Lady Inverclyde drove away.

Charlotte looked after the carriage, disconcerted. On the one hand she yearned to make a full circuit; on the other, she was embarrassed to be thrust upon the duke so high-handedly. "Take Firefly back to the stable, John, and return for me," she decided. "I'll keep beside her ladyship's carriage. You'll probably find us on the far side of the sward."

"Miss Stanwood, I beg you will not believe that wicked old woman," his grace pleaded piteously. "I am entirely safe even when *not* on a horse. You have no need of a groom, particularly," with an appraising glance at John, "when I am the bigger by a stone. Send the man back to the stable."

From the corner of her eye, Sharlie could see the

groom's face purpling with suppressed guffaws. She knew her own face was pink, she felt ready to sink with embarrassment. "And I beg *you* will not feel obligated to disarrange your day for her ladyship's whims," she returned with spirit. "Your grace has already done more than enough in assisting my sister, I have no wish to incommode you farther. I am persuaded there can be no impropriety in my riding alone within view of her ladyship's carriage."

"Phoo, sad stuff," the duke grimaced. "Two paces an hour? *Mondschein* will never be content with that," ignoring Sharlie's stricken face and averted eyes at the German name, "and I wonder you will think any day could be disarranged by encountering two lovely damsels in distress, Miss Stanwood. John—go back to the stable and stay there!"

A coin spun through the air, caught dextrously by the groom. "Yes, sir, your grace!" Hacking home across Park Lane, John rehearsed his report to the servants with gusto, ending with a Golden Boy to make himself scarce—a regular right 'un, the duke! "In course, I wouldn't have left Miss Sharlie but for seein' he was known to Lady Inverclyde and had her approval to escort our ladies."

Meanwhile, Sharlie was silently trotting beside the duke, bereft of conversation and devastated by her inadvertent use of the despised *German* . . . although who could have dreamed Imbrie would understand?

"Are you still not wishing for the acquaintance, Miss Stanwood?"

"Oh, pray—I desire you will not refine too much upon my heedless words," she said with an effort. "It is ever my disgrace to speak without thinking."

"On the contrary, it is your greatest charm, Miss Stanwood," he returned quickly. "I'd no intent to tease. I'd thought this a small pleasantry between us—

one I enjoy, but forgive me if you find the jest outworn."

"No, no," she murmured distractedly, and cried "Oh, there they are!" spurring forward eagerly to come abreast of the carriage. Emily's lovely face was blooming once more, Sharlie had no fear for her, but observing the duke's attentive bow and bemused smile, she was suddenly struck by An Idea.

It occurred to Charlotte that the Duke of Imbrie was more catched by her pretty sister than she'd thought. Further, she suspected Emily was not indifferent. Her great blue eyes looked up admiringly, then lowered shyly. Her color came and went in delicate flushes tinging her cheeks, the while she prattled innocently in her fluting voice, assuring his grace she was none the worse, could not understand how Firefly came to behave so, "for you must know she is in general the gentlest thing in nature. Papa chose her particularly for her good disposition. I am not a very good equestrienne, you see. With so many riders in the Row, I thought the pace must necessarily be held to an easy gait, but however, it did not answer, and I think I shall not attempt it again."

"Oh, you could not be so heartless, Miss Emily. To deny your admirers the sight of you is unthinkable! The horse was frightened by unfamiliar surroundings and noise, but another day she will be accustomed, and your escort will be too numerous for a repetition."

"Do you think so?" Emily asked doubtfully. "But on the whole, I find a carriage altogether more comfortable, plus being able to put my whole mind to conversation. Sharlie can manage to speak and handle the reins, you see."

"Your sister is an accomplished horsewoman."

"Oh, the horse does not live that would dare bolt with Sharlie!"

"Your grace must make allowance for a sister's

partiality," Sharlie said lightly, "and do you attend Lady Abercrombie's musicale tonight, sir?"

"Why, I believe I had her card, but I had given it no thought. Musicales are not much in my taste, Miss Stanwood. I collect you mean to be present? Will Miss Emily feel able?"

"Oh, yes," she nodded sunnily, "for I am to play the harp, you know."

"Ah, the harp!" his grace exclaimed. "I *thought* that might be your instrument . . . and what do you contribute, Miss Stanwood?"

"The most welcome of all: respectful silence and generous applause," Sharlie chuckled. "Must I confess? I have no talent whatever and cannot carry a tune in a coal scuttle. Emily has all the accomplishments of the family, Duke, for besides the harp, she has conquered the pianoforte and possesses a singularly sweet true voice."

Emily blushed and disclaimed loyally, "I wish you will not, Sharlie. You dance beautifully, far better than I."

His grace laughed. "Why, it's a very charming mutual admiration society! Miss Stanwood, there is what looks to be a fairly open stretch ahead—shall we try it?"

A gentle canter brought them to the exit, where they accompanied Lady Inverclyde's carriage to Park Street. Imbrie swung from his saddle to hand Emily from her seat. Observing the gallantry with which he kissed her hand, Charlotte was more and more certain of his interest. She slid from Moonshine to the horse block with no more than a steadying hand from the groom and repeated her courtesies to Lady Inverclyde for bearing Emily home.

"Phoo, nonsense, Charlotte—enjoyed myself mightily, but don't put your sister on a horse again. Girl's got no bottom, and cow-handed into the bargain. Can't have an Incomparable fallin' off her mount in front of the *ton.*" The old lady poked her long-suffering coachman, "Go ON, Thompson—home. Imbrie, present my respects to Lady Abercrombie—ought to know better than to send *me* her card. I can't abide musicales, and at my age, thank heaven, I needn't do anything I don't wish. WELL, Thompson, why are we dawdling?"

He was moved to protest. "I was waiting until your ladyship finished."

"I *am* finished, said all I want to say five minutes past. Go ON!"

Tossing his reins to the groom, the duke escorted the sisters up the steps to their door, where Beamish looked austerely into space. "His lordship has arrived, Miss Stanwood."

"Papa!" Emily squeaked with pleasure, but minded her manners. "Oh, milord," extending a tiny hand and curtseying, "thank you once more. Indeed it was kind in you to convey me home."

Nothing could exceed the grace of Imbrie's bow. "Your servant, Miss Emily. Pray present my compliments to your father."

"Yes, indeed, but you will excuse me now." Emily was gone, leaving him to bow over Charlotte's hand. "Your servant, ma'am."

She curtseyed demurely. "Give you good day, Duke," but once into the hall, she ran lightly up the stairs to Lady Stanwood's parlor where she found his lordship standing before the fire, and his wife behind the tea tray.

With one strong arm about Emily, Lord Stanwood beckoned to Charlotte. "Eh, there's my little Diana! What's this Emily's telling us about a rescue in the Park and Imbrie taking care of all?" He hugged

Sharlie with a hearty kiss. "Lud, ma'am," to Lady Stanwood's anxious protestations, "he'll think nought about introductions! Been hunting at Blandford Park for three weeks, a bruising rider—showed us all the way! Told me he'd had a small dust-up with your carriage—apologized very handsomely, said he'd written you, had your answer, and there's an end to it, Nelly. If you insist on formality, I'll present him as soon as may be."

"Unnecessary, papa. Lady Inverclyde has already presented him to me," Sharlie inserted. "In the stress of the moment, I fear he missed any formal introduction to Emily, but what of it?"

"Yes, very well, but what happened?" Lady Stanwood insisted.

The tale was soon told succinctly by Sharlie, leading on to innumerable questions from her mama, in particular concerning Captain Sir Eustace Gayle. She was only slightly reassured by his aunt, Mrs. Ixton. "Yes, very true that I am acquainted—very true that you may have met—but we are not upon visiting terms, Charlotte."

"Nevertheless, it was he who actually rescued Emily, ma'am, and the duke congratulated him on his masterly handling of the horse."

"Indeed it was, papa," Emily said earnestly, "for he had me away from Firefly without the least trouble, and talked so kindly that I was stopped shaking almost at once. Then the duke transferred me to Lady Inverclyde. We drove once around the Park, with Sharlie and his grace riding beside. Truly, there was no impropriety, Mama."

"I am persuaded you both behaved as you should," Lady Stanwood relented. "Finish your tea and go to dress for dinner. We must not be late in reaching Lady Abercrombie," but when the girls had gone, she was still uneasy. "I cannot like this, Robert. If Sharlie was rated too shy last season, she's like to seem too free this one. She seems more dedicated to establishing Emily than herself. Her manners, while always polite, are far too unaffectedly natural for an unmarried girl. She treats the beaux as—as though they were friends of Geoffrey's! It will not do, you know it will not do, Robert. Some little reserve there should be instead of this attitude of older spinster sister."

Lord Stanwood pursed his lips and considered. "Perhaps—but I can't feel it in me to restrain her, Nelly. Stap me, but they're two different girls, Emily as well as Sharlie! You'd not see it, you've been with 'em constantly, but there's a bloom about 'em—a sort of glow. Damme, they're—they're *interestin'*, ma'am. Leave 'em alone, dress 'em handsomely as you well know how to do, milady," he grinned approvingly at his wife. "Take 'em here or there to be seen, but don't curb 'em. That's my advice you, ma'am."

Immersed in the hip bath before the fire, Charlotte's reflections were—exciting. She had no doubt that Sir Eustace would prevail on his aunt to call tomorrow morning for the correct half hour, which would permit Charlotte to accept his escort in the Row. She spent a few minutes recalling his dashing rescue, the superb chestnut horse, and dismissed Sir Eustace: it would be fun to ride with him.

More important was the Duke of Imbrie. He had been struck by Emily's beauty in Melsham, had apologized by note to Lady Stanwood and to Lord Stanwood during the hunt party. He had devoted himself to Emily on the chance-meet in yesterday's walk, instantly requested a dance—as well as from Charlotte; she did not refine too much upon that, he could scarcely do less. All was obvious that he wished to be on terms with the family. Today was another chance meeting. He'd had no way of knowing they would be riding, yet he'd quickly seized the opportunity for formal introduction.

Words and glances came back to her. The duke had "thought your sister was with you." He'd kept his eye on Sir Eustace carrying Emily all the while he was chatting with Charlotte on the sward, and had swiftly dashed forward to take Emily away from the stranger. He had protested it'd be boring for Sharlie to keep beside the carriage—yet been perfectly happy to lean down from his horse for quite half the circuit to talk to Emily.

Lady Inverclyde wasn't fooled! She'd teased him by her reference to Lady Abercrombie. He hadn't meant to be present this evening, but as she stepped out to be patted dry by Maria, Sharlie chuckled to herself. The Duke of Imbrie would be there—she'd wager on it!

He near as nothing wasn't, although Sharlie had no way of knowing this. Trotting leisurely home from Park Street, the Misses Stanwood were dismissed from Julian's mind. He flicked cynically through the day's accumulation of carefully-casual invitations in Robsey's basket and found one worth opening. "Gerry Smythe has failed, leaving me in disgrace with dinner commanded. Join me? A.V." Julian's spirits lifted. He was bidden, hopefully, to a dozen homes; he would spend the evening with his cousin. "Send word to Lord Arthur that I'll be with him at eight."

Complete to a shade in brown satin knee breeches and a swallowtail coat of dull gold superfine, Julian accepted hat and gold-knobbed stick from Robsey, refused the suggestion of a chair, and strolled from his house down South Audley to Hill Street, where he was admitted by his cousin's man. "Evening, Patch."

"Good evening, milord. I hope I see you well?"

"Well, indeed, with one of Mrs. Patch's dinners to anticipate. Needn't bother to announce me—Arthur, how are you? Hadn't expected you in town so soon."

"Why, I might say the same of you," shaking hands heartily. "What keeps you here? Not that it isn't dashed convenient, we'll settle everything in comfort. I'm anxious to know what you found at Keighly."

Lord Arthur's rooms were cozy, Mrs. Patch provided an ample dinner suited to the requirements of gentleman of quality, her husband dispensed the contents of his employer's cellar with a free hand, and the cousins lingered companionably over dinner until past ten. They were then decidedly mellow, but still fit to go out and in a mood for it. "White's?" Julian suggested. "Or the Great Go, if you prefer."

"See who's there," Arthur nodded. "If we don't like 'em, there's a place in Albemarle Street."

The crisp April air had a settling effect. By the time they reached Berkeley Square they were in shape to be aware of no less than three houses offering hospitality this evening. Arthur groaned, "Oh, damme, we should have gone the other way. I forgot Lady Abercrombie's giving some curst musicale, she's m'godmother, Julian—always deuced kind, don't care to offend her."

"Abercrombie" and "musicale" struck a faint note in Julian's memory. He halted abruptly and laughed, "Hah, we'll present ourselves—briefly, because I warn you there's a young lady with a harp."

"There is always a young lady with a harp," Arthur shuddered, "and I wish God hadn't invented 'em."

"Which—the harps or the young ladies?" Julian asked irrepressibly. "No, this is a special young lady, Arthur. I have it on no less unimpeachable authority than her elder sister that she has also mastered the pianoforte and is thought to have a singularly pleasing voice."

"Good God!"

"Oh, it is a tale of wild adventure this afternoon in the Park," Julian was laughing helplessly, sorting through cards drawn from his pocket. "Yes, here it is. Stepan always arms me with all the invitations for the night on the chance I may fancy one. Nothing will quench his hope of eventually turning me into a top gallant." Thrusting back the others, "Oh, I thought to ride today, and found myself assisting in a rescue." Rapidly he outlined the details, and had Arthur snorting hilariously at Lady Inverclyde's comments.

"Stanwood? Those same whose coach wheels you grazed?"

Julian nodded. "Met the father at Blandford Park—very sound man—but the daughters, Arthur! The elder, Miss Charlotte Stanwood, is conversable. The younger, Miss Emily," he threw back his head in a guffaw, "Arthur, she has to be seen to be believed! This will be your privilege tonight."

"What's wrong with her?" his cousin asked suspiciously.

"Nothing," Julian gasped, leaning against the lamp post. "Nothing, Arthur. She is angelically beautiful. The sight of her seated at the harp will require only wings to convince the audience they are already within St. Peter's gates. She is spoken of reverently as THE Incomparable, she fits every classic standard of the *ton*: a wealth of pure gold curls, immense blue 'orbs' for poets to rhapsodize, every indication of shy maidenhood from blushes to downcast eyes . . . and not one brain in her head!

"Arthur, I swear you cannot tear yourself away

from her for the fascination of her vapidity. You find yourself hanging upon her rosebud lips for the next bromide, wagering to yourself which she will use. The man who marries her will need either a devilish sense of humor, or no brains at all. Come," Julian pulled himself together with a final sigh of merriment, "I cannot wait, I die to see your reaction."

In the event, it proved impossible, for the musicale was long advanced, the rooms thronged and nearly all seats occupied. The cousins were swept apart by the necessities of courtesy, and when Julian finally gained the music room, Arthur was nowhere to be seen. Apparently a selection had just ended, there was a general shifting of the guests, and it was some while before Julian sighted Charlotte on the far side. She wore a gown of amethyst sarsnet with her hair dressed *à la diadème,* and he thought appreciatively that she was in looks tonight. She, or Lady Stanwood, had excellent taste; the green habit and saucy bonnet were flattering, but this was even more so. By the time he'd gained her side, the intermission was ending and the guests were straggling lethargically back to the chairs.

"Miss Stanwood, your servant." Julian bent over her hand, and was favored with a flashing smile that startled him.

"Oh, you have come!" she exclaimed. "I had near despaired of you, milord, for you must know the order of the program has been altered, and Emily plays next. You are but just in time." Sharlie glanced about quickly. "There!" she said with satisfaction. "There are still some chairs for a perfect view. Shall we take our places, Duke?"

"By all means." Julian slid forward swiftly and secured the seats in the nick of time, to the disgruntlement of a large lady in a fearfully wonderful green turban. She was inclined to make something of it, until Julian eyed her up and down, and drawled, "Oh, I beg your pardon, ma'am, but Miss Stanwood's sister plays next and she must naturally have the full view. I am persuaded you will be entirely comfortable in the adjoining chairs. The music will sound the same, you know."

He then adjusted his coat tails and resigned himself to boredom as the harp was placed. Miss Emily was led forward by an impressive escort of beaux contending for the honor of holding the chair, altering its position to her satisfaction, and accepting such precious burdens as her fan, handkerchief, reticule. Meeting Arthur's wicked twitch of an eyebrow, Julian composed his face with difficulty. He had described her more accurately than anticipated. Emily was wearing pure white *soupir d'etouffe* in a style so deceptively simple that Julian (who was no stranger to the costs of female gowns) instantly priced it as not a penny less than 150 guineas. "With wings," he told himself mentally, "it'd bc twicc as much."

Her performance was exactly as wooden and uninspired as he had feared. It was also interminable. Worse still, the enthusiastic applause of the young gentlemen led to an encore—also as feared, although Julian clapped politely. He could scarcely do less with Charlotte beside him, but from her beaming pride, she had no doubt of his pleasure. "Is she not extraordinary," Sharlie breathed. "She never mistakes a note! Ah, she is moving to the pianoforte. I hope she means to sing. Then you will hear her at her best."

"Ah? I am sure," Julian said politely, but after the first trills he began to long for the harp! Accustomed to the finest music in the great cities of the world, Julian cursed his sense of humor. He'd thought only to make his bow to Lady Abercrombie and present Arthur to the Stanwoods before retreating. Who could have dreamed they'd arrive before the girl had played? Arthur would roast him finely for this!

The instant the final note died away, Julian was on his feet, wondering how to escape. Impossible to leave Miss Stanwood unattended in the center of the room, yet where to escort? To his further horror, he realized by the movements of the company that this was the supper intermission. However, it appeared she had no intention of retaining him. In fact, he found himself abandoned in the kindest possible manner. "I am so glad you were in time, your grace. At least you were able to hear my sister, but I fear you cannot hope to join her supper table," regretfully. "I know she was bespoke from the moment of arrival, but tomorrow there is Almack's, although you will need to be prompt to claim your dance," Charlotte warned, holding out her hand with a friendly smile. "Good evening, Duke."

Julian bent automatically, feeling slightly stunned by her calm dismissal, and wildly cudgelling his memory about Almack's. Yes, there *had* been talk of it when he'd met them walking, when he'd first been struck by Emily's inanities and still thought her in the schoolroom. He was further struck that Charlotte made no mention of his engagement to herself.

"Until tomorrow, Miss Stanwood," he murmured, "and mind you save the waltzes."

She drew her hand away with a faint blush. "Oh, pray, we were only funning, milord. I do not expect . . ."

"Do you not?" he raised his heavy black eyebrows in astonishment, "But I expect, Miss Stanwood, and will not surrender to any Johnny-come-lately."

She smiled with a sudden sidewise glance. "No, but

I fancy you may wish for a release. Emily is certain to be approved for the waltz, you know."

"She will certainly have a hundred claimants," he retorted, "and you recall she assured me you were the better dancer?" Julian had no notion what prompted him to say, *"Guten abend, Fräulein, als morgender nacht."*

Miss Stanwood's reaction was—odd. She murmured automatically, *"Danke schoen, mein herzog,"*—and once again blenched, wide-eyed and stricken. "Good evening, I must go, you will excuse me . . ." and hastened away toward her sister.

"I say, Julian, let's be off," Arthur said plaintively, "or are you fixing an interest with the pretty widgeon?"

"Lord, no!" Julian returned with suppressed violence —but as he retrieved coat, hat and walking stick, he wondered: why should Miss Stanwood be so reluctant to admit knowledge of German?

CHAPTER IV

THE GREAT DAY of Almack's dawned fair and full of promise, commencing with the announcement shortly after breakfast of Mrs. Ixton and her nephew. Lady Stanwood was at first inclined to a snub, "for it is presumptuous of her to visit when I have not expressed a wish for it." However, she was easily persuaded it was her duty to thank Sir Eustace for rescuing Emily, and on their departure, she conceded it was pleasant. "Mrs. Ixton was not at all as I recalled. I believe I must have confused her with someone else."

"Then you do not object that I ride with Sir Eustace, ma'am?"

"No, but you will take a groom," Lady Stanwood decreed repressively, noting Sharlie's sparkling eyes. By a lucky chance, she found her lord in his study. "I wish you will see what may be discovered about this young man, Robert. He is altogether too pretty, AND Irish! One has not great hopes of them aside from horse-breeding, which is exactly what may catch Sharlie."

"You have other plans, milady?"

"Indeed," she agreed impressively. "Lord Wrentham, Sir Malcolm Ogilvie, and Mr. Beauchamp—and the season has not fairly begun. Who knows what may develop?"

Neither did anyone else, and the suspense in the servants' hall was nearly unendurable, what with the knocker sounding every other minute for deliveries of notes, packages, and trifles from the finest shops in town. By dressing time, the still room was overflowing with floral tributes. "It's good as Christmas," Maria said to herself, trotting proudly upstairs with Miss Stanwood's share. The bulk might go to Miss Emily, but Miss Charlotte was not forgotten, and quite half of her beaux had not honored the younger sister. Maria tucked that up her sleeve for later use in the private skirmishing with Miss Tinsdale.

That Sharlie carried the flowers accompanied by the Duke of Imbrie's card, and Emily chose Sir Eustace's, was purely dictated by their gowns. Julian had sent yellow roses mixed with bronze pansies, which were the perfect complement for Miss Stanwood's gown of figured jonquil brocade. His gift of deep red roses could not be said to agree with Miss Emily's sapphire blue crepe over palest pink. "The effect is garish!" The modest nosegay of camellias tied with long pink ribbons was exactly right, "for I cannot give Sir Eustace a dance, you know—nor Viscount Pelham, but perhaps he will not mind if I use his holder."

To set the seal on felicity, they found Geoffrey in the salon. "Lud, Sharlie, no need to set up a squawk!" he protested. "Opening of Almack's, m'sisters need an escort—came down last year for you, came down again today. I don't say I'd have done it if I'd known m'father was here, but however . . ." He surveyed his sisters critically, raising a quizzing glass, at which Sharlie hooted with amusement.

"Oh, we've an Exquisite! How d'you mince, brother dear?"

There ensued a brisk familial interchange that

caused most undignified laughter in their parents, but Emily merely revolved slowly, and fixed her brother with parted lips awaiting his verdict. "Very nice," he approved. "Fine as fivepence—does you proud, mama, not but what Sharlie's a strong contender." He raised his glass imperturbably. "A very fetching gown, m'dear. Emily's the beauty—no doubt of it—but damme, Charlotte, you're . . . you're *elegant.*"

It was the exact word, and Lady Stanwood's bosom swelled at the glazed expression of Mrs. Drummond Burrell as Sharlie passed down the receiving line. When Emily succeeded her sister, Mrs. Burrell was momentarily speechless. Not so Miss Emily! She smiled angelically at the patroness and breathed in reverent accents, "Mrs. Drummond Burrell! How happy I am to meet you, ma'am. My sister has so often spoken of you."

"Emily, how could you!" Charlotte was shaking with inner amusement as they joined Lady Stanwood.

"Why not? It is no more than the truth, Sharlie—and I did not tell her *how* you spoke of her," Emily returned militantly.

Thereafter the evening became pure delight for Charlotte. Almack's was not usually considered particularly gay. The music and supper were excellent, but nothing stronger than a mild claret cup was served and there was no card room. This was deliberate. Nothing existed to lure the gentlemen away from their duties on the dancing floor—or cause them to be incapable of fulfilling same by reason of uncertain legs. However, the opening assembly of 1812 held uncommon interest for a number of spectators. They were first electrified by the arrival of the Duke of Imbrie, for although he was known to be in England, one would never expect to see him at Almack's.

"Lud, Imbrie, do not tell me you're hanging out for a wife at last," Maria Sefton protested incredulously.

"Not at all, milady," he bowed imperturbably, "but one must keep up, you know. I like to see what's available for the furtherance of the nation."

It was then observed that his grace refused all suggested introductions by the patronesses, walked directly to Lord Stanwood, and was warmly presented to Lady Stanwood . . . that he scrawled his name on Miss Emily's card with perfect assurance, and sat talking to her mother until the sets were forming for the third dance, when he arose and smilingly claimed her hand. Well! Nothing could have been clearer, and other eyes than Charlotte's relished the widened stare of Mrs. Drummond Burrell.

There was more in store. After returning Miss Emily to her mama, the duke disappeared into the anteroom with the older gentlemen, and emerged only to bow before Miss Stanwood for the first waltz. Every eye then turned covertly to Mrs. Burrell, whose face now resembled a boiled owl. Very satisfying!

Sharlie had settled with herself to save her waltzes for the duke, on the expectation that she would thus have him available should Emily be given permission to dance. She had no doubt he would gain it quite easily, she was hoping he'd apply to the odious Mrs. Burrell, but meanwhile let her observe last year's ugly duckling with this year's prize.

As Imbrie's firm arm circled her waist, Sharlie's courage deserted her. He felt so entirely different from Geoffrey. He was taller, he did not clutch nor pump her arm but guided her with a gentle hand, and he smelled delicious: a faint scent of fresh lavendar. Perhaps his shirts were laid in it, for her nose came only to the top of his white waistcoat. His feet moved smoothly, with perfect assurance and absolute rhythm, as though he had been waltzing forever and could do it in his sleep. Probably he could . . .

For a full turn of the room, Sharlie answered his conversational attempts at random, until finally he said, "What is it in my waistcoat that strikes you dumb, Miss Stanwood?"

"N-nothing," she looked up quickly. "I am merely minding my steps."

"You've no need, Miss Stanwood. Your sister was right: you are an exceptional dancer," he smiled at her serious face. "Surely you must often have waltzed before."

"Yes—and then again, no," she confided. "It is true that I had the permission last year, but you see, no one asked me. So all my experience is limited to home parties—and you do not feel at all like my brother."

"You relieve my mind, Miss Stanwood," he sighed, "not that your family is not delightful and I should feel privileged to belong to it—but unfortunately I am cursed with my own."

She laughed aloud at that, and the duke felt an inexplicable bounce in his pulse. He'd come to Almack's only because to fail would be an affront to Lord Stanwood, whom he'd liked at the hunt party. He'd fully intended to excuse himself gracefully after this waltz, but there was a refreshing naturalness about Miss Stanwood, and she was a superb partner. Now the ice was broken, she moved gracefully to his lightest touch and chatted with a lack of coquetry that disarmed him.

For her part, Charlotte had never been happier. Convinced in her own mind that his interest was for Emily, she already thought of the duke as a future brother-in-law with whom formality was unnecessary. All was so different this year from last. Emily was a

Sensation, but Sharlie knew herself to be a modest Success. If her ball card was not filled quite so swiftly as her sister's, nevertheless it was filled without the urging of a patroness. She would have been less than human not to enjoy waltzing while Emily was forced to sit beside Lady Stanwood, although Sir Eustace had cleverly inserted himself in the adjoining chair.

At the end of the music, Charlotte's generosity came to the fore. "I hope Emily may be permitted to waltz," she said artfully, "but perhaps the patronesses may not think it advisable on her first appearance—unless someone intercedes for her."

Imbrie glanced across the room. "She seems tolerably entertained by her rescuer. May I get you some lemonade, Miss Stanwood?"

"No, thank you." Let him have a chance to talk to Emily . . . but when he'd led Charlotte back to her mother, the duke showed no disposition to linger. He nodded casually to Sir Eustace, smiled at the ladies, bowed over Sharlie's hand, said "Number six, I think?" and moved away—but perhaps her words had fallen on fertile soil. He was next seen to be flirting very agreeably with Lady Jersey before retreating again to the anteroom. So, too, did Sir Eustace whose card was far from filled due to his recent arrival in London.

He'd said in the morning, "I've not much acquaintance among the *ton,* being mostly out of the country these five years. This Almack's now—how do I present myself there, Miss Stanwood?"

"You must obtain a voucher from one of the patronesses." From the bouquets, he'd obviously managed it, and promptly secured two dances with Charlotte upon her arrival at the rooms. He'd probably used the War Office, for he was talking now with Princess Esterhazy who was sitting beside Lady Jersey. Then he presented himself for the first dance with Charlotte. At its close she felt he was the best thing yet. He was more graceful than Mr. Beauchamp, less punctilious than Lord Wrentham, and infinitely more loquacious than Sir Malcolm. He knew all about horses, and to top that, he was handsome.

Unluckily, he was also courteous. As they returned to Lady Stanwood, Lady Jersey was moving away with a smiling nod. Emily's previous partner was reluctantly taking his leave, the Duke of Imbrie could be seen approaching because the next was Number six—and *just* before he had reached their chairs, Lady Stanwood said, "Emily, Lady Jersey has given you permission to waltz."

Instantly, Sir Eustace solicited the honor and was accepted. To Charlotte, nothing was more vexatious. It later occurred to her as she whirled around in the duke's arms that he could scarcely beg off from herself so abruptly. No doubt he would manage the transition for the other waltzes, somehow making certain Charlotte had another partner. She made sure he should notice that Emily was now permitted, but he said only, "Yes, I see. Somehow I thought it would be managed . . . and do you ride tomorrow, Miss Stanwood?"

Sure enough, he had found a substitute for the next waltz, and what a substitute! No less a personage than Mr. Brummell issued from the anteroom and bowed, "Lady Stanwood, your servant, ma'am." With a faint smile, "Miss Stanwood, will you accept me in place of Imbrie? He finds himself entangled in a business conversation—not the moment for it, of course, but we hope you may be gracious."

"Why, it is yourself who is gracious, Mr. Brummell," Sharlie widened her eyes ingenuously. "To be taking on his grace's task—what very good friends you must be." Ignoring her mother's suppressed gasp at such light-heartedness to the great Beau, Charlotte rose and curtseyed blandly.

She was not to know of the anteroom interchange when the duke entered after his last waltz. "Hallo, Julian," the Beau drawled. "Who's your charmer?"

"Miss Stanwood."

Mr. Brummell took another look. "Lud, is she back again?"

"Yes, I gather it's her second season," Julian remarked, "although for the life of me I can't think why she failed last year. Sally Jersey says she's come on amazingly. Of course, it's the younger girl who'll take London by storm."

"Gold curls, blue eyes," the Beau nodded. "Prinny will adore her, but Miss Stanwood—there's a something about her."

"Definitely, although I doubt it's to your taste, Beau. She's a magnificent horsewoman—not one to turn aside to a farmhouse before the first fence."

Brummell raised languid eyebrows. "But I've the greatest dislike of soiling the white tops to my boots, Julian. I take it Miss Stanwood dances acceptably?"

"Better than that! Miss Emily is as correct and wooden as her performance on the harp," Julian closed his eyes with a delicate wince that drew a chuckle from the Beau.

"So?" he commented lazily, still watching Sharlie through half-closed eyes. "Shall I bring Miss Stanwood into favor, Julian? She's reddish-haired, tanned skin, a bit tall . . . but perhaps it is time for a change. I am growing weary of the blushing little misses out of the nursery. What d'you think?"

Julian remembered the ingenuous admission, *I had the permission to waltz, but no one asked me.* Impulsively he said, "By all means, if you can."

"Spare me your next dance, and watch!"

All of Almack's watched in a state of shock, as Mr. Brummell led Miss Stanwood onto the dance floor. Secretly certain it was a manoeuvre for the duke to emerge innocently and seek Emily's hand, Charlotte was perfectly at ease with her illustrious partner. She responded to his conversational gambits freely, and twice drew a broad smile, nor did he leave when the music ended. He insisted on escorting her for a glass of orgeat . . . stayed beside her in full view of all onlookers until Lord Wrentham approached to claim the next dance, when he surrendered her with every appearance of reluctance and kissed her hand.

And after all, Charlotte was vexed to discover his grace had not been quick enough before Sir Eustace had nipped in first. "Why could you not have delayed a little?" she murmured when she encountered her sister. "Did you not realize it was Imbrie who got Lady Jersey to give you permission so that he could waltz with you?"

Emily widened her eyes. "No, I never thought of it, Sharlie. I understood he was promised to you."

"So he was, but he got Brummell to take his place in order to be free to ask you."

"Was that it? But I think you must be mistaken, Sharlie, for he never so much as looked from the door throughout the dance," Emily said doubtfully, "and *I* think Mr. Brummell must have wished to dance with you, for it appears he never does anything upon request unless he likes."

Lady Stanwood was of Emily's opinion, and while at a loss to account for Mr. Brummell's condescension, she was inwardly near-faint with excitement. More worldly-wise than her daughters, she knew the Beau's approbation would establish Charlotte more securely than

Emily—*and what of it?* Lady Stanwood asked herself. Emily was a full year too young to be fixing her heart, only here at all in order to prevent unwise entanglements. Let her enjoy herself while Charlotte was settled, and let Emily have a second season when she would be better able to select what she wanted.

Lost in delightful dreams of Charlotte's future, Lady Stanwood did not fail to note the departure of Mr. Brummell—without a word, let alone a dance, with any other young lady. She was so flown, indeed, as to convert Lord Stanwood's mild recollection of their own youth into an invitation to join the sets forming for the supper dance—much to his astonishment. "I was only saying you've no need of me, milady, and I'd be off to Brooks', but damme, why not a dance? I'll warrant none of 'em are as accomplished as yourself, Nelly. We'll make our own set and show the youngsters the way, eh?"

Thus it was that on the occasion ever afterwards known as "The Stanwood's Night," a set for the supper dance was composed of: Lord and Lady Stanwood, Miss Stanwood with the Duke of Imbrie, Lord and Lady Sefton, Sir Geoffrey Stanwood with Princess Esterhazy, Miss Emily with Sir Eustace Gayle, Lord and Lady Jersey.

Mrs. Drummond Burrell was not solicited to join.

Everything changed after that evening, and for all her professed disdain of Society, Sharlie admitted to herself it was very different when one was *in* it rather than a wallflower. To Emily, who had been the belle of the countryside for two years, a London triumph was new only in that here her beaux were of the *haut ton*. Otherwise, London was the same as Stanbury, merely more so.

For Charlotte, to be flattered and courted was breath-taking, although she was at a loss how to behave. "What do you do when a beau says your eyes are the color of sunlit sea-water and he drowns in them?" she asked Emily in bewilderment. "Or presses your hand with a languishing smile?"

Emily trilled with laughter. She loved Sharlie dearly, was awed by her mental superiority. From childhood custom, she always did what Sharlie told her to, but here Emily was on familiar ground. "Silly!" she said affectionately. "You look *up*—so . . . and you look *down*—so . . . and draw back with a blush, if you can manage it."

"It's getting easier," Sharlie remarked a bit grimly. "The thing is that I never was a belle, and agreeable as it is, a lot of it seems absurd. I can't believe high-flown words about my appearance when we both know I'm no beauty."

Emily eyed her sister with a curious little smile, "but you are. At least, Geoffrey was right: you're elegant, Sharlie. You have a way of walking, of holding your shoulders, of extending your hand. Imbrie says you have the only straight back in London and your curtsey is the essence of grace."

"Did he say so?" Sharlie's cheeks went pink with pleasure, for the duke's continued presence in town was most *promising*. He never failed to beg a dance with Emily, sent lavish nosegays upon all occasions, and had hosted a superb small gathering for supper at Vauxhall upon learning that she yearned to visit the Gardens. Sharlie did not depend upon an offer; a premier duke would not lightly drop his handkerchief, but if given the chance to observe, Sharlie felt her sister's beauty and sweetness would certainly win him.

That it was she who actually saw the most of his

grace escaped Charlotte entirely. As Lady Stanwood had prophesied, Sharlie was riding at least once, often twice a day. Every morning she went for a turn in the Park, until by now the exercise grooms cleared aside, grinning, to allow her a full gallop with John lolloping behind. It was tacitly understood that Sir Eustace was welcome to join her on these occasions, and he turned up so constantly that he was swiftly considered Miss Stanwood's preference. On closer acquaintance, she continued to find him delightful. His compliments were outrageously extravagant, but with an irresistible twinkle that invited her to laugh at him. Yet there was also an honest simplicity that was much to her taste, and they were soon on the easiest terms.

"Faith, and ye must have a groom, Miss Stanwood," he grinned wickedly. "Ye're far too pretty to be trusted to a wild Irishman who's all to pieces. I've not a feather to fly with, for there's no money at all, at all. My father'd a weakness for deep basset, and no head for it, poor man. When the apoplexy carried him off, all was found so encumbered that m'brother is hard pressed. My mother's her jointure, but there's five sisters to be married off with nothing for dowries."

Privately, Sharlie thought that if his looks ran in the family, there'd be no trouble in disposing of the girls, but she was deeply impressed by Sir Eustace's cheerful admission of poverty. "I've no brains, y'know. The best I can do is remove myself and leave Henry a free hand."

To Charlotte's rallying suggestion of a rich wife, he shook his head with decision. "I'll have no woman without something more than a portion to keep me in comfort. 'Tis not fair to a lass to wed where the heart cannot be given. Besides, I'd not sell out until we've finished Boney."

"Will we do it?"

"Devil a doubt of it! We've Wellington, y'know." The Army suited him excellently, he was half-minded to make a career of it, "for I've no expectations. Mr. Cleghorne, my godfather, is said to be plump in the pocket, but the most he ever did was to buy me a pair of colors five years ago." Sir Eustace laughed infectiously. "He's no opinion of me at all, at all. M'mother would have me visit him when I was coming to London, I think she's *hoping*—but it won't answer, I can tell that. Nothing pleased him, from the cut of my whiskers to my batman leading the luggage horse, and when I recounted our engagements . . . Talavera, Fuentes de Onoro, Albuera and Ciudad Rodrigo . . ." he chuckled, "Mr. Cleghorne was astounded."

"He said he couldn't believe Wellington was winning, when he had *me* on his side."

"What a—a wicked thing to say, when you might have been killed!"

"Oh, aye, but he had the gout, you know," Sir Eustace said good-humoredly. "When I came away, he sent the butler for his strong box and gave me fifty guineas. That was damned handsome, you know."

Charlotte thought it a paltry sum to one who was risking his life in keeping Bonaparte out of England, and when she imparted the story to Emily, her sister was even more indignant. "Gout or not, the man's an old curmudgeon!"

The morning gallops made Sir Eustace a cornerstone of what was coming to be known as the Stanwood Court. His initial lack of acquaintance was quickly remedied. A handsome young man who danced well and was well-connected, even if known to be penniless, nevertheless was an asset to any hostess. Captain Sir Eustace Gayle was rapidly on all invitation lists, but his loyalty to the Misses Stanwood was steadfast: he went where they went, and divided his attentions between the sisters most gracefully. Shortly, he was *persona grata* at No. 10 Park Street for conversation with anyone who was at home—it mattered not who. If the girls were out, he was happy to drink tea with Lady Stanwood . . . or walk companionably to a club with Lord Stanwood . . . or wait in the salon if any family members were shortly expected by Beamish.

He was, in fact, as much at home as Geoffrey and treated very similarly by staff and Stanwoods alike. All were disarmed by his frankness, for although offered entrée to Alfred's and the Cocoa Tree by his lordship, Sir Eustace smilingly confessed he could not afford the play and would only watch. Lady Stanwood was equally undermined by his delight in being asked to potluck, "for it is good to be within a family, not that Aunt Sophy—Mrs. Ixton—is not all that is kind, but there are no young people. It is only herself and her husband."

A second cornerstone was the Duke of Imbrie, although his status was still formal as befitted his title. Lady Stanwood would not have dreamed of asking his grace to stay for dinner on five minutes notice. Nevertheless, he was adopting habits of informality, of stopping unexpectedly to inquire if Miss Stanwood or Miss Emily cared for a turn about the Park—or he had an errand in Bond Street, did either of the young ladies wish to visit Hookham's lending library?

Since it was Emily who had a fondness for novels and who held firmly to her resolve not to ride but to promenade in a vehicle, Charlotte felt certain of the real object. She thought him a bit arrogant in not dispatching a note to ascertain Emily's freedom for an engagement—after all, they were only one street apart, and on several occasions he had but *just* missed Emily.

"What a pity you did not think to send word," she exclaimed, "for Emily has only gone to Lady Kilmartin's with mama. She might easily have excused herself, it is no more than a casual call before the Promenade."

The duke would not hear of sending John-groom post-haste to intercept Lady Stanwood's coach. "No, no, I am persuaded Miss Emily would find Richmond Park a dead bore in contrast to a comfortable coze with her friends—but you do not go with them, Miss Stanwood. You have another engagement?"

"No, I meant merely to ride until I encountered our coach and returned with them for tea."

"Ah? Then perhaps you would companion me instead? I purchased a pair of greys yesterday, and am anxious to try their paces."

Nothing was a greater inducement to Miss Stanwood! She sped upstairs, changed to a driving dress and was back almost before the duke had time to sit down. To one who was accustomed to the length of ladies' toilettes, such promptness was most engaging. Her appearance was equally engaging. A dress of leaf-green was completed by a close hat of matching straw that framed her smiling face and emphasized the green of her eyes. Gloves of lemon yellow kid and a frilled parasol with a very long handle were the finishing touch.

Handing her down the steps, his grace was amused by her comments on his horses and the high-perch phaeton. By the time he'd returned her to Park Street, he was even more amused.

"Do you go to Almack's tonight, milord?"

"If you will promise me all the waltzes."

"Who will you get to substitute when you are bored tonight, I wonder?" Sharlie chuckled faintly. "I must say you've set an impossibly high standard with Mr. Brummell."

"Not I, but the Beau. He insisted on the exchange —and you have never bored me, Miss Stanwood."

She colored and looked away in confusion. "You're bamming . . . I mean," she corrected hastily, "laughing at me, Duke."

"No, 'pon rep."

That Charlotte did not believe him was clear. She smiled politely and changed the subject. "We attended the service at the Chapel Royal on Sunday. Emily was presented to the Duke of Clarence, at his particular request," she announced proudly. "He stood talking to her for quite five minutes, and said she wore a vastly fetching hat; must be the despair of every woman in London!"

"Not of yourself, surely."

"No, of course not! Nothing could be more satisfying than her success. It makes up for EVERYTHING," Sharlie said darkly, and giggled. "I do not scruple to tell you, Duke, for you must well know it: last year I was totally ignored, a positive antidote. No one looked at me twice, except to make sure he could retreat at once. I had not the least notion how to go on, you see, but this year—I have only to watch Emily. It all comes so instinctively to her, as though she were born for exalted society. Her beauty, her accomplishments, her sweet manners, make her so uniformly pleasing as to confound my insipidity . . . plus," Charlotte laughed archly, "a great many crumbs fall to my share, such as today."

"I beg your pardon?" he said, startled.

"You are not the only gentleman who, upon failing to gain a dance, a drive, an adjoining chair to my sister, is sufficiently courteous to solicit me instead," she smiled, "but today I am very glad of it, despite your disappointment. Forgive me, but my sister becomes nervous in sporting carriages. She is not at ease with horses. It is entirely different in the country, where there is nothing to alarm them. At Stanbury she rides frequently, but the press of London traffic upsets her."

"I'd gathered as much, but it holds no terror for yourself?"

"Only when there is a snarl caused by a whipster. Then I am not so much frightened as *furious* at the beaux who set up their carriages with no ability to handle the ribbons; merely to be in the mode," she said scornfully, "and they endanger everyone else."

"Very true. Do you drive, Miss Stanwood?"

"No," she sighed. "Geoffrey—my brother—once promised to teach me, but he has been at Oxford, you know, and there was not the opportunity. Besides, papa said he could not afford to replace Geoff's curricle if I smashed it—which was *most* unjust," Sharlie's brow contracted, "for Geoffrey came to splinters himself over some foolish wager."

"I collect Lord Stanwood provided another?"

"Of course, but *then* he said Geoffrey wasn't fit to teach me, and probably he isn't. The F.H.C. won't have him," with a glance for the duke's blue and yellow striped waistcoat, "as I expect you may know."

"Well, no, I didn't, but I am not on the board of admissions," he said apologetically. "Should you like to drive, Miss Stanwood?"

"Of all things! But papa says there is no point in it as yet. It would mean an extra carriage and horses. Our London stabling is already crowded, but at Stanwood he is too often from home to take time for instruction."

The duke was undermined by her wistful expression.

"Would he accept me for your tutor, d'you think, Miss Stanwood?" The glowing face turned to him, the breathless reverential *"You!"* caused that faint quiver in his pulse. "Why not?" he smiled. "I doubt I'll need do more than assure myself your hands are firm. Never tell me you do not already know the placement of the reins, and which are the leaders, which the wheelers."

"Of course, but there is a wide difference between knowing and doing," she pointed out reasonably. "I've all to learn in proper management of the whip, for instance. Oh, would you *really?"*

Reining in before No. 10 Park Street, "Yes, Miss Stanwood, I really would," his grace smiled. "Next week? I'll send you word when I see how my engagements fall out, and hope you may be free at a similar time."

"How absurd you are!" Sharlie scoffed as he handed her down. "Your grace knows full well I'd excuse myself from any commitment except the Drawing Room presentation—but that does not arise until next month." She spared a tiny nod and smile for his groom before ascending to the front door, where she extended her hand with a sparkling flash of eyes. "It was so kind in you to take me with you today, I have not words to tell you how much I enjoyed it. Thank you."

"It is rather I who should thank you, Miss Stanwood." The duke bowed over her hand as Beamish swung open the door, "And mind you save the waltzes for me! Until tonight . . ."

CHAPTER V

IT COULD NOT EXACTLY be said that Mr. Brummell was a part of the Stanwood Court. Rather, he was its unobtrusive *deus ex machina.* Throughout the season he flicked the *ton* with an occasional admiring comment on Miss Stanwood's elegance of dress. "Her taste is unerring for the colors to suit her: green, purple, bronze-browns. Superb! One grows tired of the insipid pastels, too often they indicate an equal insipidity in the wearer." Her wealth of russet hair drew his approval also, as well as its simplicity of styling.

"What you really mean is that it has no styling," she told him mischievously.

Mr. Brummell laughed. "Perhaps I do, and a great relief it is to see a young lady as Nature made her, Miss Stanwood. I commend your wisdom, for in this instance, Nature has done a most superior job. You could not well improve upon it by the curling iron."

"No, I can't," she chuckled. "My hair has a will of its own, and no matter how it is cropped, feathered or pinned, it comes apart in mid-evening, until it is drooping despondently for all the world as though I had been retrieved from a storm by the kitchen cat!"

The Beau did not always solicit a dance, but he never failed to make his bow and exchange a few words with Miss Stanwood. While he was polite to Miss

Emily, his smile was so vague that one was not certain he recalled her name. Sharlie half-wished he might just once ask her to stand up with him, although Emily had no need of his public approval. She was still the Incomparable of Incomparables, with more beaux, bouquets and invitations than she could attend. It seemed she had no preference as yet, but distributed her favors evenly among all comers.

In time it occurred to Charlotte that the Beau was a good friend of the Duke of Imbrie. Whether he was aware of the duke's interest in Emily, or merely suspected, Sharlie thought the Beau's approval was intended to establish the duke's future sister-in-law. Upon meeting Mr. Brummell in the Row, when he abandoned his companions and turned to accompany her, Sharlie asked daringly, "Are you being so very obliging as to bring me into fashion, sir?"

"Surely, that would be unnecessary if not impossible," he returned urbanely. "You have made your own fashion, Miss Stanwood. I merely follow like the proverbial moth to be scorched in your flame."

"Oh, what a whisker!"

He smiled and inquired if she had enjoyed the Florida Gardens. "I saw you yesterday—with Imbrie, if I'm not mistaken."

"Yes, he is so kind as to undertake my driving instruction," she confided. "Is it not good of him? Papa gave me *such* a lecture on my good luck that I was in a terrible quake, but however, all passed off well enough for a first attempt."

"I don't doubt it. We shall soon be seeing you on the Promenade, dashing along in great style."

"No," she shook her head regretfully, "papa thinks me too young for my carriage this year, but that does not matter. First I must learn all I can, and ten to one the season would end before I felt confident. I will *not* be a whipster, there are too many already. The duke agrees, although he predicts I shall need very little beyond practice, which he promises I may have with his own teams."

"Ah? And which does he offer for your lessons?"

"The bays for the moment. They are easiest for a novice, but after one more lesson, I am to try the chestnuts . . . and when he thinks me ready, I *may* be allowed to drive the greys!" Miss Stanwood's eyes were awed. "Is it not kind of him?"

"Indeed it is. You must be exceptional, Miss Stanwood. Imbrie does not trust his cattle to other hands in general."

Lord Wrentham joined them at that moment. He was looking *determined,* and since all hope of more confidences was ended, the Beau gracefully excused himself to return to his friends. He was extraordinarily abstracted, however. There were those in London who called the Beau a callous egotistical upstart and roundly condemned his arrogant hot-and-cold here-and-thereianism, but when he chose, Mr. Brummell was a solid friend. He'd known Julian Voss since Eton days, liked Imbrie better and better each time they met as adults. He'd been sincerely sorry at the death of his wife, and wickedly amused at the efforts of matchmaking mamas on Julian's rare appearances in London. In common with Lady Inverclyde, he had never thought Imbrie would remarry.

"I wonder if I was wrong?" the Beau asked himself, and probed the question the next time he encountered Julian at Boodle's. "Hear you're teaching Miss Stanwood to drive. Is she an apt pupil?"

"Incredibly! Got two of the lightest hands I've ever seen," Julian said cordially. "I hear you've set the *ton* in a dither over her."

"Wasn't that what you wanted?"

"Yes. She had a thin time of it last season, poor girl—undeserved, I think. She's not the standard society miss, like the younger one, but it seems a pity for her to be so completely overshadowed. If you'd heard her, Beau—saying Emily's success makes up for every snub or humiliation," Julian laughed, "and she hasn't a notion that Miss Emily is a total vacuum!"

"Is she? That's certainly not true of Miss Stanwood."

"Lord, no, she's a positive refreshment, isn't she?" Julian chuckled. "You'll not let this go farther, Beau—on your honor?"

"On my honor," Brummell nodded, his eyes sharpening.

"Well, then—for some reason Miss Stanwood has decided that I am interested in her sister!"

"Good God!"

"Exactly—but only conceive the absurdity, Beau: everyone in London is trying to marry me, except Miss Stanwood. SHE is trying to marry me to her sister. Lord, I haven't had so much fun in years!"

"So that's it. I wondered why you were hanging about town for so deucedly long. Is the sister aware of this?"

"Not she! In fact, that's the cream of it, George. She's becomingly flattered to dance with me, it increases her consequence—not that she's at all above herself, she's as sweetly honest as Miss Stanwood—but, George, BUT she hasn't the wits of a flea. The platitudes, the bromides, the tired little society comments—she has them all; it passes belief, I assure you. I can tell she considers me the generation of Lord Stanwood, hasn't a notion of her sister's design, and to cap all," Julian's shoulders shook with mirth, "I strongly suspect the man she secretly favors is the least suitable of all her beaux!"

"Who?"

"You're on your honor, Beau," Julian reminded him warningly.

"I am," Brummell assured him. "It's your divertissement, I wouldn't dream of inserting a finger. Who's the dark horse?"

"Captain Sir Eustace Gayle."

Brummell's eyes widened. "Not old Barney's son? Lord, if he hadn't dropped dead, he'd have been sold up. But—a mere captain? There can't be any money, the Stanwoods won't hear of it."

"I doubt they will, in more ways than one. I shouldn't think he'd ever ask permission to address Miss Emily, he must know he'd instantly be forbidden the house. All the same, he's madly in love with her or I'm a Dutchman, and I'm certain she's far from indifferent."

"What a fascinating tangle it is," the Beau drawled lazily. "I must and will hear every detail, old boy. It's the price of my silence. I recall you had always the knack of getting involved in romantic adventures even at Eton."

"As for that, you were never behindhand. Who was it that convinced Mrs. Robinson her Clara should be allowed to marry the linen draper's assistant because it would mean cut rates for clothing?"

"Lord, if I hadn't forgot that—and it was how I squared my account before m'father came to hear of it," the Beau chuckled. "All the same, I fancy it was you who pointed out the parlay to me, Julian. In those days, I was an innocent. I could never have worked it out for myself."

"Hah! You've made up for lost time very rapidly."

"Naturally, with such an example as my guide," Brummell agreed blandly. "Details, if you please."

"I have none, it's only a sixth sense. Sir Eustace rescued Miss Emily when her horse bolted in the park. Aside from lack of fortune, he's perfectly acceptable anywhere: well-mannered, good birth, with the added dash of Peninsular service," Julian shrugged. "He runs tame in Park Street, rides with Miss Stanwood each morning, walks or drives with Miss Emily and her mother on the Promenade—but I notice, George. I notice that whoever goes short of a dance on Miss Emily's card, it is not Sir Eustace. It is most often Sir Eustace who sits beside her at a musicale or the theatre, who conducts her to supper. Somehow he is always *there,* to one side if not her engaged partner or escorting Miss Stanwood as a party of four.

"I'll admit I wouldn't have thought he'd the brains for it—he's a pleasant chap, but no indication of a furnished cockloft. However, he's as much at home in Park Street as a relative—all of which allows him to dance attendance on Miss Emily without comment!"

The Beau's lips twitched. "Lord, what a lovely mess of porridge! Doesn't Miss Stanwood realize?"

Julian shook his head, "If anything, she looks on him as her admirer, they share a passion for horses. No, I fancy she hasn't noticed."

In this he underestimated Sharlie. It was true that in the bewilderment of finding herself a Personage, her mind was occupied. Further, from never having thought of Sir Eustace as anything but a new friend, it did not immediately occur to Charlotte that another girl might view him differently. Lady Stanwood had indeed determined his lack of fortune, but was reassured by her daughter's blithe rejoinder, "Yes, isn't it a pity! It is why he's anxious for reassignment, in the hope of gaining his majority, you know. He can talk of little else."

On her side, Charlotte talked principally of Emily's success, and it was some time before she was aware that this topic stood next to Wellington in his interest. Once awakened, she was stunned by the portents, and being Charlotte, she inquired bluntly, "Eustace, are you in love with Emily?"

"I am that," he admitted. "Head over heels at first sight, you well know it."

"Does she?"

"For what d'ye take me?" he asked indignantly. "Not a word have I said, nor ever will. 'Tis every way impossible, I'm aware and ye needn't remind me, Sharlie. Sure, I'd not so disturb the little darling. She'll make a grand match to suit her, and I'll go back to Spain, that's all."

"You're disturbance enough just *being* here! I mightn't know someone was in love with me until it was spelled out, but Emily doesn't need words," Charlotte fretted. "Oh, dear, I wish you'd get your assignment, Eustace. You're dreadfully in the way."

" 'Tis only an occasional dance or a drive," he pleaded. "Ye'd not deny me the sight of her."

"No, I suppose not, but you're very *unsettling*. How can she fix her mind on a 'grand match' when she's looking at you, Eustace? I must tell you she was all but engaged, I'm in daily expectation of a formal offer to papa, and now . . ."

"Sure, I'll not interfere," he protested. "I'm only one of dozens dangling after the little sweetheart."

"Yes, but you're the handsomest," Sharlie said crossly. "Why is it that the larger the fortune, the uglier the face?"

It was not entirely true, she thought, when the Duke of Imbrie handed her into his phaeton that afternoon. In fact, she had grown so accustomed to the heavy flaring eyebrows and black-a-vised countenance that she no longer saw them. The black eyes were expressive, sometimes serious and sometimes twinkling, but always quick with intelligence. The deep voice ranged from sharp command to dulcet badinage that made her laugh, for she took his compliments no more seriously than Eustace's, and his smile was particularly sweet.

He was still no comparison to Eustace for looks, and Emily could not be blamed if she preferred Prince Charming. Lady Stanwood had no overweening ambitions for her daughters. Good birth, social acceptability, and some money there must be, but otherwise they were free to marry where they gave their hearts. All that troubled Sharlie was the fear that unsuitable Eustace might prevent Emily from recognizing the superiority of the duke.

It took his grace no more than five minutes to comprehend Miss Stanwood's involved discourse concerning her sister's future. "You are too apprehensive, I feel sure. Miss Emily is very young, let her enjoy her conquests," he said soothingly. "It will be time enough for her to make her choice next year. She may do even better with a second season, like yourself."

"The cases are not similar," Charlotte pointed out, annoyed by his obtuseness. "Emily couldn't possibly do any better than she is doing now, and if no one makes a push to fix her interest, a second season will turn her from an Incomparable into a Citadel who is rated too self-consequent—and you know she is not!"

The duke was hard put to restrain a guffaw, but he repeated his soothing prediction of a successful alliance for Miss Emily and changed the subject. "Here is a good stretch for practice. Do you care to take the ribbons, Miss Stanwood?"

"Oh, *yes,* thank you." For the best part of an hour, she tooled back and forth, obeying his instructions earnestly while the duke divided his attention between her progress and her pretty eagerness to learn. She was more than a refreshing change from convention. In her friendly spontaneity and unguarded remarks there was no hint of the vulgar or under-bred. Miss Stanwood was certainly young in years, but his grace sensed a lively mind anxious for stimulus. Upon several occasions she had lured him into descriptions of his travels, and all her questions showed an informed interest. In fact, Miss Stanwood—*Sharlie,* as he called her mentally—piqued the duke's curiosity. She was not blue, but somewhere she had gained more than the usual education for females. He thought that not the least part of the divertissement was his acquaintance with her.

"Last lesson for this week, I fear—I must go out to Bascombe for a few days," he said when they were returned to Park Street.

"That is your estate in Kent, is it not?" she observed, stepping lightly down from the phaeton.

"Yes. How came you to know of it?" he asked, surprised.

Charlotte was equally surprised. "You told me," she reminded him, "when I asked where you had found valley lilies for Emily's bouquet so early in the season."

"Why, so I did! Must I confess?" he smiled ruefully. "Cargill—my head gardener—is instructed to dispatch flowers daily during the season. I dislike the formal florists' arrangements."

"Yes, they are dreadfully stilted—but what very large greenhouses you must have to provide such a supply!"

"I believe they are, although it is some considerable time since I have inspected them. Now you put me in mind of it," the duke frowned thoughtfully, "I wonder if any of the plants I've brought from foreign parts have survived."

"What sort of plants?"

"Principally Oriental or from the tropics—there is something called the paw-paw, much used in the West Indies, and a number of orchids grown in Mexico." On impulse, "Should you like to see them, if any still live?"

"Very much!"

His grace had no more than a vague notion of sending a carriage for her, escorting her through the succession houses, and returning her to London after a light nuncheon. The vicar and his wife would provide propriety; they ought to be asked for a social visit, anyway. But to Julian's intense amusement, he found all arrangements taken out of his hands. In a matter of seconds, Miss Stanwood had converted his idle suggestion into a party composed of herself, Lady Stanwood and Emily. However little the duke might rate Miss Emily's interest in his greenhouses, Sharlie had no doubt that all was intended as a distinguishing attention to her sister.

"How delightfully it all comes about," she exclaimed. "I collect the drive is no more than an hour, we may easily reach you by one, which allows ample time before we must start for home. I am sure it will not be too tiring for Emily, and a day in the country—there is nothing to equal it. How kind it is in you to think of it!"

"Your pleasure is my pleasure, Miss Stanwood," he said gracefully. "All that remains is to discover if there is anything worthy of the trip to be seen in the conservatories."

Having thus provided himself with an escape, the duke went off the following day. He was half-minded to send word that nothing had survived, but it would have been a monumental lie, and even if Sharlie never learned, Julian couldn't bring himself to it. So far from dying, all his exotics were burgeoning riotously under Cargill's expert fingers. Sharlie would like to see them, and the devil with Miss Emily! On the other hand, caution raised its head. Nothing led him to suppose Lord or Lady Stanwood shared Charlotte's idea, yet might it not occur to them if the ladies were invited to view one of his grace's estates? Throughout his excellent dinner, plainly dressed in the country style, the duke pondered deeply.

The solution came to him with the strawberry tarts. Sharlie had saddled him with a party—he would expand it in such a way as to remove any notion of Miss Emily as principal guest. It may have been the brandy, but by the time Julian was seated at his desk to pen the invitations, he was feeling naughty! Lord Stanwood was specifically included in the note to Park Street, and it was suggested he accompany Miss Stanwood on their riding horses; should Sir Geoffrey be in town, he would be welcome to join the party. Lady Inverclyde was begged to be so kind as to take up Princess Esterhazy in her carriage, and Lady Jersey was asked to bring any escort she currently favored. Sir Eustace Gayle was requested to accompany Lady Stanwood and Miss Emily in their carriage, and a final note went to Mr. Brummell.

"Dear George—if you care to view my divertissement, pray ride out to Bascombe beside Miss Stanwood on Monday next. Yours, etc. Imbrie."

He then filled out his list with such of his neighbors as should be recognized by the Duke of Imbrie, begging them to bring their older children who might enjoy an *al fresco* picnic. When he laid aside his pen,

Julian felt pleased with himself. Miss Stanwood should see his succession houses; he would pay off all arrears of social duties, and Miss Emily would be lost in the crowd. He rang the bell, and had just affixed the last wafer when Stepan entered.

This was Julian's Figaro, except that he was Greek rather than Italian and a much more general factotum than Herr Mozart's. Initially the duke's English staff had viewed Stepan with shock, but after eight years they were used to his exotic appearance. He might look alarmingly wild, but it was observed that he served his grace with loving competence. Where Julian went, there also was Stepan. There was nothing he could not, or would not, do for his master, from cooking a stolen Portuguese chicken to renting a furnished villa for a month of dalliance in Sicily. After wandering about the world, he spoke a smattering of many languages, but alone with Julian, they used Greek.

"Ride up to London tomorrow morning, deliver these and ask immediate answers to Grosvenor Square," the duke said tersely. "Come back when you have them."

"Ne, ne," Stepan examined the directions. "There will be six."

"Take four bunches of flowers to leave with the ladies. Give these," extending the local notes, "to the stableboy for delivery any time tomorrow, and ask Mrs. Witchett to step in to me now."

"Ne, ne," Stepan said again. "A party? That is good, we have not had one in a long while."

So long a while that Mrs. Witchett was in a pelter to learn she must prepare a picnic luncheon for twenty or more guests on Monday. "There will be ladies and some young people—you will know what to prepare, and I will have the exact number tomorrow," Julian smiled. It did not occur to him there might be refusals. When Imbrie gave a party, nothing but death or a Royal command (considered by many to be synonymous) would keep anyone away. Having dispatched the invitations, Julian put it out of his mind; Stepan would do the rest.

But just as Sharlie had no notion of Julian's machinations with Beau Brummell, so the duke had no suspicion of his factotum's. The stabling for No. 10 Grosvenor Square adjoined that for No. 10 Park Street, and since John-groom was a Stanbury man long known to Maria, Stepan had glimpsed Miss Stanwood's maid early in the season. To his initial admiration of her fresh face was swiftly added a deep interest in her mistress. Stepan was well used to the duke's female companions, but in his experience they were never so young and unsophisticated. Nor had his grace ever allowed a woman to handle his blood-cattle, let alone offering instruction. Stepan had suffered a severe shock the first time his employer relinquished the ribbons, and made haste to ripen his acquaintance with Maria.

Thus when Stepan rode away from Bascombe, he had not four, but five bunches of flowers. After obeying the duke's instructions, he boldly presented himself at the rear door of Park Street and asked for Miss Stanwood's maid. By now, he was on calling terms, Mr. Robsey having assured Mr. Beamish that there was no harm in the duke's man. This was reinforced by Anatole, Lady Stanwood's chef, who wouldn't have cared whether Stepan was a rapist so long as he talked French.

"*Entrez, entrez,*" Anatole threw open the door genially. "*Alors, ça marche? Du café ou un petit verre? Ahé,* you bring flowers! It is a courtship?"

"One has one's hopes," Stepan shrugged. "In any

case, with my master's interest in this household, it is necessary that I should know the maid to the young ladies. I will have a *café noir, merci.*"

An hour later he left, possessed of all the current gossip of Park Street. Lord Wrentham was considered a certainty for Miss Stanwood; Viscount Pelham had a slight edge over the Earl of Dawlish for Miss Emily, but Beamish revealed a dark horse. "Mr. Bigglesworth—only a younger son, but I understand there is money and a considerable property from an uncle, which must compensate for the lack of title," the butler said austerely. "A very pleasant young gentleman, a recent entry to the lists but coming up fast!"

The Duke of Imbrie was thought to be principally a friend of Lord Stanwood, and valued only as adding consequence to the young ladies. Stepan blandly agreed that his grace was not one easily to drop the handkerchief—and was heartened by a swift side glance from Maria. Patently she agreed with Stepan's secret hunch—so much so, that as soon as he'd left, Maria took her flowers up to Charlotte's room. "From the duke, miss. That foreign man brought them."

"How sweet they smell," Sharlie breathed deeply. "Put them in Miss Emily's room, Maria."

"Stepan said they were for *Miss* Stanwood."

"Nonsense, he's confused the names. Of course they're for Miss Emily."

"I don't think so," Maria insisted. "I think perhaps they are some of the flowers you are going to see."

Sharlie took a closer look. "Perhaps you're right, Maria. I don't recognize those white blossoms. What a delicious scent!"

"Fair goes to your head, don't it, miss." Unobtrusively, she set the vase on a table. It was still there when Charlotte came up for an afternoon bonnet, but when she opened Emily's door, meaning to transfer the flowers, that room was so full of nosegays another vase would be too much. She returned it to her own chamber; Emily would never miss it, and the perfume was irresistible. It quite made up for the faint disappointment of learning that others had been asked to Bascombe, although as the guests were identified, Sharlie could not entirely understand what the duke was about.

Lady Inverclyde and Princess Esterhazy were welcome additions; Lady Jersey was less so, for having chosen Viscount Pelham as her escort, and the discovery that Sir Eustace was to accompany Lady Stanwood was a decided facer. "Surely, you cannot accept? It would not be in your power to be absent from the War Office."

"Faith, and they'd be glad not to see me for a day," he returned cheerfully. "I've naught to do but run errands. 'Tis sick of my face they are."

Charlotte debated refusing to ride, saying she preferred to go by carriage, which would leave no place for Eustace, and for two days Fate played into her hands: Lord Stanwood regretted he was engaged. "Damned if I want to ride fifteen miles in order to look at some dashed flowers, Nelly . . . don't know why you do."

"Sharlie has rather set her heart on it," his wife answered placidly. "You know her interest in conservatories, Robert, and it appears Imbrie has a number of exotic plants. I don't doubt she'll cajole the gardener into giving her seeds and cuttings for MacLean."

"Probably, but it's not the outing I fancy. Take the girls and make my excuses, Nelly."

Lacking her father as escort, Charlotte must go in the carriage, and let Eustace ride if he insisted on coming —but her sigh of relief was frustrated by a polite note from Mr. Brummell.

No more than Miss Stanwood did the Beau know

what Julian would be about, but the implication was that she was wanted at all costs, and on horseback. "Hmmm," said Brummell to himself, and lazily excused himself to the Prince Regent for Monday. "Imbrie, you know, sir—we were at Eton together—and there's nothing so fascinating on the Calendar, after all. Why don't you do some work for a change—sign some laws or receive some deputations or something? I shall be back in ample time for whatever's afoot for the evening, sir. You'll not miss me."

His Highness pouted slightly, but reluctantly conceded (under the Beau's expert cajolery) that there were indeed tasks that could not be shared by his friend George. Yes, he might as well get them out of the way, Monday was as good a day as any other, and he applauded George's loyal friendship for an old schoolmate. Accordingly, Miss Stanwood was neatly trapped—for Mr. Brummell cleverly dispatched his note to *Lady* Stanwood, who instantly wrote back that she could answer for her daughter's pleasure in Mr. Brummell's company upon this occasion.

Informed of the arrangement, Charlotte was moved to heated protest. "Mama, you did not! Oh, how could you?"

"Why should I not?" Lady Stanwood raised her eyebrows in astonishment. "If you have taken Mr. Brummell in aversion you should have told me."

"No, no, of course I haven't. He's quite delightful and one cannot wonder the Regent makes a pet of him," Sharlie returned impatiently, "but mama, if I ride to Basçombe, it leaves a place in the carriage for Eustace."

"What of it? Don't tell me you'd rather drive than ride? I think it very pretty in Imbrie to arrange an escort. He must have guessed your father would fail."

"You don't understand, mama," Sharlie said desperately. "Eustace is in love with Emily."

That did give Lady Stanwood pause. "I thought he was *your* beau, riding every morning," she exclaimed. "Are you *sure?*"

"I'm sure. He won't say anything to her, he knows he's ineligible." Sharlie repeated the conversation, ending, "Don't you see, Mama? Imbrie is trying to fix his interest with Emily. Why else are we asked to Bascombe? And she likes him, Mama, but because he's too mature to be dangling, I don't think she realizes her chance, and he isn't apt to make a push without some encouragement. If only we'd not made Eustace into a family friend!"

Lady Stanwood reflected briefly. Her reading of the situation with Imbrie was quite different from her daughter's. In fact, Sharlie would have been astounded to learn that her mother nursed a growing suspicion that Imbrie's real interest was in *Miss* Stanwood. Since Lady Stanwood was as shrewd as she could hold together, she was playing her cards extremely close to the chest. A very shy bird was the Duke of Imbrie, and she wanted him for Charlotte, but in the suppressed excitement of watching Sharlie, Lady Stanwood had taken her eye from Emily. Charlotte's revelation was a distinct jolt.

"Yes, I must agree," Lady Stanwood said slowly, "but for his sake rather than Emily. I thought him a pleasant riding companion for you. Your father finds him conversable, we know him to be lonely with his relatives. Mrs. Ixton is deeply grateful that he has some young society—but I am sorry for it. It was not kind to be exposing him to the unattainable."

"It's even less kind to expose Emily."

Here Lady Stanwood differed. "Do not be matchmaking, Charlotte. It never answers," she warned, "and often addles a hatching egg. If his grace has an interest, nothing could more certainly delay his declaration than a suspicion that it is expected . . . and if Emily's heart is touched by anyone at the moment, it is more than I engage for, I assure you! You may safely leave Emily's matrimonial future in the hands of her parents."

Sharlie winced and hung her head—exaggeratedly. "Oh, WHAT a set-down," she mourned. "What a complete hand you are, mama!"

"That," said Lady Stanwood austerely, "is a whisker!"

Nevertheless she was perturbed, and the outing at Bascombe increased her alarm.

The Duke of Imbrie's guests left London at ten in the morning by Lady Inverclyde's dictate. "I've no mind to drive out, turn around and drive back," she stated. "*I* will start at ten, and if there's anyone too finicking to eat her breakfast at nine-thirty, she'll find herself left at the post."

It was a goodly company that set forth on Monday with her ladyship's postillion blowing up for the toll at Reisgate before the turn to the Sevenoaks road. With little traffic to interfere at such an hour, the coaches moved along at a spanking pace and were entering the grounds of Bascombe by half after eleven. Sharlie looked about eagerly, admiring the stately elms lining the curved drive and exclaiming at the glimpses of flowers and rolling park land. A stream meandered through an oak woods in the most natural manner possible, with a wide shady walk following along beyond mossy banks. "How lovely it is!"

"Yes, I consider this the most charming of Imbrie's

properties. Rickaby is too far out of the way, and Calydon Towers," Mr. Brummell shuddered delicately, "there can be no more uncomfortable pile in all England! Scotland, perhaps—but nowhere in England."

"Of course—I had forgot, but you must often have been coming here."

"In college days," the Beau nodded, "but it must be quite seven years since I've seen the place. It is not vast, Miss Stanwood. What one sees is nearly all there is; the rest is farmland, although I believe that is fairly extensive. The house is comfortable, but too small for permanent residence. You will get the full view when we top this rise, if I remember correctly. Yes," reining in while the carriages were making their way forward, "now you have a perspective."

From their position, the building was seen to be snugly placed in a slight dip, surrounded by modest lawns and somewhat confined by the nearness of the stream. It was of Tudor design, well hung with ivy that was trimmed away from the windows, and Charlotte judged there could not be more than ten chambers, if so many. They would be disastrously low-ceilinged, too. "What a pity," she said regretfully. "It is quite charming, and so conveniently placed with respect to London, but to remodel or enlarge would be a monumental task. All the stables and succession houses would have to be moved, and there is the question of whether that would even be possible because of the rocky outcrops."

"The stream prevents expansion to the side, too, and an attempt to divert into a new channel is not like to succeed. Water is stubbornly determined to go where it will, particularly here. As you see, it runs extremely free; it probably rises in higher ground. Yet it would be a pity to dam it entirely, for the stream is quite half the beauty of the place. Do you not agree?"

"Absolutely." Mr. Brummell eyed her inscrutably. "You speak very authoritatively. I collect you are well versed in country matters?"

Charlotte colored faintly. "Must I confess? My father entrusts most of the small estate details to me. It relieves the bailiff of petty problems, and I enjoy it. I fear I am a milkmaid at heart, Mr. Brummell," she said valiantly, "and you are at liberty to despise me."

"On the contrary, I applaud your competence," he returned gravely. "I wish I shared it, for the proper management of land is always praiseworthy. Unfortunately, the opportunity has not come in my way. You see, I have no estates." He rose slightly in his stirrups and gestured with his crop. "Our host is waiting to welcome us, looking anxious."

Julian was indeed anxious when he'd bowed formally over the feminine hands extended by one after another of his guests, and turned them over to Mrs. Witchett for removal of cloaks and bonnets, while the carriages drew away to the stableyard. By the time Lady Stanwood was descending, his grace merely sketched his bow before asking, "Miss Stanwood is not with your ladyship?"

"She chose to ride with Mr. Brummell. I fancy they may have stopped to admire the prospect," Lady Stanwood said with outward placidity and inward glee. *Hah, I was right: it's Sharlie he wants.* She was confirmed by the duke's quick glance to the road, the untensing of his shoulders at Mr. Brummell's wave. He certainly smiled as he bent over Emily's hand, but nothing indicated more than kindliness. His grace was entirely willing to relinquish her to Eustace and Viscount Pelham, who had flagrantly abandoned Lady Jersey in favor of hastening to Miss Emily's other elbow. She was looking quite distractingly pretty, too, in a flowered muslin the color of wild hedge roses—but the duke's eyes were turned to Sharlie, cantering forward with the Beau beside her.

For Julian, the day began at that moment. The demands of a good host made it impossible to stay for long at her side, but as he moved around among his guests he was conscious of contentment. However ill-assorted they might have seemed at the outset, the company blended swiftly with the local families. The older ladies were comfortably established beneath shady trees; their husbands paid ponderous compliments to Lady Jersey, who flirted outrageously with all of them, and after five minutes of shyness, Miss Emily was absorbed into the schoolroom group, "where she belongs," his grace said to himself amusedly, noting the bewilderment of Eustace and the Viscount.

"All the same, I never liked her so well as today," he told the Beau privately. "You see? She's an Incomparable, she's two attentive beaux from London beside the eagle eye of Mr. Brummell—but does she care what you might say to the *ton?* Not a fig!"

"Neither does her sister," but the duke had turned away to Princess Esterhazy without hearing, and the Beau continued to stroll from group to group with lazy politeness. It was far removed from his usual taste in social gatherings: bucolic squires and florid-faced knights, over-plump wives and adolescents in all the agony of ill-tied cravats. There was even—good God!—the vicar and his helpmeet, but Mr. Brummell found more interest in Julian's "divertissement" than anticipated.

He was not the only one to observe how frequently his grace had a smile or a word for Miss Stanwood.

Julian's unobtrusive but expert removal of Sharlie while the guests were engaged with digestion of Mrs. Witchett's monumental luncheon was not lost on Lady Inverclyde. "Where's he takin' Sharlie?" she demanded abruptly.

"To the greenhouses, I fancy. I collect there are exotic plants from his travels which he promised to show her," Lady Stanwood returned composedly.

Lady Inverclyde watched their disappearance into the conservatories in silence. "Hmmm, she's a good girl. I like her. Think she'll get him?"

There was never any use in feinting with Lady Inverclyde. "I've no idea, although I believe it to be not in her mind," Lady Stanwood looked squarely at the old lady, "and I beg you will not suggest it to her, Flora."

Lady Inverclyde stared a bit haughtily, and suddenly cackled. "Lud, I'd not stir the omelet, Nelly. You know me better." Her face became reflective. "It'd be a good thing, Nelly," she said after a few minutes. "There's sound blood in you and Robert, she's got a respectable dowry—not that Imbrie lacks money. It's time he stopped wandering. Yes," with a decided nod, "I hope you pull it off."

"I am not trying."

"Let nature take its course?"

"Yes."

"Hmph! What'll you do with the other one? I suppose you've had offers?"

"Nothing of consequence," Lady Stanwood shrugged. "Robert considers her too young to settle this season, unless she should show a decided preference. So far she has not."

"She never will, she's a pea-goose, Nelly. Get rid of her as soon as you can," Lady Inverclyde stated.

"Sharlie, now—if Imbrie don't come up to scratch, she'll hold for another year or two, and be twice as well worth a major title. She's young enough to gamble on how she matures. I suppose she's shown no preference?"

Lady Stanwood shook her head. "I sometimes think, with only a twelvemonth between her and Geoffrey—that is, they were more close than the others. It causes her to treat young men . . . not that Charlotte ever passes the bounds of propriety," she inserted hastily.

"No, but she ain't coquettish, either, Nelly. Well, I won't say that mightn't be the very thing to catch Imbrie."

His grace was not thinking quite so analytically in the tour of the conservatories, but he did find it rewarding. Miss Stanwood lost no time in getting on terms with Cargill. Before the duke's incredulous eyes, she had twined the dour Scot around her finger and was briskly discussing the merits of chicken versus cow droppings for plant feeding! This was a completely new and different Miss Stanwood from any Julian had hitherto encountered. Wandering through his succession houses in Sharlie's wake, Julian thought that *if* he were not so content with bachelordom, he might be in danger of succumbing to her pretty spontaneity.

She had forgotten him entirely, he thought with wry amusement. He was merely the owner of these superb greenhouses, with a gardener from whom she could learn. Occasionally she threw a comment over her shoulder, as one might toss a titbit to a pet . . . but each attested her memory, her interest in what he'd told of his travels. "Are these the orchids from Mexico or from Brazil, Duke?" or "The red blossoms—are they the jasmine or the hibiscus?" It was very disarming, but began to be tiresome. Apparently Sharlie meant to examine each individual plant in all four of the houses, and the duke owed attention to his other guests. "If you would excuse me, Miss Stanwood? You're in expert hands with Cargill, and I should see that all is well with the rest of the party."

"Yes, of course," she said absently. "You must not be lingering here. I am persuaded you are bored already, and Cargill can tell me all I want to know."

"I am sure he can—and will." Julian's lips twitched at her dismissal. "Cargill, you will give Miss Stanwood whatever she fancies, and perhaps," he added courteously, "when you have completed this inspection, you may like to ride a short way along the fields and pasturage? I will return in a while."

"That would be delightful," her voice was still absent. "What is that odd purple-leaved plant on the farther bench, Cargill?"

Sic transit opulens, Julian said to himself as he closed the conservatory door. He was torn between faint annoyance to be so expendable to Miss Stanwood—any other young lady would have been flattered and fluttered to be personally escorted by Imbrie—and an amused admiration for her single-mindedness. Striding back to the lawn, he encountered the Beau.

"Why the heavy frown? Don't tell me you've received a set-down?"

"No, no, for I didn't ask anything," Julian replied impatiently. "Merely—oh, devil take it," he snorted ruefully, "I did! Miss Stanwood prefers my gardener, if you please, and is not at all heart-thumped to be asked to ride out for a view of the pasturage."

"Oh, a decided leveller!" Brummell drawled. "Well, it is a successful outing, Julian. Everybody likes everybody else. The children have gone down the lane in search of wild strawberries and daisies. Sally and the

Princess are ruralizing with your local bucks on the paths beside the stream, the other ladies are gossiping comfortably on the woodland benches, and Lady Inverclyde is enjoying a cat nap with her odious pug snoring in the grass at her feet."

"We won't disturb her." Julian led the Beau on a circuitous route to reach the bridge across the stream. After a half hour of courtesies, he thought Sharlie must have exhausted the possibilities of the greenhouses, and turned back. "George, will you come with us?"

"Good God, no! And for the Lord's sake, don't overtire her horse. We've still to get back to London."

"I'll mount her on one of mine."

He had timed it perfectly, Sharlie was just taking leave of Cargill and turned to Julian with sparkling eyes. "Have I teased you by delay? But it was so delightful, I could not bear to cut short. Besides, now I shall appreciate a ride the more for being able to observe Cargill's new strain of wheat—and I hope you will not mind?" she looked at him hopefully, "but Cargill means to send us some for a trial. We are not certain it will do as well at Stanbury because of the different climate, but MacLean will like to experiment."

"Of course you may have it," Julian smiled. "I see you have completely conquered Cargill, which is no mean achievement."

"I'm fully sensible," she laughed, "but there is a peculiar fraternity among *gardeners,* as opposed to competitors. I daresay he would not mention his wheat to MacLean, nor give him so much as a mignonette seed, but when he saw I was knowledgeable, all was different . . . and if Cargill's wheat survives in Northhamptonshire, he will be odiously above himself, I promise you!"

"I shall take care to depress his pretensions," Julian

assured her. "There is obviously more to horticulture than I realized. Oh," as she paused in surprise at the saddled horses, "you will not object to ride one of my country hacks? I think we should not weary Moonshine before your return to town."

"Of course not. What a beauty he is," Sharlie stroked the soft brown nose and murmured approvingly. "What is his name?"

"Pacifico. He was used to be a hunter, but now he is too old for a full run. You'll find him as placid as his name."

With a final pat, Sharlie came back to set her foot in Julian's hand and be tossed up to the saddle. The horse snorted and sidled, tossing his head while she gathered the reins and leaned to pat his neck. "Yes, you're a fine fellow—indeed you are!"

She continued to be entirely natural as they ambled along the farm road. Nothing escaped her observation, she was unhesitant in asking questions and frank in her comments on Julian's property. Miss Stanwood in London was a superb dancer, always becomingly robed and correctly behaved. Miss Stanwood in the country was at home, and unafraid of anything. "Where had you that saddle, Duke? It seems a very unusual design."

"It is a type much used in South America, by the stock men called gauchos. There is a considerable concentration on cattle and animal husbandry in general. The herds are very large, roaming over the plains for forage, and the gauchos accompany them for protection against predators."

It was a subject to interest Sharlie; she had a dozen questions on the cattle strains, their specific superiorities and disadvantages, how large were the herds and how many men were needed. Since Julian was equally absorbed by the South American methods, he readily answered and explained—but when they had gained a small rise for a sight of his cattle, it occurred to him (with a faint shock) that once mounted on his hobby, he had been talking to Miss Stanwood as freely as to a man!

"There they are," Julian gestured to the cows grazing in the farther field, "and those great black fellows are my 'criollos' from the Argentine," he pointed to the right. "My herdsman has been crossing them systematically with every English breed, but it is too soon to tell which may produce the best beast."

As he spoke, the two bulls suddenly raised their heads alertly, gazing to the end of the field that was hidden by a stand of trees. One of the bulls seemed uninterested and returned to nibbling grass. The other was more curious. He sauntered forward at leisure, until he could get a good look, and apparently what he saw was disturbing. Slowly at first, then with increasing urgency the bull went from a pace to a trot, and with an exclamation the duke was cantering down the lane. Pacifico moved automatically to follow, and as Sharlie in her turn rounded the curve for a complete view, she was horrified.

Unaware of the field's tenants beyond the rise, Emily was innocently picking hedge flowers along the inner side of the lane. Eustace was precariously poised on a fence rail, reaching for a spray of roses, and they were both an appreciable distance from the gate standing half-open.

"Good God!" Sharlie applied her crop vigorously. "Pacifico, you were a hunter, there must be some *go* left in you."

There was, but not much. Useless to scream, her voice would never carry so far and too much agitation would only increase the danger. The bull was not yet at the gallop, he was principally curious and might still be calmed. Far ahead of her, Sharlie could see the duke thundering along on his black horse. Stablehands, alerted by the noise of the hooves, were running out to peer in bewilderment . . . shrinking back as Pacifico approached, and surging out to follow when he'd passed. By now there were warning cries from the young people straggling along the lane. "Emily—the bull, the bull! Come out quickly!"

Several of the older boys vaulted into the field and tried to assist her in climbing over the fence, but in her terror, Emily was unable. Instead she tried to run for the gate and promptly tripped on the uneven ground. Eustace had leapt down from his rose-gathering, and was shouting indistinguishably to the would-be helpers, while he tore off his coat and ran forward, waving it in an effort to distract the animal . . . but it was the Duke of Imbrie who held Sharlie's eyes.

In one fluid spring, his horse was into the field and the coiled ropes that had looped from the foreign saddle were in his hand. They were suddenly elongated, whirling and flying through the air in a circle that settled over the bull's head. It stayed the beast's rush, but failed to halt him; he staggered, went to his knees and was up with a roar, to turn on the duke. Sobbing under her breath, Sharlie pounded down the lane until she reached the fence corner where Stepan was sitting, another coiled rope dangling from his fingers. "Oh, can't you DO something?" she cried wildly. "He'll be killed!"

"Not milor'," the man said positively, without removing his eyes from the scene. "I have the rope if he needs, but you will see . . ."

Unconsciously, she'd brought Pacifico to a stand.

Below, at the field gate, all was confusion; Sharlie scarcely saw Eustace lifting Emily into his arms and bearing her to the lane. Her eyes were only for the man on the black horse, turning and twisting, always moving the bull away. "See? *Magnifico,* yes?" Stepan murmured softly. "He tire the bull because the horse move faster. Many time I have see him do this, Mees. When is safe, he come out. You will see."

"But if the bull should charge?"

"It do not catch the horse. That is Ajax, who is used . . . He is from the Argentine, Mees. See how he enjoy to sport with bull? That Ajax is one fine horse, he take care of milor' like myself. We know is no finer master in world."

"I'm sure," Sharlie said mechanically. She'd thought Eustace's rescue of Emily in the park was excellent horsemanship; it was nothing compared to Imbrie. Reassured by Stepan's confidence, her breathing steadied, her heart stopped pounding, and she could revel in the duke's expertise. Time and again he pulled Ajax into rearing on a turn that avoided the bull's horns, until at last the animal was on its side. Then, before it could struggle erect, he abandoned the rope and gracefully leaped the fence into the farther field.

"So. He does not need me." Stepan slid from his seat on the fence and bowed to Sharlie with a flash of white teeth. *"Au revoir,* Ma'amselle."

"Au revoir, à tout à l'heure," she said absently, setting Pacifico forward and missing the gleam in the servant's black eyes.

The duke's guests were in turmoil. Alarmed by the shouts of the young people and the commotion of attempting to get Emily out of the field, the older people had hastened back to the house and came pouring over the sward exactly as Eustace was tenderly bearing Emily across the bridge. "Good God, what has happened? Oh, Lord—not dead, is she? Tom, make haste to the doctor." The chorus of faint screams, shocked outcries, threatened swoons by Princess Esterhazy and the vicar's wife, awakened Lady Inverclyde, who demanded, "Merciful heavens, what's to do?" The pug sat up and barked vociferously, while Lady Stanwood thrust through the crowd with a ruthless maternal hand.

"Eustace?" she asked fearfully.

"No, no, milady—all's safe enough," he reassured her. " 'Tis only fright, not a swoon. Let me place her in this chair—if ye'd stand away, please? There, now—open your pretty eyes, macushla, the way your mama'll know ye're all right." Obediently Emily's lashes fluttered upward. "Ye'll try for a smile to convince everyone," he crooned coaxingly. Emily's lips quivered, her eyes filled with tears, but she managed the smile—directly to Eustace. She then burst into strong sobs, and wailed, "Oh, mama . . . mama . . ."

"Yes, my love." Lady Stanwood dragged the vinaigrette from her reticule and directed it at Emily's nose. "Compose yourself, darling. Shhhh, it's all over."

Lady Inverclyde shook herself erect and straightened her cap. "WHAT is over? Be *quiet,* Cupidon," she cuffed the pug militantly. "Emily's makin' enough noise, you needn't help her."

The company had withdrawn into small groups, where the younger people were informing everyone of the circumstances which—since Emily was seen to be unharmed—were now productive of most enjoyable shudders. Eustace still knelt on one knee, alternately soothing her and rapidly explaining.

"Faith, no one told us of cattle, much less a bull! We'd been gathering flowers along the lane, and Emily saw some prizes beyond the rails, so we made bold to enter. We only saw the animal when the others called for us to leave. 'Twas too much for Emily to climb over the fence, she tried to reach the gate and tripped. By then, Imbrie was into the field on his horse, and engaging the beast while we lifted Emily and brought her out."

Sharlie was in time to hear this, having abandoned Pacifico in the stableyard and run around the drive to the lawn. In her relief at finding her sister undamaged, she had her mouth open to deliver a scold, but simultaneously the duke strode over the stream bridge and came direct to Emily. His face showed his exertions in disarranged hair clinging damply to his forehead. He was breathing heavily, and his expression was anguished anxiety as he bent over her. "My dear Miss Emily, are you all right? Lady Stanwood, I would not have had this occur for the world! But what has been done for her comfort?" His grace possessed himself of Emily's hand, softly stroking it and murmuring solicitously, "My poor girl! Gayle, desire Mrs. Witchett to give you a cordial and prepare tea as quickly as may be."

Under such soothing ministrations, Emily's sobs died away to a series of tiny gulps and she made a strong effort for composure. The duke produced a handkerchief and gently mopped her tears. "Ah, that's better!" Emily gave him a watery smile and tried to sit up—then she sank back with a faint moan.

"My foot—oh, my foot!"

His grace hastily released her hand and knelt down. "Lady Stanwood, with your permission . . ." but when he'd exposed Emily's thin kid half-boot, it was seen to be tight about her ankle. "This must be cut off at once. Stepan?"

"Yes, milor'?"

"A razor, please." When the servant brought it, "I'm sorry, I know it will hurt badly, but try to be brave." Emily gritted her teeth and clung to Sharlie's hand with closed eyes from which tears trickled silently down her white cheeks. He was incredibly deft, the shoe was freed in a matter of seconds, or so it seemed, and Emily relaxed briefly. "I fancy it is merely a sprain," his fingers probed delicately while Emily suppressed a groan. "Yes, there is no break, but it is badly swollen and should be bandaged. Lady Stanwood, shall I summon the doctor or will you trust to me? The stocking must be cut away."

"Then cut it away," Lady Inverclyde commanded testily, leaning forward to peer at the ankle. "This is no time for missishness. The girl's in pain, and no knowing how long before the doctor can arrive. Give her the cordial for courage, strap it up, and she can have it looked at in London if need be—although Imbrie and that rascally man of his are as competent as Halford, Nelly."

"Please do whatever you can, Duke," Lady Stanwood agreed.

Sharlie was scarcely aware of Emily's painful grip on her hand as she watched the duke swiftly slitting the rose-colored silk of Emily's stocking, drawing away the foot section to reveal flesh already puffed and livid. She was only half-aware of Stepan, squatting beside his master with a basin of warm water, a sponge, a bottle of some evil-smelling dark fluid, a roll of lint—handing them in silent progression to the duke. Vaguely, it occurred to her that Imbrie had given no instructions; Stepan had instantly been at hand with what was needed, knew what to extend when the duke waggled his fingers, and already Emily was easier, sighing with relief.

At last Imbrie sat back and smiled at his patient. "How very brave you were. Now you shall sit quietly and drink the tea Mrs. Witchett is bringing, and we shall contrive a footrest for the carriage," and if, to Lady Stanwood's ears, the duke's voice was that of an affectionate uncle, Sharlie had no fault to find. Almost, she could forgive Emily for her stupidity in opening a *closed* field gate—which anyone reared in the country must *know* indicated animals, whether or not they could be seen.

Emily had regained her color a little, and was beginning to smile and shyly utter thanks combined with abject apologies for thoughtlessness, "for I would not have overset the bull for anything. Sharlie will ring a peal over me for it and say I am well-served to have sprained my ankle."

"No, no, I am sure she will not. She will be far too happy there is nothing worse than a fortnight's discomfort for you," he smiled into her eyes, patted her hand and moved aside for Stepan to set a footstool beneath the bandaged ankle. "Ah, here is the tea." His grace stood up, adjusting his coat sleeves and said to Stepan in Greek, "Saddle Athena; I will ride to London with them."

"No, no, I beg you will not disturb yourself, Duke. There is not the least need," Sharlie protested absently. Occupied in settling her mother in a chair, she was unconscious of the startled flick of glances between the duke and his servant. Miss Stanwood comprehended *Greek?*

"French, also," Stepan remarked five minutes later, innocently staring into space as he helped the duke exchange sweaty shirt and coat for fresh clothing. "Do you still wish Athena, milor'?"

"Have her readied, we will see what Lady Stanwood desires."

It was not on his agenda to ride up to London tonight, with a return tomorrow that would delay his plans for the day, but when Lady Stanwood firmly refused any escort, he was conscious of frustration. He did insist upon accompanying his guests as far as the turn into the London turnpike, but by then he'd realized there was no point to continue. With Brummell riding beside Miss Stanwood, the conversation was necessarily impersonal. Julian made his most graceful farewells to each carriage—ignoring the Beau's bland assurance that he would protect Miss Stanwood with his life, "which is a very safe risk, for I have not lately learned of any lions or tigers in this vicinity."

Equally he turned aside Lady Inverclyde's comments on his Party. "Very pleasing, happy to see Bascombe again. I liked that vicar's wife. She knows what needs doin'—very sound woman! Give her the money for it, Imbrie, and my compliments to your cook for the *pigeons en gelée*. Don't doubt I'll suffer for 'em, but not her fault," her ladyship stated. "All the upsetment of that ninnyhammer, Emily—Incomparable she may be, but in MY day we'd have called her *shtupid.*"

"Fashions change," Julian murmured apologetically, but Lady Inverclyde merely snorted, eyeing him up and down.

"Not for you," she said with finality. "Well, invite me again when you've a hostess to welcome me."

"Not," said his grace irrepressibly, "if you insist on bringing that odious pug, Cupidon—and a more unsuitable name I never heard."

Lady Inverclyde had the last word—as always. "Cupidon is twelve years old, and at the rate you're goin', he'll be *dead* before my next invitation." She poked the coachman with her cane. "Go ON, Thompson, or we'll never reach London in daylight."

Chuckling to himself, Julian rode back to Bascombe at an easy pace, but the house seemed strangely empty after the cheerful babble preceding Emily's mishap. He threw off the formal country clothing, impatiently shrugged into rough coat and long gaiters with a dark concentration that Stepan knew better than to interrupt. "I'll be out in the fields. Tell them to set dinner back to seven."

"Ne, ne," Stepan bowed, but observing the duke's stride and his walking crop slashing at the hedge weeds along the path, Stepan was uneasy. Which Miss Stanwood was his grace's objective?

CHAPTER VI

EMILY'S ACCIDENT altered everything, and Lady Stanwood could not be blamed for feeling seriously annoyed with her Incomparable. Although Sir Henry Halford majestically approved the duke's bandaging, and a night's repose induced by his soothing draught restored Emily's sunniness, it would certainly be some time before she could venture to walk more than a few paces. Dancing was entirely out of the question, as was her presentation at Court, and the season was drawing to a close. Sharlie was for cancelling all engagements, but this her mother flatly refused to permit.

"Emily suffers nothing beyond mild discomfort, which is entirely her own fault, for nothing could be more idiotish than to be entering unfamiliar fields, not to mention oversetting Imbrie's party. I vow I am afflicted by some wicked christening fairy! Last year *you* contracted mumps, not that you could help yourself, but it ruined all—and *this* year Emily contrives an end to her reign as a Belle by sheer silliness."

"It seems so—so unfeeling to leave her at home while we enjoy ourselves."

"Save your sympathy," Lady Stanwood advised tartly. "Emily is very well entertained, I assure you. Every Tulip, Pink of the Ton, and Nonpareil infests my salon. It is so thronged I can scarce find a chair for myself. I shall be glad when she can wear a shoe again. Then she can accompany us—and sit on the sidelines to be admired."

Lady Stanwood had a deeper reason for desiring Emily to be ambulatory. She was, in fact, quite distracted by the situation. On the one hand, nothing could be more dangerous than Eustace, who arrived as soon as his duties at the Horse Guards were finished—and who *stayed.* Viscount Pelham, Lord Dawlish, Mr. Bigglesworth and others called frequently, sent floral tributes, or stopped en route to some mandatory engagement, but Eustace was simply *there.* Her ladyship half thought of returning Emily to Stanwood Hall for these final weeks, but Charlotte protested vehemently, and Algy Whipsnade was more of a threat than Eustace.

On the other hand, Lady Stanwood was determined that Sharlie should have the last measure of her season. There was still the Drawing Room, followed by the Prince Regent's gala at Carlton House. There were three more assemblies at Almack's, and half a dozen private parties before one after another of the great houses would be put into holland covers for the next six or eight months. Lady Stanwood's practiced eye told her that of Sharlie's original three suitors, Lord Wrentham would come up to scratch, providing there was anyone at hand to receive his offer, which there was not. Lady Stanwood considered it all of a piece that at this precise crucial moment his lordship should have departed jovially for Newmarket—and upon falling in with some kindred spirits, have departed for northern trout streams instead of returning to town.

It was not that Lady Stanwood particularly favored Lord Wrentham, although he was highly eligible. It was merely that, after all the dash of Sharlie's second season, her mama would have liked a formal application from *somebody*, even if she rejected it. Already four engagements had been announced in the Gazette, and two other mamas were smiling with sweet anticipation of glory to come. Lady Stanwood could tell herself with perfect truth that no one of the men was much of a catch, but in her darker moments she admitted that if she had to take Sharlie back to Stanbury without even one offer, she really could not BEAR it.

A daily bouquet arrived from Bascombe "with his grace's compliments to the ladies of the household." Initially Lady Stanwood took this as an indication of continued interest, but as time passed she became perturbed at the absence of Imbrie in person. Recalling his party in detail, she was at a loss to guess what could have gone wrong, "for nothing could have been more promising, even Flora noticed." Had Charlotte said something that indicated her belief of his interest in Emily—and when forced to bandage the ankle, Imbrie feared the ministration might give rise to hope? Could Charlotte somehow have convinced him she had no wish for him? "Did *I* say or do something to give the impression I thought him a possible for Sharlie?" Lady Stanwood wracked her memory, but could not honestly accuse herself of any tinge of complacency, any inadvertent word or glance.

Sharlie was equally uneasy at the duke's non-appearance. Bascombe was no more than an hour's ride on Ajax. The duke had spoken of estate matters, but what on earth could take such a concentration of time? Had he been seriously annoyed that Emily's stupidity had unsettled his *criollo?* Perhaps the bull had been injured when he was forced to draw off the animal. Sharlie fretted and fumed privately, was inclined to sharpness with her sister when at last Emily could be shod and accompany them to Almack's.

Leaning on a small gold-handled Malacca cane scaled to her inches (presented by Mr. Bigglesworth), and resting her hand on the arm of Viscount Pelham while carrying the posy of Lord Dawlish, Miss Emily was the cynosure of all eyes. She was tenderly settled beside her mama and instantly surrounded by beaux. Her card was quickly filled by those desirous of sitting out in her company, upon whom she smiled impartially.

A single glance told Sharlie that Imbrie was not there. He might yet appear, she kept the waltzes free until the musicians were starting the opening flourishes, when she was sitting unbespoke. Upon Emily's innocently remarking that his grace seemed not to be present and she wondered what could be delaying him, "for I thought it was a standing engagement between you for the waltzes, Sharlie," Charlotte replied with asperity that she was not surprised. "Considering all, I am prepared for his dropping our acquaintance."

Emily blushed with distress, and Lady Stanwood said, "Nonsense, Charlotte," in a firm undertone that recalled Sharlie to her surroundings. She was shortly asked to dance by Lord Wrentham, but despite relief that she was not seen to be left at the post, he was a very indifferent substitute for Imbrie. So, in fact, was every other man in the room, and to Sharlie's fear that Emily was rolled up was added the secret admission that quite half the pleasure of Almack's had been waltzing with the duke.

On the morrow all was explained: the duke had left Bascombe unexpectedly for Calydon Towers. "I supposed you knew, miss. That Stepan who brought the flowers told Anatole," Maria revealed. "There was an express arrived early one morning that his grace was urgently required. Stepan was to pack clothing from

Grosvenor Square, and they drove direct from Kent. The duke never came back to London at all."

It was some consolation, but not much. How long would Imbrie remain in the north? Would he ever return to London, or suppose the Stanwoods to have left? Already the fourgons were rolling away from town. The older people without daughters to present made haste to withdraw before the summer heat, and daily the knockers were off new doors. Lady Stanwood could not decide on her course. Logically she should return to Stanbury, but she doubted Imbrie's fancy was sufficiently caught to cause him to journey to Northamptonshire. No matter if he had a legitimate reason for being in that locality, to visit Stanwood Hall must betoken some positive interest which Imbrie was far too wary to arouse.

More and more it seemed she must contrive a casual meeting. Otherwise, he would forget Sharlie or recall her merely as a pleasant young woman with something more of intelligence than the usual society miss, and it was no solace to Lady Stanwood that Charlotte would not be unhappy or humiliated. She had never realized the duke's interest was in her, and neither had any member of the *ton* aside from Lady Inverclyde.

It was she, however, who provided a solution. "Takin' my leave," she announced in a morning call. "I'm off to Bath on Thursday, although I don't know why. Loathesome waters don't do anyone a particle of good. Place used to be entertaining, watching the flirtations and manoeuvrings, but now it's infested with old tabbies like Laura Voss—Imbrie's mother, y'know." She wrinkled her nose distastefully. "She was a Daintry, made her come-out with me—one of your die-away misses. Hah, did she want Inverclyde!" the old lady chortled, "but I got him."

"I'm not surprised," Lady Stanwood smiled absently.

"Do I understand the Dowager summers in Bath?"

"House adjoins mine in Queens Crescent," Lady Inverclyde nodded, "and which is infuriatin', she chooses to consider us bosom friends. Often thought of selling, but there's nothing so comfortable in as good a location. Besides, Inverclyde liked it—the baths helped his sciatica in the last years."

"I wonder," Lady Stanwood mused. "Emily's ankle does not strengthen as it should—perhaps the waters would be helpful for her." She ignored Lady Inverclyde's sharp glance. "That is, if any suitable lodgings could be discovered at this date," she added with dignity. "I must own I had not thought to do more than return to Stanwood Hall, but the uneven country terrain—the least garden pebble might lead to a second sprain and cause irreparable damage."

"Not to be risked," Lady Inverclyde agreed blandly. "I should consult a house agent at once, Nelly. I doubt of there being anything left on Royal Crescent, but in any case Camden Place would be better for Emily's foot . . . and what d'you hear from Imbrie?"

"Why, nothing," Lady Stanwood shrugged. "I believe he is in the north on family business, from something a servant let fall to Beamish. You must know that a fresh bouquet is sent us daily from Bascombe."

"Hmph, very pretty of him." Lady Inverclyde arose to take her leave. "Let me know when you settle in Bath. You can send Sharlie to call—not Emily; it'd be unwise for her ankle. Besides, she's afraid of Cupidon, the silly goose."

Lacking any exact address for her piscatorial husband, Lady Stanwood sent a dozen notes in various directions to inform him that she was removing to Bath where Emily could enjoy a water cure. She was not disturbed by lack of response. The present crisis, she felt, was not one in which he could be useful. It would be time enough for him to learn they were in Camden Place when he reached Stanwood Hall. With no notion of ulterior motives, Sir Geoffrey heartily agreed that all must be done for Emily's preservation, while firmly pleading prior engagements that would prevent him from accompanying the ladies to see them settled.

"Lud, ma'am, *Bath*—y'know it's dull stuff. I'd as lief not go, you'll not do this in a single day."

Lady Stanwood's expression was mulish. "Eight hours," she stated, "and Emily can survive on tea and toast."

"You've still no need of me," he protested. "If a man you must have, here's Wrentham, panting to be asked." Sir Geoffrey polished his quizzing glass casually. "Think Sharlie means to have him?"

"I've no idea," his mother replied repressively, "nor do I wish for his escort. We shall manage very well with the servants."

"He's a good fellow, I don't mind him," Sir Geoffrey observed, "but for myself, I think she'd do better with Imbrie. Thought it seemed in the wind—pity if it's gone off."

Lady Stanwood eyed her first-born with suppressed hatred, and deflected his mind by a request for his direction, "not that I suppose I shall wish for you, but since your father appears to have lost himself, I would appreciate a general idea of *some* male of the family."

"Can't see that," he said, surprised. "If ever anyone was up to snuff, it's you, mama. Don't tell me you'll ever be under the hatches, and if you were, I'd be no use."

"That," said his mother, "I can well believe."

Miss Stanwood's curtsey to the Queen was exceptionally graceful, and the Princess Mary smiled at her. Miss Stanwood's appearance at the Prince Regent's dress party was a marked success. His Highness, with Mr. Brummell at his elbow, distinguished her by inviting her to view his conservatory, although he did not (as usual) attempt to kiss her—blondes were his preference, and he asked most solicitously for Miss Stanwood's sister of whom (he said) he had heard much. It was noticed at the final assembly that Lord Wrentham had secured all the waltzes and the supper dance with Miss Stanwood. Those ladies whose daughters were already fixed ventured to smile at Lady Stanwood and observe, "I fancy we shall soon see an interesting announcement in the Gazette."

"I can't say, Lord Stanwood is from home, you know," was all she could reply, but the general expectation somewhat raised her spirits. Only Mrs. Drummond Burrell had the power to disquiet Lady Stanwood by remarking, "What a pity! So often these promising situations come to nothing for lack of the right moment. I wonder Lord Stanwood should not be at hand to settle matters."

Lady Stanwood ground her teeth silently, but clung to her hopeful gamble: let Sharlie be in Bath—quite certainly he would learn of it. If there were any interest, he would shortly arrive to visit his mother—and if he did not, Lady Stanwood had lost her private wager.

For a full three weeks, it seemed that she had, and it was taking all her stamina to face the succession of days. Emily was beginning to droop at the morning footbath, and in truth there was no need for them. She was perfectly fit to walk through Russell Street to the Circus and the Pump Rooms. While the gentlemen who had set their names on Mr. Guynette's subscription list at the New Assembly Rooms were instantly gaining presentation to Miss Emily, she found them less amusing than her London beaux. Sharlie was happier only in being able to ride Moonshine out to the countryside each day with John-groom, but otherwise she also found Bath rather boring.

As for Lady Stanwood, she was so weary of gentle drives, tea parties and mild dinners that she felt her face would crack with smiling. Nevertheless, she persevered grimly, even going so far as to endure the dowager Duchess of Imbrie's company for a full four hours' drive to the Abbey. That lady's querulous conversation very nearly caused Lady Stanwood to call the whole thing off and accede to Emily's sighs for home. She could not feel that Sharlie would prosper with such a mama-in-law, particularly as she lost no opportunity to introduce Emily to the dowager's notice.

To cap all, there was but too much reason to fear Imbrie would *not* learn Charlotte was in Bath. Lady Stanwood could not discover that any communication existed between Lady Imbrie and her son. Her companion—a distant relative of wilted appearance and chirruping manners—appeared to be the sole link with Calydon Towers, "whereby," Miss Clapham simpered, "I am able to keep Cousin Laura abreast of the news." She then put her hand over her mouth and blushed, aghast at the ungenteel word. Aside from a weekly report by Lucinda's governess, the Calydon budget consisted of a sort of serial detailing the machinations by which the doctor's wife was attempting to entrap a local widower for her extremely plain daughter. Lady Imbrie's disapproval of such duplicity was not calculated to cheer Lady Stanwood at the moment. Of the duke there was no mention, and she ventured to observe, "I wonder his grace should not interest himself in the matter, since the man is one of his best tenants."

"Oh, as for that, Imbrie would feel it not his concern. He thinks it very good fun to see his friends ensnared, but if it were HE—he would leave for the Antipodes at once," the dowager sniffed. "He has no consideration for the claims of his motherless children, or the strain on *my* health to be charged with their care. I am *mazed* he should remain so long, quite confounded with what Flora tells me of his taking his place in the season. I collect the seas are unsafe due to the wars, but I assure you, my dear Lady Stanwood—had any mama come within a yard of attaching him to her daughter, Imbrie would have taken to his heels at once, pirates or no pirates!"

This, and similar animadversions upon Imbrie's character, was deeply discouraging. Lady Stanwood settled with herself that if the duke did not arrive within ten days, she would return to Stanbury. "Emily's ankle is greatly improved, and Sharlie is moped to death."

"Don't be in a hurry," Lady Inverclyde said bluntly. "I've something you'll like to hear. Imbrie's either in London or on his way. I'd a letter from Maria Sefton—said they'd been stayin' with the Wainfleets, mentioned she'd seen Imbrie at a dinner party and he was for town the next day. That's where he'll learn you're here, Nelly." Lady Inverclyde grinned triumphantly.

She was quite right, although it was still some days. A peculiarly unsavory local scandal had required Julian's presence in the north. Once verdict was given, he spent a few days at the Towers, found it as uncomfortable as always, and readily accepted an invitation to try his cousin's streams near Spitsby. On impulse, he took his children with him.

Lord Arthur's family was entirely different from Imbrie's, and roundly condemned by the dowager as a "ramshackle lot. Your father deplored the marriage. 'A mere Miss Georgina Upton with nine thousand pounds? And who may SHE be?' I remember him saying, but when you were born, it no longer mattered. Your Uncle Lionel was not heir, and I believe Imbrie later came to think her not a bad thing, for your Uncle Lionel was sadly unstable, as you must know—and now we see the result: six surviving children, of which five are *girls,* before an inflammation of the lungs prevented further increase!"

The duke could not entirely agree with her strictures. It was true that Lionel Voss had done little to expand the fortune of a younger son, but upon his death all was found well to pass. Arthur's only encumbrance was those five younger sisters, and Julian's first act at his majority was to assure his Aunt Georgie of five thousand pounds for each of them. Farther he could not go, it would not have been accepted. He was able to assist by offering Grosvenor Square for the come-out of his young cousins; what Lady Voss would have refused for herself, she would instantly take for her children. A further assistance lay in asking Arthur to supervise Imbrie estates, although this was worth far more to Julian than the fee he paid his cousin.

"An independent lot, we Vosses," Arthur said with his father's light-heartedness—but it occurred to Julian that the care of two lively ten-year olds would provide his Aunt Georgie with exactly the chance of repayment she would most like, while simultaneously offering a major treat for his twins.

So it proved, and induced his grace to linger a full two weeks at Spitsby, although the fishing was indifferent. Nevertheless, he found himself in a family life he had never known. For the first time he saw his son and daughter as *people* with distinct personalities. At Spitsby they suddenly began *talking* to him, and Julian was stunned by Giles' grasp of land and estate management. Lucinda was not far behind, although her father suspected it was principally emulation of her adored twin. Still, it would serve her well. She would listen knowledgeably to her husband, instead of falling asleep in the middle—like Isabella.

Time and again, with the twins tagging at his heels, his mind turned to Miss Stanwood. A chance word from Giles or Lucinda, and he wished Sharlie could have shared his amusement . . . or what she'd have contributed to their comments and inquiries, how she'd have instructed Lucinda in flowers and plants. Even, Julian could visualize Sharlie beside him, watching eagerly for the rise of a trout to his cast.

"What's amiss, Coz?" Arthur drawled one evening when Julian had silently poured a fourth glass of port.

"You won't roast me?" Julian asked after a moment.

"You know me better!"

"I think I'm in love."

Lord Arthur opened his mouth to say "Cheer up, you'll recover," or some such pleasantry, but a glance at his cousin's serious face changed the matter. "That is good news," he said sincerely. "Do I know the lady?"

Julian shook his head. "That is why you would roast me. It is Miss Stanwood . . . Sharlie," his grace murmured affectionately, while his cousin stared at him. "She understands French, German and Greek, Arthur. She rides like Diana Artemis, she waltzes like a feather in the arms; she has the knack of dealing with servants, gardeners, country folk. She listens, asks to hear more, and never forgets what she is told. She is eager, and teachable, sincerely interested. She says what comes to her mind, and then blushes for fear it is too out of the mode, but even when she is minding her manners, Sharlie is . . ." Julian's voice died away dreamily.

"Miss Stanwood?" Arthur repeated cautiously. "Well—well, I'm sure I wish you very happy, Julian. She's a most beautiful creature, I hear she had all London at her feet."

"No, no, that's the little widgeon with a harp. All the same, she's a complication."

"How so? It's expected the older sister will go off first."

"Not by Sharlie. She is convinced my attention is for Emily. To say truth, I'd no special attention for either of 'em, Arthur, beyond amusement. They're a pair of nice youngsters, I like the parents, it tickled my fancy to get Brummell to give Sharlie the nod, but I'd no real thought beyond helping her to a successful second season. Thing is," Julian said moodily, "I didn't wake up in time, Arthur. I should have made it clear to Sharlie at the outset that I had *no* interest in Emily, and was only a friend of Lord Stanwood, but it didn't seem to matter. I could see Lady Stanwood was under no misapprehension, she welcomed me as a London neighbor known to her husband—hence, an entirely acceptable escort for either daughter.

"But now—damme, what a coil! I've no reason to suppose Sharlie's ever thought of me except as a possibility for her sister. If I ask permission to address her, the Stanwoods will give it. I fancy they'll be amazed, but they like me very well—and in that family, titles and money are less." Julian smiled faintly, "Oh, they'd be alive to the coup of catching Imbrie, but if she rejected me, she'd not be devilled for it."

"She wouldn't reject you."

"She very well might. God, what am I to do?"

Lord Arthur regarded his cousin with concern. This was a man he'd not suspected. In common with the rest of the world, he'd come to view Julian as a dedicated bachelor with a low opinion of wedded bliss, but his dreamy catalog of Charlotte Stanwood's virtues betokened lovesickness of no mean order. "Consult m'mother," he decided, tossing off his wine and pushing aside the bottle. "M'mother has a good head for this sort of thing. Come along, Julian."

Lady Voss opened her grey eyes very wide at her son's *prècis* of the situation. "Julian's in love—unexceptionable girl, but hasn't a notion, thinks he's after her younger sister. What's his course, mama?"

It could not be supposed that his Aunt Georgie would instantly render a verdict. All must first be explained in great detail, "for it is in the highest degree unlikely that she would promote your pursuit of her sister—yes, I *know* you have not, Julian, but she thought you were. I wish you will not interrupt," Lady Voss said severely. "Now I have lost my train of thought, where was I?"

"Julian's supposed pursuit of Emily."

"Oh—yes, she would not promote that if she did not like you very well for yourself, Julian, for from what you say, she is not at all *worldly* minded. Sharlie—what a cunning name! I long to know her, I feel sure I shall like her excessively which, if you will forgive me, I could *not* say for Isabella, but however—Sharlie does not sound at all the girl to wish for an unsympathetic brother-in-law, no matter how rich he is."

"Very true, but how shall I make her wish for me as a husband?"

Lady Voss pursed her lips, and sipped her tea while her son and nephew regarded her hopefully. When mama (Aunt Georgie) pondered, SOMETHING useful was bound to emerge. At last she said, oracularly, "You must contrive to be at hand wherever she is. You must devote yourself to her, and by your conversation let her know that you have never thought of the sister as anything more than a sweet little schoolgirl."

"In heaven's name, how will he do *that,* mama?"

"Oh, he will inquire particularly for her beaux, which does she favor, give his opinion that so-and-so would be a very good thing," Lady Voss stated. "First, let Sharlie realize that he has no intentions whatever for the sister. Then, when she has accustomed herself to the disappointment of her plans . . . then it will be time for Julian to show his real objective by a few pretty speeches, a glance, a pressure of the hand." She shrugged, "by that time I fancy Lady Stanwood will see how the wind blows and afford some discreet assistance. It is really very simple, Julian, although it may take you some time to convince Sharlie that you are not hanging out for the sister . . . and I may say," severely, "you've no one to blame but yourself if you're rolled up.

"You've been far too will-o'-the-wisp for too many years. By now you've been written off as a prospect by any wise mother. Small wonder your divertissement has caught you amidships, and it will do you good to be uncertain! That is all I have to say." Lady Voss finished her tea with austerity.

"Yes, ma'am," Julian replied meekly, but upon reflection, he felt the advice to be sound . . . although how was he to contrive to be at hand when he'd no idea where Sharlie was? London would be a good starting point; unlikely the Stanwoods would still be in residence, but a servant would certainly know where they had gone.

Two days later he returned his children to Calydon

Towers, stayed the night and set out for London at an early hour. Sitting beside his master, Stepan covertly observed the silent set-jawed determination and occasional reminiscent smile with a hopeful heart. "We shall have a mistress. *Kahloss!* It is time to stop roaming," Stepan said to himself, "and that Maria suits me very well."

By a circuitous route, his grace managed to drive *up* Park Street and round the corner to drive *down* Grosvenor Square. A swift glance to the Stanwood residence showed it darkened but for a basement light. Well, he'd expected nothing more; London would be well nigh deserted in late July. Some word might be gained from one of the clubs. "I shall be content with the simplest of dinners," he informed Robsey, "at nine if this can be managed—or at ten, if it cannot."

"Very good, your grace," Robsey bowed imperturbably. "Will there be guests?"

"No, I doubt I shall stay longer than tonight." Julian went up to his chamber while Robsey was murmuring, "Very good, your grace," and stripped off his driving clothes. "I'll bathe now, Stepan—see what's in the study, and go to a club after dinner." It did not get so far. The instant the duke had closed the study door, Stepan hastened to the rear door of No. 10 Park Street.

"'Allo, mon vieux! J'y suis," he said jovially to Anatole. "We are here for only a little—and where is milady and *les demoiselles?"*

"They have gone to Bath, which is a detestable place that gives no scope for art," Anatole replied. "Once I have been there—it is many years past, with a relative of milord's to whom he offers a house and servants. *Mais, figurez-vous:* no one has heard of *l'escargots* or *les rognons oporto!* All that is wanted is a chicken, a joint of beef or lamb, with a *Gateau St. Honoré*—in *August. C'est impossible!* I hope I never see the place again—and where have you been, Stepan?"

"Here and there," the Greek shrugged airily, "and what news of *les beaux?* There are engagements, *hein?*"

"Not that I hear. For the little one, *n'importe*. It is too bad she has the accident, she cannot make the curtsey to the Queen, but she will come again next year. For our Mees, one supposes it will be Lord Wrentham, but nothing is announced."

Stepan lingered long enough for politeness, made his excuses and rapidly slid back through the mews to the stable entrance for Imbrie's residence. The duke was at dinner. "Very good," Stepan said to the butler. "I think we leave tomorrow. Please to tell milor' I have a need to speak with him before he go to club."

As it chanced, Julian discovered a lack of snuff box and went up to his chamber before Robsey could deliver the message. He found Stepan bustling about with open valises, obviously engaged in packing. "What the devil?"

It was the moment for honesty. "They have gone to Bath," said Stepan. "No engagement has been announced but one expects it will be Lord Wrentham." He allowed a slight pause to fold an evening coat tenderly. "At what hour do we start, milor'?"

"Nine," said Julian automatically. "Damn you, Stepan—who told you to play Cupid?"

"No one, milor'—but I think it comes out well. That Maria is one very nice girl for me," Stepan grinned ingratiatingly, and took heart as his master first snorted, then chuckled, and finally roared with laughter.

"Good God, am I to marry because you've an eye to the girl's *maid?*"

"No, no!" Stepan protested. "But I think it will be more comfortable that we are all married together, *ne?*"

"Yes—and what if they refuse us?"

"Maria does not refuse me when her mistress accepts you," Stepan said confidently.

"You lay a heavy responsibility upon me."

Nevertheless, the servant's attitude was heartening, and his grace was further cheered by the discovery that Wrentham was gone into the country to attend his father's possible death bed. Even if this came to anything and he became Earl of Waxe, he was bound to be immobilized by all the details of funeral and succession. Illogically, Julian was furiously insulted on Sharlie's behalf. Wrentham had had months in which to come to the point. Did he expect her to have no other offers, to be waiting hopefully until Wrentham got everything else settled and found time to drop his handkerchief.

"Hah, we'll see about that."

CHAPTER VII

JULIAN SET OUT for Bath next morning, and accomplished the journey in rather less than Lady Stanwood's time, since he was travelling light. Despite a good rest for his team, Julian was sweeping from Guinea Lane through Bennet Street into the Circus, and able to draw rein before his mother's house by half after four —or exactly as Miss Charlotte Stanwood emerged from Lady Inverclyde's establishment. Her reaction at the sight of the duke removed the last lingering reservation in his mind. But for the presence of onlookers, Julian would have leapt from the phaeton and dashed up those steps to clasp her in his arms!

She was utterly adorable, he had forgotten how graceful her figure, how sweet her smile, how charmingly natural she was. A moment she stood transfixed, lips parted in recognition. Then she was hastening down to the walk, holding the riding habit out of her way and stretching out her hand. "How delightful this is!" she exclaimed. "We had not the least notion . . . that is, your mama said nothing of a visit."

"She could not, for she did not know of it," Julian held her hand tightly and smiled the charming Voss smile. "I'd heard you were here, but had not hoped for the luck of encountering you so immediately. How do you go on? Are you enjoying Bath and those horrid waters? Where do you stay?" Impulsively, "Send Moonshine home with the groom and allow me to drive you. We must catch up on these past weeks."

"Yes—but ought you not first to inform Lady Imbrie of your arrival?" she asked doubtfully.

"Since I am not expected, it will be time enough to tell her when I return from . . . wherever you live."

"Camden Place." She hesitated briefly, then with a mischievous twinkle she walked toward the phaeton. "I know very well I should not. Lady Imbrie will come to cuffs with me for delaying your arrival, but it is so good to see you. Hello, my beauties," Sharlie crooned, patting the noses of Julian's greys. "Ah, you are tired, but still full of pluck, are you not? How good you have been to bring him all the way from London. But there is not much more before you will have a rubdown and a bag of oats, and tomorrow you'll be full of frisk again."

Julian stood bemused while the greys—reputed to be his most difficult team—snorted and sidled, ducked their heads and delicately pawed the ground, for all the world like bashful debutantes. He came to himself as she moved away to smile at Stepan, and swiftly tossed a coin to the waiting groom. "Take Miss Stanwood's horse back to the stable, please."

"Yes, your grace!" Another Golden Boy, but John-groom was struck with An Idea, as he watched the duke assisting Miss Stanwood into the phaeton. John was a cautious soul. Jogging homeward, he thought he would consult Maria before he said anything—but if he was right, "Eh, it'd be a hem set-down for they Londoners if our Miss Sharlie catched a duke!"

Meanwhile, Julian was taking the reins from Stepan, who sprang to the rear step as the phaeton began to move. "Oh, it is good to see you," Sharlie said again, "and all falls out so well, for you must know that

Emily's ankle is greatly improved by the water baths and she can venture to dance again. Only the minuets and simplest country dances for the present, but in time she will be able to waltz."

Julian nearly said "The devil with Emily!" but recalled his aunt's advice. Instead, "That is good news. I suppose her card is as crowded as ever? Who are her principal suitors in Bath?" It was the right line, for Sharlie looked a bit taken aback at his calm avuncular voice.

"Well—well, of course there are no beaux to compare with London," she said. "The Bath assemblies do not equal Almack's, and the entertainment is necessarily more quiet, to suit the tastes of older people. I am able to get away for a ride in the country, but Emily is as near to boredom as I have ever seen her. You must know the sweetness of her nature, in general she would be happy wherever she found herself . . . but now you are come, all will be different."

"Yes, indeed," Julian agreed. "We must continue your driving instruction. The countryside around Bath is the very spot for it, and it will be several days before my horses arrive *fur ein gallopp mit Mondschein.*"

She blushed faintly, and then laughed. "Oh, I am finely caught, am I not? But I am truly not at all *blue,* Duke—only that papa allowed me to study with Geoff when he was preparing for Oxford, and mama feared I should gain that reputation. However, it no longer matters, does it?"

"It never did, to me," he smiled. "I find it pleasant to meet a young lady who is not ashamed to admit some education—doubly pleasant in reminding me of my travels. Should you object if we practice our languages while we take our drives? I grow rusty."

She looked startled. "No—but I fear I never had

sufficient command to be helpful," she murmured.

"Which have you studied?"

"German, Greek, Latin, a little Italian, and French, of course, but Emily only knows some French."

"I suppose," he nodded comfortably. "She is but little removed from the schoolroom, after all. There is plenty of time for her to advance, although I fancy she is having too good a time to care for study. Meanwhile it will be good to hear the foreign tongues again. Which shall we practice first?"

"Oh—it matters not, whichever pleases you."

"Then let it be Italian," he decided, smiling. "It is a long while since I have used it, but I once was fairly fluent. Perhaps I can help to expand that 'little' of yours."

"It would be kind of you, Duke," she said with an effort, and noting the faint bewildered frown, Julian congratulated himself on having made a good start via Aunt Georgie. It was even better in Camden Place, where they found Emily surrounded by young ladies and gentlemen, occupied with parlor games. She certainly jumped up and ran forward with a broad smile, hands outstretched, but her welcome was for a family friend. "What a lovely surprise! How glad I am to see you, Duke, for you must know that Sharlie is moped to death with no riding companion."

Julian chuckled to himself at her reaction, but could not be sure that Sharlie had grasped it. He excused himself from introduction to her companions on the score of traveller's dust, bestowed a general fatherly smile on the group and withdrew to the hall, where Lady Stanwood was coming down the stairs. "Milady," he bowed over her hand, "it is shameful of me to present myself in all my dirt and dishevelment. I beg your pardon! But the luck of encountering Sh. . . . Miss

Stanwood at the very moment of arrival—it was irresistible to pay my respects."

"Indeed, no apology is needed from any acquaintance of my husband," she said warmly. "I collect it is a surprise for Lady Imbrie? I hope you will find time to accompany her to dine with us."

"Most assuredly," Julian smiled, turning to Sharlie. "I must not stay, it is kind in you to receive me at all, but what are your engagements for tomorrow, Miss Stanwood? Can I take you up for a driving lesson?"

"I believe—that is, there is a scheme for driving to Wells, but you will scarcely wish to leave Lady Imbrie on your first day."

"Wells, eh? Oh m'mother will see more than enough of me," he returned cheerfully. "At what time do we start?"

From a place of dullness, Bath suddenly became great fun . . . particularly for Lady Inverclyde. She bestirred herself daily to keep abreast of the situation, having her chair carried to the Pump Room for observation and chuckling to herself wickedly. Julian was assiduously accompanying his mother—and abducting Miss Stanwood for a driving lesson as soon as he'd got Lady Imbrie settled. Emily was enlivened by the arrival of Mr. Bigglesworth, come to pay his respects to an aunt who was much bewildered by such courtesy. Lady Stanwood preserved a calm demeanor that gave no hint of her inner glee, and Lady Imbrie was totally unaware of *anything*.

But by week's end Julian was growing impatient. Daily Charlotte polished her driving technique, then returned him the ribbons for a conversation in Italian, "for I do not yet trust myself to handle the team without putting all my mind to it." When they resumed

English conversation, however, Sharlie was still stuck fast to the concept of his interest in Emily, and the more he tried to indicate his opinion of Emily as a schoolgirl, the more earnestly she emphasized her sister's sterling qualities. Dash it, why the devil couldn't Sharlie realize that she herself was his objective? He rather thought everyone else did, aside from Lady Imbrie who never saw anything unless she saw it first.

Reinforcement arrived on Friday in the person of Lord Arthur. Lady Imbrie certainly widened her eyes with astonishment at such an influx of uninvited guests to what was, after all, her personal establishment. She *wondered* that Arthur should not have thought to send word, she *wondered* what might be amiss to require instant consultation with Julian, "for it cannot be dire," she informed Lady Inverclyde. "Julian was excessively pleased to see him, and I must own that Arthur apologized very prettily for his laxity. He always does, which does not prevent his doing it again the next time—a shag-bag lot, Flora! However, I could not hear of his removing to a common hotel when there is ample space here—and on the whole, one cannot dislike Arthur. It is what one most particularly regrets."

Julian had no regrets at all. "By Jove, you're the very man I need!"

"So m'mother thought," Arthur grinned. "Sent me off to superintend, says you're bound to make a muff of it on your own—and how goes it?"

"It doesn't," Julian said grimly. "I begin to think I'll never have a chance until I'm rid of Emily—which is why I'm devilish glad to see you, Arthur."

"Hold hard!" his cousin protested in alarm. "I'm not ready for the altar, Julian. There's a limit to what I'll do for family solidarity."

"Lord, if I thought you'd be bowled out, I'd forbid

the banns," Julian returned scornfully. "No, all that's wanted is to engage the girl's attention sufficiently for Sharlie to see for herself. Emily hasn't a thought of me, Arthur. She hasn't a thought of anyone as yet. She's simply enjoying herself. The more conquests the better, she's flitting like the honeybee, and you're the very person to flutter her. Will you do it?"

"Yes, but damme, Julian—I've no wish to raise expectations."

"You won't. You'll see for yourself at the Assembly tonight."

However, it was his grace who saw—not merely at the Assembly but subsequently, for in the space of one cotillion, Lord Arthur and Sharlie were on the best of terms. True that Emily blushed becomingly at Arthur's compliments and permitted him to sit beside her during a country dance which Lady Stanwood declared too strenuous for the injured ankle. True that he cleverly obtained the adjoining seat when the company went in to tea, and drew such smiles as bitterly annoyed Mr. Bigglesworth on her other side. On the morrow he delighted Miss Emily by shamelessly emptying her cup of the famed water into a nearby potted palm, and in the afternoon he gained Lady Stanwood's permission to form a boating party on the Avon—but as Arthur had somehow seated himself to face Sharlie, the conversation was necessarily general.

Lady Stanwood's dinner party placed the duke to her right, with Lady Inverclyde beyond; to her left was General Pocklington, the perennial extra man of Bath, with Lady Imbrie beyond. Observing the cheerful group of young people below the salt, Julian had never been so irritated by the protocol required for his title. Lady Inverclyde held an informal gathering two nights later, "merely old friends for a few tables of whist," she said blandly, "and perhaps the children may be able to make up a set for dancing, if you will lend us Miss Clapham for the music, Laura."

From his seat as Lady Inverclyde's partner, Julian was enabled to watch Sharlie tripping the light fantastic with his cousin, and the sight of her laughing face caused a revoke for which his hostess took him to task with all the freedom of one who had known him in diaper days. Julian transferred her strictures later to Lord Arthur.

"Damme, I told you to concentrate on Emily. What the devil are you doing, dancing attendance on Sharlie?"

"Emily's chockablock with the sprigs, there's no getting near her," Arthur countered suavely, "so I'm emphasizing that to Sharlie and telling her what a fine character *you* are."

"She already knows that," Julian snarled. "It's why she thinks I'm perfect for the ninnyhammer."

Arthur chuckled. "Afraid I'll cut you out, old boy? It serves you right for dawdling about. All's fair in love and war, every man for himself—it's even our family crest: *Sauve qui peut.*"

Matters were not improved by Lady Imbrie's sudden recognition of A Situation. "Flora tells me that Arthur is becoming most particular in his attentions to Miss Stanwood," she observed. "I would not have thought him to have so much sense as to look to his own advantage, for you must know that Miss Stanwood has a very pretty fortune of her own, aside from her father's portion. Well, well! I believe it would be a very good thing upon the whole, do not you, Julian?"

"No, I do not," her son snapped curtly.

"Ah? How so?"

"Considering your disapproval of my aunt, I wonder you will condemn Miss Stanwood to deal with such a mother-in-law."

But just as it was difficult to introduce Lady Imbrie

to an idea, it was impossible to eradicate it once planted, and she continued to give it as her opinion that it would be a very good thing for Arthur. In furtherance of his supposed romance, she invited Lady Stanwood and her daughters to dinner, together with such members of the *haut ton* as were to be found in Bath. This placed Julian at the head of the table between Lady Inverclyde and Lady Stanwood, set General Pocklington and a septuagenarian earl beside Lady Imbrie, and filled in the middles with an assortment of lesser importance—but she had not failed to accord Arthur the honor of taking Miss Stanwood in, whereby Julian could observe their friendly chat.

It quite destroyed his appetite. He took three mouthfuls of the *Soupe à la Reine,* toyed with the *escalopes de foie gras* and the *fillets de Turbot* with Italian Sauce, ate half a slice of the beef, a roasted potato, a single *suprême de volaille* with two spears of asparagus, and rejected the glazed parsnips, the baked ham, the cold partridge, the broiled mushrooms . . . all of which caused grave concern. The servants hastened to tell the chef that his grace didn't seem to fancy his dinner, whereupon Jean-Pierre uttered various Gallic opprobriums which (luckily) only Stepan understood, and swiftly expanded the menu by certain temptations for presentation in the second course.

Useless!

While the others relished omelets, various jelly shapes and stewed fruits, baskets of pastry, a dish of spinach with croutons, and some anchovy toasts (among other things), his grace was content with a *crême Bavarois,* a morsel of sponge cake and a peach. He was quite unaware that his refusal of the *attereaux de ris de veau* was creating a crisis belowstairs, where Jean-Pierre threatened to suicide himself!

Julian himself was more murderous than suicidal, and took the earliest opportunity of telling his cousin to hedge off. "Lud, Julian," said Lord Arthur easily, "there's nothing in it—you know me better. She's a damned fine girl, I'd think myself lucky if I could find something similar, but frankly, old boy—she's a bit blue for my taste. You may understand her, but I haven't the education."

"She is NOT a blue-stocking," Julian roared.

"I never said she was," Arthur replied, surprised. "Simply, if the young'un don't know how to spell her name, the old'un knows twice too much. Makes me uncomfortable."

"Then why don't you go away?" Julian growled. "Heaven knows, you weren't invited to turn up here. Aunt Georgie never told you to interfere."

"No," Arthur admitted. "She said you should have a private word with Lady Stanwood, disclose your budget. Once she knows you're serious, she'll assist. You'll see," he clapped his cousin on the shoulder jovially. "Wish you good luck, Coz!"

Thus emboldened, Julian arrayed himself with care —and an unaccustomed nervousness—the following day, and presented himself at Lady Stanwood's residence, begging the favor of a word with her. Beamish looked dubious. "Her ladyship is preparing to drive out for the afternoon. If your grace would step into the salon, I will enquire whether she can receive you."

The salon contained Sharlie penning a note at the desk. She rose to her feet in confusion, changing to her friendly smile upon seeing who entered. "Oh, I am so sorry," she exclaimed, extending her hand. "Emily has but just gone to walk with some friends, what a pity."

The touch of her hand in his . . . the clarity of her

eyes reflecting the green of her Italian crepe walking dress . . . the frank smile of welcome . . . all were too much for Julian. "I don't come to this house to see Emily, but to see you," he said huskily, holding her hand firm and drawing her a little toward him. "Miss Stanwood—my dearest Sharlie—will you do me the honor of marrying me?"

For a moment she stared at him, open-mouthed. "What?" she murmured faintly.

"My darling dear, I am asking—*beseeching*—you to marry me." Julian sought to draw her into his arms, but she resisted.

"But you can't," she protested. "I mean, you want Emily, but she has gone walking."

"No, I do NOT want Emily. I *never* have wanted Emily."

Charlotte's eyes widened. "What do you mean? You're in love with her, from the first glance at Melsham."

"I am not, I never have been, in love with Emily!"

To Julian's astonishment, Sharlie went from shocked incredulity to anger. "But you *were*, you definitely WERE," she insisted, "and if you changed your mind, you should have said so instead of taking up all my time. You've made me odiously conspicuous to all of London and Bath if you didn't mean to offer for her. Nothing but a future engagement could excuse my being seen with you constantly. Everybody will think *I* was trying for you, and you didn't come up to scratch. Oh, the humiliation!"

"But I have come up to scratch," Julian pointed out.

"What of it? I can't very well *explain* to Society."

"Why not?"

"Because nobody'd believe me. You're much too eligible for anyone to believe you'd be rejected."

"There's a simple solution: you can marry me."

"That," said Charlotte, "is the silliest thing you've said yet. I don't want to be a duchess, I never wanted a second season in the first place, all I want is to stay at Stanwood and help to manage the estate."

"In that case, what difference does London opinion make?"

"Well—I might wish to marry *sometime,* but who'd have me now?"

Julian felt his mind beginning to spin gently, he had never thought there could be so much involved in a simple declaration, but he persevered. "I've just said I'll have you—and what's wrong with me? Sharlie, my dear one," capturing her hands once more, "I thought we dealt extremely well together. If you yearn to manage estates, I've got lots of 'em. You can stay in the country and never go to London if you don't wish."

"I don't want to manage *your* estates, I don't know anything about them," she returned stormily, "and if I stay in the country, the *ton* will wonder why you're ashamed to produce me."

"Very well, you needn't manage anything. I've already got excellent agents and stewards. We'll open Imbrie House and live there, if you prefer."

"I don't—and I won't be buried at your horrid castle when you're off traveling," Sharlie cried, trying to release her hands. "Mr. Brummell says it's the most uncomfortable pile in all of England."

"I'll pull it down and build whatever you like, wherever you like," Julian promised recklessly, "and I'm through with travelling. It isn't safe these days, and besides, I've already been everywhere. Now I want to settle down—with you, my darling."

"Oh, very good!" Sharlie snorted. "You mean you

will never take me anywhere because *you* are tired of voyages."

"Nonsense," said Julian impatiently. "I wish you would stop twisting my words, Charlotte. In plain English, we will live wherever you wish, do whatever pleases you. If you've a fancy for travel, I will take you around the world—if you prefer country life to city, you may have it. Damme, what a pother you're making, considering you've been perfectly happy with my company for weeks!"

"Damme, yourself! I won't be married off just because you've put me in an odious position and are trying to be—to be a gent."

"Oh, the devil with it!" Julian said vehemently, dropping her hands. "I did *not* propose in order to save your face, and I've never been a *gent* about anything. What's more, if you have your eye on Arthur, you'll never get him."

"If you think I can't do any better than you, I'd rather be a spinster forever!" Sharlie burst into tears, precisely as the door opened to admit Lady Stanwood. "Mama, you tell him . . ."

"Shhh, my love," Lady Stanwood held her daughter's shaking form. "Indeed there is nothing to cry about."

"Oh, yes, there is," Sharlie wailed. "Oh, mama, it was all a hum! How are we going to tell Emily?"

"Never mind Emily. I wish you will compose yourself, Charlotte." Over her daughter's shoulder, Lady Stanwood raised her eyebrows commandingly at the duke.

"All I did was ask her to marry me, ma'am," Julian said wrathfully, twitching his coat sleeves into place, "and she's enacting me a Cheltenham tragedy, claiming her exquisite sensibilities are bruised beyond recall."

"Yes, yes, no doubt. My dear Imbrie, I wish you will go away for a while until Charlotte is more the thing—and she does have sensibilities, although I shouldn't call them exquisite."

"Neither should I," Julian replied grimly. "Good God, ma'am, the things she said!"

"Well, you might have expected she would. It's one reason you love her," Lady Stanwood remarked severely. "Do, for heaven's sake, go away, Imbrie. In round words, you've made a hash of it. Charlotte, stop bawling like a sick calf! Nobody will make you do anything you do not wish. No, you do NOT have to live in a castle, and yes, everyone WILL believe Imbrie came up to scratch as soon as Beamish gets down to the local alehouse. It will be all over Bath by dinner time, and if anyone is humiliated it will be Imbrie."

Julian had never felt so helpless in his life, while Sharlie clung to her mother and sobbed disjointedly.

"Never mind Emily—I told you long since she was *not* your concern," Lady Stanwood said with asperity. "Stop crying, Charlotte! I must say I feel you might have shown a little more restraint upon this occasion, my love. It is one thing for Beamish to overhear your calm rejection at the keyhole, where you may be sure he had his ear—and quite another for the entire household to be aware of a scene so tempestuous that he came in haste to fetch me."

Behind her daughter's back, she made flapping motions at Julian, who seized up hat and gloves, made for the door and sketched a bow. "Y'r servant, milady."

Flinging it open, he nearly fell over Beamish who was standing as close as possible in the hall. The butler moved away with what dignity he could, to open the entrance where he stood looking expressionlessly into space until the duke strode forward. With a fulminating glance, his grace extended a coin. "That should be enough to wet your throat for a full recital."

"Yes, your grace. Thank you, your grace." Beamish gently closed the door and examined the coin: a guinea. *Very handsome,* he said to himself, but after considering for some hours, Beamish concluded it could not be allowed to weigh, "for this would give rise to garbled accounts." It was, Beamish decided, his positive duty to issue a correct statement.

While Lady Stanwood was soothing her daughter until she could be got up to her chamber for repose of her agitation, Julian drove at a reckless pace to Queens Crescent, where he tossed the reins to the stableboy and strode into his mother's house with Stepan silently at his heels. As luck would have it, the dowager was descending the stairs with Miss Clapham in attendance, burdened with parasol, fan and vinaigrette. Lady Imbrie stopped short and eyed her son's thunderous countenance with astonishment.

"Good gracious, what has happened? Where have you been?"

"To Lady Stanwood."

"What in the world did she do to put you in such a temper?"

"Not she, but her daughter," Julian said bitterly. "I wish you will come down from the stairs, mother. I should like to go to my room."

"Her *daughter?*" Lady Imbrie stared. "Which one?"

"The elder. Will you move out of my way, madam?"

The dowager continued to stand stock-still. "Miss Charlotte Stanwood? A very pretty-behaved young female. Why have you taken a pet against her, Imbrie?" she inquired in the voice of one determined to get to the bottom of matters. "I thought it was settled she would be an excellent choice for Arthur, one I should be happy to welcome into the family."

"I regret you will not have that opportunity," he said icily. "Miss Stanwood has rejected my hand in marriage."

"*Your* hand?" Lady Imbrie's eyes popped.

"Yes, madam," he said coldly. "Why so incredulous? God knows you've done your possible to marry me off for years. It would appear I am not so desirable a *parti* as you thought. Now, IF you please—or shall I use the servants' stairs?"

Speechlessly, his mother tottered down to the hall, her face glassy with shock. Miss Clapham scurried forward to thrust the vinaigrette beneath the dowager's nose, while Julian strode upward and vanished. Then with a moan she clutched her companion's arm. "Did he really say what I think he said?" she asked faintly. "Good God, *rejected?* No, no, he must mean Arthur."

Miss Clapham was bright-eyed, quivering with excitement, the while she assured Lady Imbrie her hearing was not deficient. Nothing so titillating had occurred in all the years of her association with the dowager. "Oh, no, Cousin Laura—it was never Arthur. I must say it has been quite clear from the moment of Julian's arrival," she tittered. "Why else did he come but to fix an interest? It was not just certain which girl had caught his eye, but very shortly it became obvious—all that riding and driving together, you know. Oh, yes, everyone in Bath has been expecting. I wonder you should not have realized."

"Everyone has expected . . . ?" Lady Imbrie repeated dazedly. "And he is refused? Oh, lud, the humiliation!"

His mother's discomfiture was nothing compared to Julian's, and Arthur was no help. "Good God," he exclaimed exasperated, "if ever there was a gudgeon. I despair of you, Julian. Why must you plunge in without warning, why could you not enlist Lady Stanwood's aid first?"

"I meant to do so," Julian admitted. "That's why I was there, but she was being dressed and when I was shown into the salon . . . well, Sharlie was there, and I lost my head." He shrugged moodily.

"Hmph!" Arthur snorted. "Well, what's to do now?"

"Damned if I know. My hopes are quite cut up and I don't need you to tell me it's my own fault. The thing is that she not only never thought of me—she wouldn't have had me if she *had* thought of me. I see that now: I never had a chance."

"I don't know that," his cousin observed. "I fancy your chances were better than you realized, if you had not been so impetuous. She may be more receptive when she's reflected."

"Not she," Julian shook his head. "It was as flat and final as she could find the words, Arthur. I could not discompose her by any repetition—nor face a second such scene. The butler heard. It will be all over town by morning. How can I encounter her again? I shall have to leave Bath."

"Yes," Arthur agreed. "Pity, but there it is: you're dished for the moment, old boy. Go away until it blows over, which it will as soon as the next titbit comes along."

"In Bath there won't be another titbit to equal this!" Julian prophesied grimly.

"There's *always* another titbit, even in Bath!"

Lady Inverclyde concurred that evening when Julian entered the salon before dinner. "What's this I hear about you, Imbrie?"

"I've no idea, ma'am. There seems always so much

to engross the gossips in my rather ordinary pursuits that I fear you must give me a clue," he returned stiffly.

"Pish-tush, don't think to give ME a set-down," she snorted. "She wouldn't have you, eh? That's a new experience for you, I'll wager."

Julian compressed his lips. "As you say, ma'am."

The old lady relented. "She'll come about, you'll see. Go away, Imbrie. Give her time to miss you. She will; she's found no common pleasure in your company, she'll not find another beau to equal it," Lady Inverclyde nodded brusquely, "and I suppose you heard that Wrentham's father is dead?"

"I had not. My information service does not equal yours."

"Don't look so castaway," she cackled maliciously. "Sharlie won't have him, either—that's if he offers, which perhaps he won't now that he's succeeded. If I know Caroline Waxe, she'll want something better than a baron's daughter as her successor. Go away, let Sharlie think it over; you be thinking it over, too—and that's my advice to *you*."

After enduring an evening of escorting the older ladies to the play, where he retreated to the rear of the box and observed that the Stanwood's stall was unoccupied, Julian felt the advice was sound—particularly as Stepan was already packing. "At what hour do we leave, milor'?"

"Nine," Julian said curtly. "We'll make for Warwick and try for Calydon in a day. Have the horses set to follow."

"Yes, milor'." Stepan worked silently for a few minutes, while the duke leaned against the window and despondently viewed the moonlight. Finally, "That Maria," Stepan observed, "tell me Mees is very full of crying, but already all advances. The little one talks to her, Maria does not hear, but Mees does not cry any more. They do not go to theatre because visitor comes from London."

Julian started and swung around. *"Who?* The Earl of Waxe?"

"No, no, is Captain," Stepan reassured him. "The friend of little one, Maria say she is *very* glad to see him. Excuse interference, milor'," Stepan hung his head ingratiatingly, "but we think—Maria and me—Mees will be sorry if we go away. Then we come back later, *ne?"*

"Perhaps. I doubt it will answer. My poor Stepan, I have cut up your hopes as well as my own, have I not? I am sorry, but perhaps 'that Maria' will marry you anyway."

"No, she will not," Stepan shook his head positively. "She insist to stay with Mees. So: we must have them both, milor'—that is, if you still want Mees."

The Duke of Imbrie stared absently at his feet, twisting the seal ring on his finger. "I want her," he said tersely. "We leave at nine . . ."

CHAPTER VIII

WHILE THE DUKE was setting forth for Calydon, Sharlie was drinking her morning chocolate and pondering the events of yesterday. Her head felt heavy from the prolonged spell of weeping followed by a restless night, during which she woke repeatedly to a sense of bewilderment. "This cannot be true, I must have dreamed it."

Had the Duke of Imbrie really thrown the world at her feet, asked her to be his wife, sought to draw her into his arms? Her initial shock was compounded by a growing humiliation. How stupid she had been! Mama had warned her not to attempt to promote, that Emily's affections were not settled on anyone. She had been right. When Emily returned from her walk, her reaction to Lady Stanwood's simple statement confirmed all. "Imbrie has made your sister an offer, which she refused, but she is naturally unstrung."

"I should think so!" Emily's blue eyes positively flashed with the light of battle. "The dreadful ugly old man, how did he *dare* approach Sharlie. What could he mean by it?"

"He meant to marry Sharlie," Lady Stanwood remarked, "and he is not old, Emily—no more than thirty-three or four, I judge."

"That IS old—and he's a widower, too. Poor Sharlie," Emily crooned, stroking her sister's hand and kissing her gently. "Of course you couldn't bear him. Shhh, darling, we won't let him have you, will we, mama?"

"No, of course not, and I wish you will go away, Emily. You are making her worse," Lady Stanwood said distractedly, as Charlotte burst into tears once more.

"Oh, mama, he said . . ." and "I was so sure it was Emily, and she doesn't even like him!" and "Everyone will think . . ." she wailed.

"That will do," her mother said firmly. "I am surprised at you, Charlotte. There is no need for an attack of the vapors merely because of an unanticipated offer of marriage. Imbrie has declared himself, you have refused. I am sorry for it, I have long thought you might be well-matched, but if you cannot like him, there is no more to be said."

Sharlie gulped and stared at her. "You have long thought?" she repeated. "You never said so, mama. Why didn't you warn me?"

"Because *I* am not a matchmaker," Lady Stanwood said meaningly, and laid a cloth soaked in lavendar water over Sharlie's eyes. "Pray compose yourself, my love. We must strive to refute gossip by continuing as though nothing had occurred, which swollen red eyes will instantly defeat. I shall take Emily with me for tea, and on our return we shall proceed as planned, with dinner and attendance at the play."

"No! Oh, mama, I cannot!"

"You must," Lady Stanwood stated superbly. "You will wear the violet spider gauze with the fluted velvet pelerine—and if necessary, Tinsdale shall rouge your cheeks, but you will *appear,* Charlotte, and you will hold up your chin with perfect unconcern."

That the Stanwoods did not attend the play was due

to the arrival of Eustace. All three ladies were in the salon, sternly holding the conversation to trivialities, when Beamish announced "Captain Sir Eustace Gayle, milady." Emily's glowing face set the seal on Sharlie's disillusion. In a trice, Emily'd manoeuvred Lady Stanwood into the offer of dinner, the abandonment of the play, "for we must hear all the latest *on dits,* mama, and the play is not thought to be particularly entertaining. Miss Parton viewed it last night, and declares she was never so bored. Do let us remain at home for a comfortable coze?"

For herself, Charlotte asked nothing better, and it was certainly a pleasant evening, but . . . Even Lady Stanwood was looking rather serious as she bade Eustace goodnight.

Setting aside her chocolate cup, Charlotte reminded herself that she was no longer concerned. "What a coil I've made," she shuddered unhappily. "Why did I let him know what I thought, expected? Emily never did; if he had offered for her, she'd have been dismayed—but he doesn't know that. He'll think she was trying to attach him—so I've humiliated her as well as myself. Oh, my wretched tongue! How can I ever hold up my head again? If only we could go home . . ."

She drooped against the pillows until Maria bustled in to remove the tray. "I'll wear the demi-toilette of mulled muslin, I'm not riding today."

"Yes, miss." Silently Maria assisted her mistress to dress, but Sharlie's doleful face wrung her heart. "Oh, please, miss," she said impulsively, "don't take it so hard. There'll be someone you can fancy—not but what his grace is a feather for your cap, so rich and handsome as he is."

"I suppose so."

"Oh, yes, miss. The way he sits his horse, the way

he drives his carriages," Maria sighed. "He's more than a Nonpareil, Miss Stanwood—but you'll not have to see him again. They left Bath early this morning. Eh, what have I said to make you cry?" Maria asked, alarmed.

"Oh, Maria, you don't understand. I never expected . . . I mean, I thought he wanted Miss Emily," Charlotte said despairingly, "and now we are all undone. He thinks she was trying for him, and he's had to leave Bath to avoid embarrassment."

"For *you*, miss," Maria said, extending a handkerchief. "Don't fret yourself, please. 'Twas always *you* in his mind, he never thought either of you was trying for him, miss."

"How do you know that?"

"That Stepan told me," Maria looked a bit conscious. "He'd come through the stableyard and talk French to that Anatole in the kitchen. By what he said," she murmured artfully, "the duke was more interested in our house just because he knew he could be comfortable with our young ladies. Our family wasn't trying to marry him, miss. No, he didn't misunderstand, you've no need to worry."

"I see." Charlotte eyed her abigail in the mirror. "What else did Stepan tell you?"

"Oh—he thought it would be a very good thing, miss, if so be you took to the idea," Maria blushed furiously and hastily turned to gather up Sharlie's bedgown and wrap. "If that's all, miss?"

"Yes, you may go."

Steeling herself to composure, Charlotte accompanied Lady Stanwood to the Pump Room with Emily, where their entrance caused a general turn of heads and pause in conversation, until Lady Inverclyde beckoned imperiously. Head in the air, Lady Stanwood sailed forward, distributing nods and smiles to her acquaintance, and established herself beside the old lady. Further rescue emerged in the person of Eustace, hastening forward to attach himself to their group. By the pressure of his hand and his meaning glance, he was now in possession of the gossip, and anxious to assist by devoting himself to Sharlie as soon as Emily was surrounded by her friends.

It went off surprisingly well despite the peering eyes and muted buzz of voices. There was no sign of Lady Imbrie and her companion. Intense avid curiosity certainly existed, but no indication of social censure. In time, Sharlie stopped shaking inside and was able to chat composedly, to laugh at a quip from Eustace, and look about the room with a smile for her friends.

"Good girl!" Lady Inverclyde said gruffly. "Mind, I think you're a fool, Sharlie. If ever a pair was made for each other—but I don't mean to tease you, child. You'll think it over for yourself . . . and how d'you fancy Biggleswoth for a brother-in-law?"

"If Emily fancies him," Charlotte said with an effort.

"She don't," Lady Inverclyde stated. "Got her eye fixed on Gayle, or I'm out in my reckoning. Pity there's no money, but at least he's not a half-pay officer and the children will be angelic. They won't have any brains, but neither has Emily. Mind, I'm fond of her—you can't help it—but she's a silly goose. Afraid of poor Cupidon, who's lost half his teeth and snores louder than I do!"

Now that the veils were stripped from her eyes, Charlotte saw that Lady Inverclyde was right. Eustace was far more suited to Emily than the duke. Emily would consider him a font of wisdom, where the duke would have been incomprehensible. It was still not wise for her to give her heart so openly. Riding with

Eustace the following day, Sharlie asked bluntly, "Why did you come? How could you so disturb Emily?"

His face was unwontedly grave. "I am for Spain within the month," he said. "Marmont was *rompéd* at Salamanca, Wellington's heading for Madrid to drive King Joseph out—but there's still much to be done before the country's free of Frenchies. We'll see a few engagements before we get them over the mountains."

Sharlie caught her breath, "Does Emily know?"

"No, and ye'll not tell her," Eustace stated firmly, "but 'tis my last chance to see her. Faith, how could I stay away?"

"I suppose you couldn't, but it is not kind to her, Eustace. I—was mistaken about Imbrie's interest," she said with difficulty, "but you are still hopeless. Even with a majority, you cannot conceive of Emily following the drum."

He shook his head, "I'd not ask. The darling must have the best of everything. Sure, she'd not know how to go on," Eustace muttered. "War is no place for a lady—the sights and sounds, and never enough food nor any money. No, I don't think it, Sharlie—but this little time I must have. 'Twill put heart into me for facing the cannons again."

After a moment, Sharlie raised her chin arrogantly. "You will NOT be killed," she stated. "I won't have you even be wounded, Eustace. I shall pray for your protection every day, and so will Emily when she knows . . . and perhaps you'll come home a general."

"I doubt it," he said wryly. "I've not the brains, but 'tis like ye to want my success." Eustace reached for her hand and kissed it affectionately. "Ye're as much a dear as your sister, Sharlie me darlin', and if we're not to be sister and brother-in-law, I'll wish ye the happiest marriage for yourself."

Charlotte looked away with a faint blush. "I doubt *that,* but we'll make a pact to wish good things for each other, shall we?"

"We will!" Eustace kissed her hand again, released it. "Shall we have a gallop?"

"By all means." Sharlie flicked Moonshine lightly and dashed off, oblivious of a solitary rider trotting toward them.

It was Lord Arthur, and he had not missed the horses walking sedately side by side, or the hand kisses. Reining in and turning back, he was conscious of a slight jolt. Did Miss Stanwood really prefer that handsome military *clod* to the Duke of Imbrie? Arthur could not believe it, but certainly he must find out as soon as possible. That evening he drove to Camden Place, and upon observing every sign of a gathering, presented his card to Beamish, after first inquiring whether Lady Stanwood held a party.

"No, milord," Beamish bowed majestically. "Merely a few friends of the young ladies, quite informal."

He was shortly shown into the salon to be welcomed most pleasantly by Lady Stanwood, and to find a group of young people excitedly playing at Lottery Tickets. Sharlie's face was certainly shy, her greeting was a confused murmur, but in a single glance Lord Arthur saw that the dashing captain was seated beside Miss Emily. Inside of two minutes chat with Lady Stanwood, he was reassured. "After the little 'un," he told himself thankfully, and laid himself out to charm his hostess until the game was finished. Then he excused himself and cleverly inserted himself beside Sharlie for Speculation.

When the noise was at its height, he said casually, "I am sorry you are not to be my cousin, Miss Stanwood."

"Oh, pray, do not speak of it. I am so ashamed for my behavior," she murmured. In her agitation, she made a reckless bid and found herself the gainer, which unnerved her even more. "You must know I had not expected . . . and I fear I said a great many things —but so did he."

"I'll be bound Julian did, he holds himself very high, Miss Stanwood—not that he took success for granted." Lord Arthur made a bid for himself and lost. "I must tell you that he was as bashful as a boy, asked m'mother's advice . . ."

"Oh, no, pray," Sharlie said faintly. "Do not speak of it, you cannot know! Why, he actually said that if I wanted you, I'd never get you."

"No more you would," Arthur said cheerfully. "Julian warned me off as soon as I reached Bath—not that it was necessary. I like you very well, Miss Stanwood, but not to mince words, you aren't quite what I have in mind for myself."

"Sharlie, it's your wager," Emily called.

"Oh—I do not bet," Charlotte said at random, oblivious of the exposed king that augured well for capturing the game. She was occupied in controlling herself.

Lord Arthur passed in his turn, and said in an undertone, "Forgive me, I do not mean to overset you, but I must tell you that my cousin is not given to impulsive starts. What he has said, he will mean. If it is abhorrent to you, that is the end of it—but I beg you will reflect." Leaning forward, he examined the exposed card and said, "I bid," while Sharlie looked blindly at her fingers. He said no more for the remainder of the evening, changed his position when a new game was begun, and merely pressed her hand gently with a level glance from his brown eyes before taking his leave.

Lady Stanwood had not failed to notice Sharlie's agonized expression while Lord Arthur sat beside her, but she found herself in a coil. On the one hand she would prefer to remain in Bath, where Imbrie's cousin might cause Charlotte to reverse her attitude—and on the other, she was deeply distressed by the presence of Eustace. If only he had some money! Emily's portion was substantial, but not sufficient without some addition, however modest. She could not make up her mind what best to do. To stay in Bath was to allow Emily to fix her heart—to return to Stanwood Hall was to allow Sharlie to slip back into her spinsterish estate management, to say nothing of Algy Whipsnade lurking in the background.

The question was settled for her: measles had invaded her nursery, and communicated themselves to Geoffrey who had been spending a few weeks at the Hall. An express arrived from Lord Stanwood, saying that all the children had the disease. Since he had never had it, he was removing at once to Park Street, and trusted it was in time to avoid infection.

"Good God!", exclaimed his wife. "Measles? Of all mischances that Geoffrey should have contracted them, for they are much more uncomfortable for adults. Well, there is no help for it. We must go home." She frowned slightly, "I forget—you and Emily have had them, have you not?"

"No, I think not," Emily began, but Sharlie bore over her.

"Of course we did, Emily—at Aunt Eliza's when we were about ten. She was vastly annoyed with us," Charlotte said severely, "not but what she was always annoyed with anything we did."

"Yes, I suppose so," Emily agreed weakly, "but why must we leave Bath, mama? There is Miss Dunning and Mrs. Fawcett and Dr. Ambrough—and it seems as though we would be more trouble than assistance. Extra meals and chamber service, after all, when they already have so much to do."

Lady Stanwood eyed her sharply, but she said only, "When you have children, my love, you will understand better. I daresay, Georgie, Edmund and Louisa might go on satisfactorily without me, but it is a different matter with Geoffrey. I am sorry, but I cannot be easy to be away from him at this moment."

"Yes, mama," Emily sighed, dolefully.

For her part, Sharlie was never happier than when they set forth early the next morning. By seven o'clock they were turning through the modest gateposts of Stanwood Hall, and wearily seeking their chambers for freshening before dinner. Lady Stanwood had instantly visited the sick rooms, and when at last they sat down at table, she was as dismal as her daughters had ever seen her.

"Geoffrey is so full of measles, I don't know where it will end," she said, "and here is your father gone to London to be out of the way of infection—but will he think to send Sir Henry Halford? It is his heir, after all, but depend upon it," bitterly, "your father will be enjoying a snug dinner and a look-in at Watier's or Boodle's."

"Well, but if the measles are dangerous at twenty-three," Sharlie pointed out, "how much more dangerous at papa's age . . . and you know Dr. Ambrough is very sound. Papa has every confidence in him."

"Yes," Emily put in softly, "and everything will go on more smoothly tomorrow when Beamish and Tinsdale and Maria arrive, Mama. It is every way sad they could not make our pace because of the luggage, but Sharlie and I are here, and I will brush your hair at bedtime. You know that always makes you ready to sleep."

"Yes." Lady Stanwood looked at her daughters with sternly controlled lips. "You're good girls," she said abruptly. "No woman could ask for better. Let's have tea and go to bed."

Sharlie was out to the stables and riding over the estate before breakfast next day. Within two days (though nothing was said) all of Stanbury knew that Miss Sharlie had received an offer of monumental distinction, and rejected it. The village was riven in twain, although loyally behind her. One half was proud she'd had the chance for a rejection, and the other half was sad he hadn't suited, while agreeing that Miss Sharlie wasn't to be married off like a sack of meal.

"She might change her mind," Maria confided. "He takes getting used to before you see he's right handsome, and he startled her like, but he understands horses and all those languages she learned with Sir Geoffrey."

"Wot about Miss Em'ly, then?" Maria's mother inquired. "You wrote she was the Belle of Lunnon, but she looks peaked to me. Is she sickening for summat?"

"She's unhappy to leave Bath," Maria admitted. "She was the belle there, too. Eh, the house was never quiet unless they were out. Mr. Bigglesworth and the Captain were for riding escort to her ladyship, but Mr. B. had never had the measles and the Captain's leave was ended—he had to return to London." Then, *very* casually, Maria added, "If so be there's a letter for me, Ma, you'll take it in and keep it safe till I come. 'Tis a friend I made in London, I'd not like to lose word of the news from her."

"Letters? Eh, very grand we be with our Lunnon friends!" Her mother pretended scorn, but Maria knew she was in high gig over her daughter's success as an abigail. Few of the Stanbury locals had ever been privileged to visit the metropolis. Maria's descriptions cast glory on her family, as well as affording absorbing details of town life to their friends . . . but she was still not giving anything away, such as the guinea Miss Emily had slipped to her, "for your trouble in watching for a letter. I know I should not," Miss Emily's eyes filled with tears, "but he is going off to that horrid war, and you do see how I shall be agonized unless I have some word?"

The first weeks were necessarily restricted. Lady Stanwood devoted herself to her measle-y offspring, Sharlie plunged into the estate affairs left unfinished by his lordship's precipitate departure, and Emily drooped disconsolately. Only a few of the neighbors had had the disease and might dare to call. She missed the busy excitement of the past months, desperately missed Eustace, and was altogether useless. There was literally nothing Emily could *do* to amuse herself, aside from sewing and embroidery. She was no great reader, could not tell one card from another for a game of Solitaire; the heavy late summer heat made walking uncomfortable, nor did she care to stroll without someone to talk to. Lady Stanwood felt very sympathetic for her loneliness, while at the same time exasperated. There was not even the bugaboo of Algy Whipsnade; the Squire's wife had instantly informed Lady Stanwood of his betrothal to a suitable young lady from Oundle.

Despite her relief at being away from Bath and constantly busy, Sharlie was less happy than she'd expected. It was certainly good to supervise byres and barns or ride the land among old friends who made no reference to romance, but she found herself recalling the duke far more often than was comfortable. She missed his astringent comments that always threatened to cause unladylike giggles under the eyes of Almack patronesses. She wondered what he would advise in this or that estate matter; his knowledge was greatly superior to hers. She remembered the way he sometimes took her seriously, and sometimes laughed at her gently. The deep voice, expressive eyes, charming smile, were all too clear in her mind, as well as the hand guiding her in a waltz or instructing her in handling the ribbons. Most of all she remembered Bascombe and his mastery of Ajax when drawing off the bull.

If she had been going to marry him, Bascombe was the house of all she'd ever seen that she felt would be a happy home. It would be too small to contain an adequate nursery—Sharlie blushed at her thoughts—but Julian had said he would build whatever she wanted wherever she liked, he'd even tear down his horrid castle and replace it.

Julian—was a nice name, it suited him and his air of authority. Lord Wrentham's Christian name was Cedric. "Good God, it's as bad as Eustace," Sharlie said to herself—not that it mattered. "What's in a name? A rose by any other . . ."

The nursery recovered from the measles. Geoffrey took another ten days and was disastrously limp when pronounced cured. His convalescence proved more onerous than his bed of pain. Sir Geoffrey was impatient, imperious, demanding, and—said Sharlie—an utter beast!

"Merely because he is not yet fit to be in the saddle or walk as far as the stream in search of a fish, why must he fuss and disapprove? Demanding an account of what *I* have done," she said hotly, "when papa trusts me implicitly! Mama, I wish you will remind him he has no authority. Stanwood does not yet belong to him—thank God!"

"So say I," her brother retorted, "and you'd better marry someone, because I won't have you telling me how to go on! I'll tell you what, Sharlie: you're a shrew!"

"How can you say such a thing," Emily cried, running to put her arms about Charlotte. "Papa does trust her, he depends on her, which is more than can be said for you, and she is NOT a shrew. She's the sweetest, dearest, person in the world, and you are lucky to have her, because you would *not* know how to go on, let alone being weak as a kitten."

"That will DO!" said Lady Stanwood, awesomely. "If you wish to quarrel like children, you will remove to the nursery. I have the headache."

"Oh, poor mama! Of course you do after nursing this ungrateful monster," Sharlie sympathized. "Come away, Geoff, and let Emily take care of her. If you've the strength, I wish you would walk to the stables with me. I fancy one of papa's hunters is throwing out a splint."

"Oh, very well," he agreed ungraciously. "I collect you admit there are *some* things I understand better than your highness?" But he followed her from the room, and Sharlie contrived to keep him amused for an hour of consultation, until they returned in perfect charity with each other. The happy suggestion from Emily, of teaching Sharlie the intricacies of piquet—"because I am hopeless with cards"—filled the evening.

Nevertheless, Stanwood Hall was on edge in a way formerly unknown. The staff walked warily and avoided loud voices. It was understood that Sir Geoffrey was fretting with inactivity. "Resty is what 'e is," said his

Tiger wisely. "We'd ought to be orf to town, where 'e'd find a few larks, but there—'e ain't got the strength yet."

The one letter Emily had received, smuggled by Maria, completely unstrung her with the news that Eustace had reached Lisbon en route to join Wellington. This caused her to cry herself to sleep, and arise with such a dismal face as agitated her mother. "No, I have not the measles, mama. I've already *had* them." For Emily her tone was snappish.

Charlotte was equally snappish. "I suppose it's Eustace being posted again," she said privately to her sister, "but you know full well neither papa nor mama would allow you to throw yourself away on him, charming or not."

"No," Emily suppressed a sob, "but at least he is *young*. All you've got is that ugly old widower, and perhaps Lord Wrentham, if he ever offers."

"Imbrie is NOT old and ugly," Sharlie flared, "and if I wouldn't have him, I certainly wouldn't have the Earl of Waxe."

"Girls!" Lady Stanwood's voice cut across the melee. "Calm yourselves! What has put you in a tweak? I declare I do not know how I shall survive. Here am I, worn to the bone—my children squabbling, and your father arrives this evening for dinner. I am not prone to the vapors," she said with dignity, "but your behavior may easily induce them."

"Oh, poor mama!" Both girls ran forward penitently. "How hateful we are, forgive us?" Sharlie said remorsefully. "Emily, take mama to her chamber and brush her hair. You are so clever at it, where I am all thumbs—and I will send word that we must have *all* her favorite dishes for dinner, as well as MacLean's finest blooms for the centerpiece."

Under such soothing ministrations, Lady Stanwood allowed herself to be led away for a few hours of repose—but it did not answer, for upon Lord Stanwood's arrival, Sharlie attacked him on the grounds of selfishness. "You think only of yourself—what about Mama, who has had to deal with everything?"

Lord Stanwood opened his pale blue eyes very wide. "Damme, what else should she do? That is the wife's responsibility. Lud, you don't expect *me* to run the risk of infection?"

"No, I've no wish for your illness, sir. I doubt not it would overset all of us," Sharlie shrugged. "Merely, it would be *helpful* if you returned to Park Street, taking Geoffrey with you, and allowed us time to regain our strength."

"Well, 'pon my soul, that's a pretty welcome!" his lordship exclaimed indignantly. "What's come over you, Sharlie?"

In the connubial bedchamber, Lady Stanwood told him. "She's in love and doesn't know it," she sighed. "So is Emily—and she *does* know it. God knows what's to be done, Robert."

Nor was his lordship of any assistance when his lady poured out the facts. "God bless my soul," he muttered. "Rejected *Imbrie?* Good God, Nelly!"

"Well, she did," Lady Stanwood could not repress a faint sniffle, "not but what I'm positive she regrets it already, for she is so impatient and waspish as passes belief—but what's to be done?"

"Lud, Nelly, how should I know? It was agreed you'd do what was best for the girls, but I must say you've managed very ill," Lord Stanwood frowned. "Here's Sharlie rejecting the first catch in England, and Emily fixing her mind on a penniless nobody."

Lady Stanwood's eyes filled with tears. It was the first

time in twenty years he'd seen his wife weeping. Naturally, he went to pieces at once. "Now, now, my little love," he patted her shoulder anxiously, "we'll come about. You'll see."

Such affectionate condolence sent his wife into suppressed sobs. "Sharlie *told* me Eustace was in love with Emily," she sniffed against his stalwart shoulder, "and I *told* her Imbrie didn't care for Emily, nor Emily for him, but it didn't answer. Oh, Robert, it is all my fault, and I should have consulted you at the outset."

"Well, why didn't you?"

"Because you'd have put your foot into it somehow —not that it matters now, and I suppose they will both get over it, but it is very lowering to my spirits, Robert, even though my strategy was right. Imbrie did follow her to Bath, where he *never* goes and I am sure I cannot wonder at it, for his mother is a most dismal female—but however, he did come and he did make Sharlie an offer."

"What of it, if the silly chit won't have him? Had you given me a hint, I'd have talked her round."

"Exactly what I feared, for you must know that it was her utter unconsciousness that attached him," Lady Stanwood said. "I own that had you returned to us from Newmarket, been available to receive Imbrie's offer, all might have been different."

"Lud, Nelly, I'm to blame for going *fishing?* If you needed me, you'd only to send word."

"Send it where? You gave me no direction, Robert. In any case, I had no certainty of Imbrie's sentiments, and the presence of a father kicking his heels in London would be the very circumstance to cause Imbrie's retreat. All my object was to make him feel there was no expectation."

"You did too good a job of it!"

"Yes, but how could I dream he would address her without a prior word?" she sighed. "Had he so much as asked where you might be found, given me the least indication of wishing formal permission to speak, Robert—*then* I could have ventured to prepare Sharlie. Now all is at a stand. I'm certain she's unhappy for it, but he'll not renew his offer. No man would after such a set-down," she winced, "for it could not be suppressed, everyone in the house was aware. It was all over Bath within hours, and Imbrie left next morning. He'll not try again."

"Good God, of course not. So that's why . . ." his lordship muttered. "Heard he was in town, didn't happen to run across him, but I fancy he's going to Greece."

Lady Stanwood closed her eyes faintly and moaned.

"Well, it may have been someone else," he said hastily. "I wasn't paying close attention. Somebody's going somewhere, and from what you tell me, it's like to be Imbrie—always off to some devilish foreign place or other, even when he hasn't been rejected."

In fact, it *was* Julian and he was thinking of going to Greece—a destination devoutly wished by everyone at Calydon Towers, particularly his children. "Or at least," amended Lord Giles with a scowl, "I don't care where he goes, so long as he leaves."

"That is not a proper way to speak of your father," said Miss Tolliver severely.

"Oh, stuff," he retorted. "You wish he'd go away, too, after his raking you over the coals about Cinda's 'deplorable accent in the French language,' and don't deny it, Tolly."

"And what is so unfair is that we've learned more

from Tolly in six months than ever before!" Lady Lucinda agreed indignantly. "Even you, Gillie, because you said yourself she makes it interesting."

"Thank you," the governess bowed to her charges with an austere countenance that cast them into giggles. "May I suggest that further application to your arithmetic problems will reveal vistas of interest hitherto undreamed-of?"

"Why?"

"How will you know whether your steward is managing your estates properly unless you can figure the ratio of profit for yourself? How will you know when you can afford an expensive improvement to your lands?" Miss Tolliver asked, surprised. "How will Cinda know whether her housekeeper is efficient and whether the chef is pocketing a percentage for patronizing the most expensive purveyors? Why, you would not know how to place your bets and count your winnings at Boodle's, or for silver-loo at a lady's morning party. *Anyone* could cheat you—and let me tell you that indifferent, incompetent masters make lazy, thieving servants. Take up your slates—how much is 13, plus 14, plus 15?"

"All the same," said Giles when the sums were completed and they were grouped about the globe, "I wish he would go away. I quite liked him at Aunt Georgie's, he told me all sorts of things and showed me how to cast. He didn't even mind Cinda tagging along, it was regularly splendid—but now it's all different. He just grumbles and glooms, and tells us he hasn't time, but I can't see that he's *doing* anything very particular."

"He's been crossed in love," Cinda reminded him. "I *told* you, Gillie. The Clapham wrote the Vicar's wife all about it. I couldn't hear it all, because they discovered me sitting outside the window and sent me away. But however, there is no doubt—and I think you should not have asked him if we were to have a step-mamma, Gillie, nor said 'you mean she doesn't want you, either,' when he said we would not."

"Phoo!" Giles said valiantly. "Very probably we shouldn't have liked her in any case. Let's choose a place for him to visit," spinning the globe. "Close your eyes, Cinda, and point. Any place will do."

That her finger rested on the Nipponese Isles—on the other side of the world—was thought by the twins to be an exquisite joke!

CHAPTER IX

AUGUST WAS GONE, together with Lord Stanwood and Sir Geoffrey, who departed for Scotland, grouse and salmon. "Damme, milady," said his lordship irately, "between Sharlie's sharp tongue and Emily's vapors, I've no appetite for the best dinner you'd set before me. I'll be off to Kirkcudbright in the morning."

"I pray you will take Geoffrey with you," Lady Stanwood returned, and sailed out of the room with her nose in the air.

While the atmosphere of Stanwood Hall was less sulphurous with their absence, discontent remained. Charlotte was irritable, Emily was disconsolate, and Lady Stanwood was at her wit's end with both of them. She was positive Sharlie pined secretly for Imbrie, yet how to get him back? Before Bath, it was merely to allow Imbrie to learn where Miss Stanwood was to be found, and hope that he would follow. Now, Sharlie must somehow physically cross his path, and apparently by accident. It was far easier to state the problem than to solve it at this time of year. Could they have remained in Bath, a word to Lady Inverclyde would have passed to Lord Arthur who would (she was certain) have informed his cousin that Sharlie appeared to regret her words. *If* Imbrie's interest had survived, he could have returned to Bath . . . or come to Stanbury when Lord Arthur informed him of their removal.

At this season, gentlemen ruralized; their ladies visited relatives, like Lady Inverclyde. When Flora left Bath, she traditionally descended upon her two daughters and three sons, striking terror in all hearts. Even the Sixth Marquis of Inverclyde quailed under his mother's piercing eye, "and what is so *unfair,*" his wife remarked bitterly, "she never says *when*—she simply *arrives,* and one has no possible chance to arrange previous engagements . . . and she has no fixed schedule. One year she visits youngest to oldest, and another year she reverses it, and just as we think this time it will be by ascending age, she makes a circle tour—going to the next nearest, you know."

"And what is more," her sister-in-law added, "she will never say who gets her when she leaves you; we cannot even send an express warning, and at this time of year one has always so *many* arrangements to be made for hunting and holiday houseparties, but *all* must be put aside, or she will insist upon seeing the guest lists—and changing everything about. It quite puts one in a frenzy!"

Lady Stanwood herself, despite her preoccupation with Imbrie, had similar parties to be planned that would carry country society through the winter months. She thought and thought, but could discover no solution. The Duke of Imbrie was undoubtedly catching fish or shooting game birds at the moment, but he could be doing this anywhere in England or Scotland . . . and upon reflection she devoutly hoped he would not accidentally encounter Lord Stanwood. It was a groat to a shilling that her spouse wouldn't make some disastrous reference to Bath! Yet if something were not contrived rapidly, the Duke of Imbrie would be gone travelling again, if Lord Stanwood was right . . .

In the face of Charlotte's unhappiness, Lady Stanwood was inclined to impatience with Emily's dolor. "Had I realized a single taste of Society would so impair your former enjoyment of simple pleasures," she observed tartly, "I would have sent you to your Aunt Eliza. I wish you will cease these sighs and tears for the cessation of past glories. You will have them again in six months."

"Y—yes, Mama," Emily gulped, and ran from the room with a sob.

"It's Eustace," Sharlie remarked. "I told you how it would be, Mama. He's gone back to Spain, that was why he had leave to come to Bath."

"Oh, dear!"

"I don't know that he told her, he didn't intend to do so," Sharlie sighed, "but she must suspect, particularly when there is no word of him. He was used to being so much in our family that I'm certain he would have written to us to say how all goes on, if he were still in England, don't you think so?"

"Oh, I suppose," Lady Stanwood agreed unhappily, "and I admit you were right in your warning, my love, but I hoped . . . That is, out of sight out of mind, and she's still so young. One would expect she would get over it."

"Not," said Sharlie, "when one has recognized love, Mama."

The Stanwood males returned from Scotland, bearing two fine fat salmon wrapped in thick layers of seaweed, and several brace of grouse. For a while their presence created sufficient diversion to draw the girls out of their glooms. There were shooting parties for local gentlemen; county society entertained at dinners, arranged picnics and modest balls. Lord Stanwood directed Geoffrey to lend his curricle to Sharlie, and personally accompanied her for an estimate of her competence—which he declared adequate for setting up her own carriage. *That* indulgence produced such joyous squeals and kisses from his daughter as required her to be sternly called to order.

Lady Stanwood began to breathe more easily. Sharlie was sparkle-eyed at the promise of a curricle. Emily was revived by the increase of social engagements. Geoff was enjoying his status as the local buck, fluttering all female sensibilities, and finding Georgie grown enough for endurance on a ride, or fishing the local streams when nothing better offered for amusement. Lord Stanwood rode his land, approved of Charlotte's decisions in his absence, and Edmund and Louisa did *not* do anything outrageous—such as coating various church pews with fresh glue.

The inhabitants of Stanwood Hall were in perfect harmony for a full two weeks—after which all reversed itself to such a point that Lady Stanwood had recourse to her vinaigrette on every occasion.

There was first a formal missive delivered to Lord Stanwood from the new Earl of Waxe, requesting the hand of his elder daughter. "Lud, Nelly, what's to do about this?"

"She won't have him," his wife said flatly, "but you'd better leave it to me to get her answer."

"Why?"

"Why *what?*" she countered impatiently. "If you mean why won't she have him, it's because she's finally realized she wants Imbrie."

Charlotte put it more simply. Summoned to her father's study and apprised by Lady Stanwood, "My love, your father has received a request for your hand from the Earl of Waxe—but it is agreed you are to make your own choice," Charlotte was first astounded and then distressed.

"No," she said succinctly.

"Why not?" her father inquired.

"Papa, you cannot wish me to marry someone called Cedric!" Sharlie said desperately.

"Good God, what has that to say to anything?" he demanded, bewildered. "It's a family name, all the Wrenthams have a Cedric. It was his father's name and his grandfather's, and it'll go to his oldest son, and what of it, Sharlie? Man can't help his name . . . I must say."

"Not *now,* Robert," Lady Stanwood said firmly. "Charlotte refuses him, you must write a rejection—and if you are uncertain of the phrasing, I will assist you later. Come, my dear."

"Is Papa angry with me?" Sharlie asked fearfully.

"No, indeed," her mother assured her. "I fancy he may be surprised, for you seemed to like Wrentham very well in London, but no one will give you a scold."

But when this was shortly followed by Emily's refusal of Viscount Pelham, Lord Stanwood was somewhat more than surprised. "God bless me, Nelly, what is wrong with your daughters? Are they meaning to turn down every member of the peerage in descending order?" he asked in astonishment. "So far we've had a duke, an earl and the heir to a marquis—I don't know how it will end. In heaven's name, what do the girls want?"

In a burst of temper two days later, Geoffrey said he didn't care *what* they wanted—*he* didn't want two aged spinsters in his future establishment.

"Do not worry," Sharlie retorted with spirit. "If you are meaning to offer for that platter-faced daughter of the Harbisons, I wouldn't live in the house with her."

"Elizabeth is *not* platter-faced," Geoffrey flushed furiously.

"No," his small sister Louisa agreed, "*I* think she looks more like a fish, don't you, Emily?"

"A tench," Edmund added helpfully. "It's your turn to deal, Louisa."

Matters were not improved by Sharlie's involuntary giggle, but worse was to follow. Upon entering Emily's chamber unexpectedly, Lady Stanwood discovered her weeping over a sheet of paper. "What have you there?" she asked suspiciously, and twitched it from Emily's fingers to identify—a letter from Eustace! That it was remarkably ill-spelled and contained no word of *love* did not mitigate the shock of an illicit correspondence. The uproar in Bath was nothing compared to Lord Stanwood's explosion; even Beamish trembled, while Miss Tinsdale took pains to keep out of his lordship's way.

Everybody wept, but Emily most of all. "You don't understand," she moaned when Sharlie sought to console her. "I *am* glad he's safe, but—but he's *enjoying* himself in Madrid!"

The sight of his favorite daughter in constant tears became too much for Lord Stanwood. "Good God, Nelly, I can't stand this curst weeping," he said irascibly. "Geoff can remove himself to friends, but I'm fixed here for the Bench sessions and Assizes. Send Emily to Eliza and for heaven's sake, let us have a little peace."

Lady Stanwood heartily agreed, she was sick of the girls, too. For good measure, she sent Sharlie with her sister, "and I do not want you back until you have stopped crying," she said severely, "so you may as well take Moonshine and Firefly."

Charlotte was able to face the visit with fortitude. Her father's sister was domiciled near Grantham which was Melton country and considered the best hunting in England. On Moonshine's back, she could always get away from Lady Eliza's caustic remarks. Emily was not so fortunate, although, between the devil of her aunt and the deep blue sea of riding, Emily would take Firefly. Her lamentations and protests against the removal were in vain, however.

"Nonsense," said Lady Stanwood, bracingly. "One would think you were being cast out of heaven. A change of air will be good for you."

"Stanbury is no heaven," Emily muttered sulkily, "but Grantham is certainly hell."

"WHAT did you say?" her mother demanded, awefully.

"I beg your pardon, Mama," Emily stuttered, and burst into tears exactly as her father entered the room.

"Oh, good GOD, not *again!*" said Lord Stanwood violently, and departed without pausing.

Lady Stanwood's heart was touched by Emily's misery, she was half-minded to send the girls to her own sister near Oxford, but the riding horses had already been despatched to Eliza. Best to leave it as it was—but had she known, she would have sent her daughters to Lady Eliza long since, for Calydon Towers was no more than eight miles away.

The Duke of Imbrie was not presently in residence, to the unabashed relief of his children. As Lady Stanwood had surmised, Julian had shot birds in Aberdeen, fished in Inverness and Argyll, gone north to Moray and south to Roxburghe—moving restlessly from one host to another, and finding himself hard put for civility. He was in no humor for the evening wine and gambling of male parties, but even less inclined for the conventional insipidities of the young ladies introduced to his notice. Neither was solitude to his taste after a week at Rickaby. By the time Arthur joined him for the sport of Calydon coverts, Julian owned to desperation.

"I'll be off on the first boat out of Portsmouth," he shrugged, "preferably to the Mediterranean. It should be safe enough by now; the latest dispatches indicate Wellington's pushing Joseph ahead of him up to the Pyrenees, and Boney's too far to the North to reinforce in Spain."

Arthur nodded. "I'm sorry," he said quietly, "but maybe it's best you should go away entirely for a time. It may be easier among total strangers."

"It'll never be easier," Julian muttered. "Damme, I'd got used to her, Arthur. I could talk to her, I'd no need to guard my tongue or confine myself to chitchat. I'm too old for the ninnyhammers, I found them boring from the moment I returned last year—and after finding one female with a mind, how can I endure a return to simpers, blushes, social pretenses?"

"You don't feel like trying again?"

"How can I? I would not so embarrass her. I've had my answer. It would be the same if I made a formal offer to Lord Stanwood. I hoped perhaps, if I went away, you might have noted a change," Julian sighed, "but it didn't answer."

"There was not the time, no more than ten days before Lady Stanwood was forced to remove by illness in her nursery. I wrote you."

"Yes, but I'm not upon such terms with her parents that I could venture to call without a formal invitation. Depend upon it, she will have Waxe," Julian finished gloomily.

"Now *there* I'm positive you're out," Arthur observed. "I fancy he's been rejected, too. Saw him at Boodle's a while back, he was looking almighty pleased with himself that evening—saw him again about a week later, and he was definitely glum when Miss Stanwood's name was mentioned."

"What of it? Doesn't mean she'd have me," but Arthur thought his cousin looked faintly cheered, and since he was sincerely fond of Julian, he set his mind to discovering some way by which to determine Sharlie's possible change of heart. The simplest procedure, when he'd located Stanbury on the map, would be to call upon Lady Stanwood, on the pretense of discovering Stanwood Hall was on his way to a friend. Luckily, before he had set forth, a chance houseparty word revealed that Lord Stanwood would be at home for his duties in local justice—so *that* was ruled out: Arthur could not call informally at the home of a man with whom he was unacquainted when the man was in residence. It would have been brash enough to visit Lady Stanwood on the strength of no more than a few weeks in Bath, but under the circumstances, he had thought he might risk it.

He debated a letter, but again, the acquaintance was too slight. The incident at Bath had not been mentioned between them, and while she must know he was aware—how could he be ignorant of what everyone in Bath knew?—might she not be affronted by any reference to it? He did not know, could not judge her reaction to a blunt inquiry, and dared not chance setting her back up.

His next idea was the possibility of encountering some of Lord Stanwood's friends in the London clubs, and in this he was successful. Unfortunately, those whom Arthur knew at all well were all bound for shooting parties far away from Northamptonshire. In desperation, he sought information on Sir Geoffrey, but while he turned up the names of a few cronies, none was at all familiar. After four weeks of asking casual questions, Arthur had nothing but the general statement that Lord Stanwood was a sound man, and the son was satisfactory.

Unaware of his cousin's efforts, Julian was busily arranging his trip, and if Arthur was discouraged, Stepan was even more so. Every time they reached London, he slipped over to the rear of Park Street, but Anatole had no news. Not even a groom had been sent down from Stanbury since the end of the measles. "At this season it is never," said Anatole comfortably. "*Alors*, it is as good as a vacation. Have another slice of this *tarte de pigeonneaux, mon vieux*."

Stepan began to feel desperate, this constant moving about was very unsettling. They had now been more than a year in England, and Stepan discovered within himself a reluctance to resume the old life of ships and rented villas. He thought that the duke's heart was not in it, either. They had been once to Plymouth and thrice to Portsmouth without milor' finding a voyage to suit him. For some reason he was determined on Greece; at last, grudgingly, he settled for Malta, to weigh anchor in early December, but despite commanding suitable clothing for southern climates and being fitted at Weston's whenever they were in town, Stepan was by no means sure they would actually take ship.

On the other hand, Lady Imbrie had returned to Calydon from Bath, and in the duke's present frame of mind, Stepan was glumly certain that a week of his mother would cause milor' to depart whether he really wanted to travel or not.

If only it were possible to consult Maria, but Stepan's penmanship was limited to Greek. Robsey could write for him and read the reply, but what could Stepan say that would not be a breach of discretion? From the stable maps, he painfully located Stanbury; he judged it to be about a four-hour ride from Calydon. In the old days, he would have asked for the loan of a horse and some free time "to improve an acquaintance, milor'," and his grace would have granted it at once, "On condition you report progress" or perhaps, "If she has a sister, I'll come with you."

He would probably still give permission, but Stepan shrank from the appearance of dalliance when the duke was so far from it. He had decided to chance it when they were at Bascombe. "Here, all reminds him, why must that stupid Cargill insist on telling milor' the report from Miss Stanwood's gardener? Definitely, I must see Maria; I will do it when we return to Calydon. . . . we must certainly return; milor' would not depart with a personal leave-taking, would he?"

November arrived, and they were still in the south going back and forth between Grosvenor Square and Bascombe. The duke's new wardrobe was completed; he was going over financial affairs with his Uncle Biddulph and outlining estate work with Lord Arthur. Stepan was more and more anxious, but finally his grace said, "We leave for Calydon tomorrow. Arrange about the horses, I'll get in some hunting, and we'll go direct to the ship. Robsey can send what's here to meet us in Portsmouth."

"Very good, milor'."

The instant his grace had left for his club, Stepan slipped over to Anatole, where at last good fortune awaited. *"Ahé, mon copain,* you find us *affairé.* Sir Geoffrey arrives *sans un mot.* Tomorrow he goes, *grace à Dieu,* but for tonight there must be the 'snoog dinnair,' " the chef snorted wearily. "*Alors,* they have eaten, they have gone to lose the money on the cards. *Asseyez-vous,* Stepan—and do you know Jemmy, who is the Tiger?"

"No, I have not had that pleasure," Stepan bowed politely, to which Jemmy choked on his coffee.

"Coo-er, 'oo's this cove?" but once the amenities were observed, Jemmy was a mine of information—except that his English was Cockney interlarded with boxing cant and various expressions better known to Bow Street than to gentlemen's servants. Luckily Anatole did not understand Jemmy any better than Stepan, and was so insistent on having things explained that Stepan returned to Grosvenor Square with the gist.

"Why are you still packing at this hour?" the duke demanded.

"Because I have visited a friend this evening," Stepan replied cockily, "and there is a development."

"I trust you have not left your calling card with any maid belonging to my neighbors," Julian grunted, tossing his neckcloth aside.

"No, no, it is not that sort of development, milor'—merely that Mees and her sister have made refusals, and all becomes so uncomfortable they have gone to stay with an aunt."

"WHAT?" Julian whirled, his eyes blazing. "Where had you this?"

"From the Tiger of the brother who comes unannounced for a day before a shooting," Stepan shrugged casually, "I do not know which aunt. It is a Lady Alden."

Julian stared at him transfixed. "Good God," he said in a hushed voice. "Good GOD!"

"Please?" Stepan widened his eyes alertly.

The duke made no answer. Slowly he disrobed, his eyes fixed on space while Stepan quietly removed discarded clothing. At long last Julian turned to his servant and clapped him on the shoulders. "Be of good cheer," he grinned. "You may yet have 'that Maria.' We leave at nine."

Immolated at Alden, Emily had no cheer at all. Her eyes filled with tears on the slightest excuse, until her aunt roundly censured her for a stupid pea-goose. "Do not be putting on these lachrymose airs to be interesting," she advised. "You are far too young to wear the willow, particularly for a young man who—from what I can discover—has been treating you as a sort of younger sister."

Emily's tears then became resentful, until Charlotte got her alone, and said "Aunt Eliza is right, you know. It will not do. My dearest sister, do but consider the embarrassment for Eustace."

"How so?"

Sharlie steeled herself against the widened blue eyes. "Darling, he never said he loved you, never hinted at an offer. In fact, there was no word in his letters that might not just as well have been addressed to the entire family," she pointed out, "and it was sheer folly for you to be making a secrecy of it that has cost Maria her job. I do not know why Eustace should have lent himself to such idiocy, except that he is very easy-humored and would accede to whatever anyone suggested.

"It must be embarrassing enough for him to receive the set-down which I doubt not papa sent him for 'illicit correspondence,' when he'd meant no more than to give news of his well-being to a family that had, in some sort, treated him as a relative, but how much more embarrassing to discover that you have taken this as a distinguishing mark of attention for yourself alone! Emily, dear," Sharlie went on earnestly, "only think of his position. You must not—you really must *not* give him the reputation of a heartless betrayer, for nothing is more easily believed than that a handsome officer has trifled with a young lady's affections and blithely departed to the wars. It could ruin him for further promotion in the only career he has."

"Oh, no!" Emily protested aghast.

"Oh, yes," Sharlie said firmly. "If you care for Eustace, you will strive for composure, and at once, Emily. Thus far, your tears seem merely shame for naughtiness, but let them continue and the servants will gossip—once that begins, the fanciest tales will fly about. What's more," grimly, "the worse they are, the more they'll be credited. Remember Bath!"

"It was not the same thing at all," Emily shook her head, "and in any event, it all blew over—but I shall never see Eustace again. Oh, Sharlie!"

"I don't know," her sister said slowly. "I wish you would be sensible, darling. Think! It was always hopeless at this moment, but let Eustace return with preferment, and if you have found no other preference, I fancy papa would entertain his offer. That is, should he make one." Sharlie eyed Emily's rosy blush suspiciously. "What makes you think he will? Has he said so?"

"No—but I know," Emily said simply, "and I shall not find any preference, no matter how many seasons I have."

"I suppose not," Sharlie agreed ruefully. "I remember now: you were always the most stubborn brat imaginable, constantly tagging after Geoff and me when we were trying to escape from Miss Dunning."

"I expect I was a nuisance, I could never walk as fast or as far as you," Emily smiled reminiscently, "but it was so wonderful to be with you. I thought you were grown-ups, you know, because you used to be sent for after dinner, and you seemed to know so much more than I did. You still do."

"By no means," Charlotte muttered drily. "At least you know your own mind—but however, if you are fixed on Eustace, I can tell you how best to go on, for you have made a sad hash of it so far. First, you must *stop* crying and put Eustace aside for the moment. You must make every effort for normal happy enjoyment of every day, until it appears you are recovered from your attachment."

"And then?" Emily asked, lips parted in earnest attention.

"You must go through your London seasons, accepting flowers and favors, with just enough flirting to convince Mama you are willing to bestow your heart. The more offers, the better. Papa won't force you to accept," Sharlie pointed out, "but then, when Eustace turns up, it will be obvious to Papa and Mama that you will have no one else, so they might as well agree."

"You make it sound simple," Emily said after a moment, "but that could take years, Sharlie—and what if he were to be . . . killed?"

"That is a risk all women take, I fancy," Sharlie replied. "Mama is often uneasy when Papa goes hunting or competes in a private race . . . and how would it be different if you were Eustace's wife? Would it not be worse to lose what one has known, become accustomed to love, than never fully to have known it at all?"

"Do you really think so?" Emily asked doubtfully.

"Of course. How horrid to be a widow!"

"Yes—look at Lady Inverclyde."

"By all means," said Sharlie. "She is the perfect example, for she was not at all as she is now before Inverclyde's death. Mama says she was the sweetest, dearest, most delightful person in the world."

"Lady *Inverclyde?* Charlotte, you're bamming!"

"No, I am not. Ask Mama."

Emily was very thoughtful for the rest of the day, but by dinner time she had regained composure and made a valiant effort to join in the conversation. Unfortunately, her aunt had also been cogitating, and the outcome was that Emily was not sufficiently occupied. "The devil finds work for idle hands. Keep her too busy for repining," Lady Alden said to herself—and forthwith unloaded all her less agreeable chores on her niece. Let Emily attend the Sewing Circle for Orphans . . . let Emily supervise the games for Johnny's birthday party . . . let Emily finish the embroidered altar cloth Lady Alden had started in a burst of piety (and a siege of gout).

"Good God," said Emily desperately, "she has a new notion every time I enter the room, Sharlie. I've scarce time to dress for dinner or wash my hands, let alone think."

"I fancy that's what she intends," Charlotte returned, "but I can't be sorry for it, darling. You're looking better every day. Do admit you don't really mind caring for the children."

"No, of course not. They're such darlings," Emily smiled fondly. "Did I tell you what Johnny said this morning?"

"No, and I beg you won't," Sharlie said forcefully. "If ever there was an ill-conditioned brat!"

"Now, that is not fair—merely because he spilled the paints over your riding boots," Emily protested.

"He did it deliberately, because I wouldn't delay to

play spillikins with him—but he won't do it again. I went as I was, and told Uncle George *why* my boots were soiled."

Nevertheless, life became calmer when Emily was busy, and Sharlie often accompanied her with the children, for which Emily was devoutly thankful. "They mind you so much better, I don't know why."

"It's because I don't ask, I *tell* them, and if they disobey, I give them no sympathy."

"But that makes them afraid of you."

"And so they should be, the silly gudgeons. You'll notice they think twice when I say 'don't' after Johnny fell into the stream because his legs couldn't manage the stepping stones," Sharlie said impatiently. "I suppose you'd have comforted and cosseted, but it was far better for him to be forced to lose the rest of the treat by going home for dry clothes, as well as having to explain to Aunt Eliza *why* he wasn't with us when we returned."

Sharlie spent most of her time on Moonshine's back, and as much as permissible with her Uncle George. He made no objection to her riding his land with him, but he was a taciturn man who lacked Lord Stanwood's ready laugh and easy humor. His decisions were always the letter of the law, and lacked any forward vision. Time and again Sharlie bit her lips firmly to suppress protest against his refusal to try a new way . . . and yet, she began to see that if Lord Alden moved slowly, his movements were sound. His land was more varied than Stanwood: his people were different, but he knew them as well as her father knew his tenants. Where Stanbury was used to impulsive change and trial, Alden Manor was happier with *status quo*.

Hacking home one day, Sharlie mistook her road and found herself in unfamiliar woodland. She continued along placidly; the road was bound to lead somewhere, and she'd be set back on her track for Alden. For some time she saw no sign of life nor any cottages, and she began to be anxious that she might have come into the farther reaches of Alden Manor—she was not acquainted with all her uncle's estate. Then ahead of her was an obvious nutting party: two small children with an obvious governess, engaged in whacking such tree branches as she could reach with a sturdy stick. Beyond was a pony cart, waiting on the road, and she realized she must somehow have strayed onto another estate.

Reining in thankfully, she called, "I beg your pardon, but I fear I am lost. Can you set me on the road for Alden Manor?"

"O'course," the boy said scornfully, "but you'll have to jump and go through the fields—that's if you can."

"I assure you I can," Sharlie said amusedly, "but when I have jumped, in which direction shall I ride? Right, left, or straight ahead?"

The boy scrambled out from the tree shadows and came up to the lane with his sister beside him—and Sharlie caught her breath. There was no mistaking those slashing black eyebrows, nor the black eyes fixed unwaveringly on her. These were Imbries, however miniature!

"I think we should walk beside her until we reach the proper place for a jump, Gillie," said the girl. "It isn't far, and we've already got all the nuts we can reach."

The governess had now got up the bank and was surveying Sharlie critically. Apparently she was satisfied. "You have strayed into Calydon Towers," she observed in a deep contralto voice, "and I fancy you might be better advised to follow the lane until you reach the first fork, when you bear right, although it is a longer ride. The adjoining property belongs to Mr. Ridgeway, who has the greatest dislike of strangers riding across."

"So he's said repeatedly," Sharlie chuckled, "but I fancy he will not shoot *me* if I am careful to follow the outer edges of the fields. I am Miss Stanwood, you see, and Mr. Ridgeway would not wish to fall out with my uncle, Lord Alden, until he has got that extra acre for his pasturage." She smiled mischievously at the two children regarding her, wide-eyed. "I'll take my chances on the short cut—and to thank you for your help," she pulled Moonshine a few paces back and raised her whip to thrash at the higher branches, sending a shower of nuts down to the bank.

"Oh, I say!" the children shrieked excitedly. "Oh, *please*—could you just get down and around to the other side? The branches are so full, but the squirrels get them. Even the longest sticks won't reach. Oh, Tolly, look—we never had so many before."

"Let that suffice," the governess commanded. "Do not be delaying Miss Stanwood, or she'll be late for tea."

"Oh, phoo!" the boy grumbled.

"Phoo, yourself," said Sharlie. "Show me where to get down from the verge, and I'll get you so many nuts YOU will be late for tea."

Twenty minutes later, she was carefully short-cutting through Mr. Ridgeway's fields, leaving (had she known it) three devoted adherents behind her. "I suppose she couldn't bear him," Cinda mourned, "but if she only could! Oh, Gillie, wouldn't it be wonderful to have someone to—to play with us."

"For you," Gillie scowled, "but I have to go to Eton, so what difference does it make whom he marries."

"That will do," said Miss Tolliver austerely. "I have told you before that your father is not a subject for gossipy speculation. You know nothing but what Cinda overheard—and if it stemmed from Miss Clapham," she cleared her throat meaningly, "I would hesitate to give it credence."

Cinda did not agree. "This time I think she was right, and what's more, you'd like Miss Stanwood for our step-mamma, Tolly, because all would go on more easily. Do admit: you liked her, too."

Miss Tolliver made a show of surprise. "Why, of course: a very pleasant young female with all that was correct in her manner. It was a charming condescension for her to turn aside and help you to gain the extra nuts—but scarcely all that your father would require for a life-partner."

Four black eyes regarded her unwinkingly. "Oh, stuff!" said Giles disgustedly. "I didn't think it of you, Tolly."

CHAPTER X

ALL THE WAY BACK to Alden Manor, Charlotte was appalled. That Imbrie's principal seat should be so close! There could be no doubt that her aunt and uncle were known to him, even if not intimate due to difference in age. She could not recall they had ever mentioned Julian, but until the past two years, she was always in the schoolroom if they were entertaining during her visits. Lord Stanwood had judged her old enough to hunt the recent seasons, but Julian had been out of England. Papa himself had never chanced to encounter Imbrie until his sojourn with Beaufort. No, it was not remarkable that Sharlie should never have realized Calydon Towers was in this vicinity. Even Brummell had not pinpointed an exact location, merely described it as "in the North—the most uncomfortable pile in all England."

By the time she had delivered Moonshine to John-groom's hands, Sharlie was totally unstrung. She could not think what best to do, and hastily went in search of her sister. Emily was in the garden, playing battledore and shuttlecock with the older cousins, and considerably hampered by Johnny's determination to assist, but one glance at Charlotte's wan face, and Emily thrust her racket on the governess. "Please take my place—I must help my sister to change her dress."

The instant they had gained their chambers, "What is it, darling? What has happened?" Emily asked in alarm.

"The very worst!" Charlotte said tragically. "Imbrie lives not ten miles away! Emily, what am I to do?"

When she had related her meeting with the twins, her sister frowned thoughtfully. "Of course he must be known to our aunt and uncle, but Sharlie, we have been here near four weeks with no word of him . . . and from something Lord Arthur said, I feel sure he comes here as rarely as he can. Why should you run away to Stanbury, when Papa comes next week and you have looked forward to hunting?"

"Exactly! It is the very place of all others I am like to face him without warning," Sharlie said distractedly, "and what must he not *think* to find me here? Oh, the embarrassment!"

"I don't see that," Emily returned stubbornly, "and in any case, you cannot spend your life avoiding the duke merely because you refused his offer. Some slight awkwardness there must be, I admit, but is it not better to settle it as soon as possible, Sharlie? What is it papa says? 'Always get over heavy ground as lightly as possible.' You cannot fear Imbrie would deliberately discomfit you; he may be an ugly old widower, but he is most truly a gentleman. He would never renew address he knew to be distasteful to you."

"Yes," Sharlie agreed, but in such a forlorn voice that Emily widened her eyes sharply, but beyond recommending her sister to consult Aunt Eliza, she made no comment.

"Aunt Eliza? Good God, I *cannot!*"

"You must," Emily said with unexpected firmness. "If you cannot, I will. Do but consider, Sharlie: she must be apprised, lest she or Uncle George innocently invite Imbrie to dinner. You know she has it in mind to entertain for us when Papa comes, and if Imbrie is known to be at Calydon, nothing is more likely than to include him. *That* would be to embarrass our aunt and uncle, as well as yourself and the duke."

Charlotte felt all the commonsense of Emily's advice, but she was still agonized. "You know Aunt Eliza —she will have a deal of unpleasant remarks, or rake me over the coals for missishness, or something."

"No, she will not," Emily stated militantly, "for I shall come with you, and if she says anything to overset you, I will tell her to be quiet."

"You?"

"Yes, me. . . I . . . whichever it is," Emily said impatiently. "Come on. She'll just be finished dressing, and we can be sure of finding her alone."

Stunned by Emily's command, Sharlie allowed herself to be thrust trembling into her aunt's dressing room, where Emily said, "Aunt, there is a private matter—if you would spare us a few minutes when your dresser is dismissed."

Lady Alden's slightly prominent pale blue eyes widened to something approaching a pop at Emily's authoritative manner. "That will be all for the moment, Robbins," she said promptly. "I will ring when I want you. Now," as the door closed, "what is this private matter?"

Charlotte's voice deserted her, she could only twist her hands together and look pleadingly at her aunt, until Emily took charge. "Sit down, darling. There is nothing to be frightened of," she pushed her sister gently to a chair, and turned to Lady Alden. "The thing is that Sharlie has just learned that Calydon Towers is in this area, and while we believe the duke is not often in residence, we think you should know that Sharlie refused his offer of marriage in Bath this summer," Emily said calmly. "In general, one would not disclose such an incident beyond the immediate family—I daresay Mama may not have told you that Charlotte has also rejected the Earl of Waxe and I have refused Viscount Pelham—but the circumstances surrounding Imbrie make it necessary to inform you. We should not like you or Uncle George to be embarrassed."

"God bless my soul!" Lady Alden fumbled for her vinaigrette and took a deep sniff. "God bless my soul, Imbrie? And Charlotte *refused* him? Well—well, and why should she not, if she had no fancy for him?" Lady Alden pulled herself together with a vigorous shake. "Lud, child, there's nought to be so dolorous about. You were right to inform me, although we rarely encounter. Your uncle sees him, of course; they sit on the Bench together when Imbrie's home, and I believe they are sometimes in company at a club or a shooting party, but I cannot abide Laura Voss! A dismal female!"

"Yes . . . but the thing is that I doubt anyone knows about Waxe or Pelham, but *everyone* in Bath knew about Imbrie, because—because . . . well, I'm not sure what happened because I wasn't present," said Emily, "but . . . but . . ."

Sharlie roused herself. "I—didn't expect a declaration," she said feebly, "and—and I made a scene, Aunt Eliza . . . and Beamish heard me, and summoned Mama, and," her lips quivered, "it was a *scandal*."

"Good God," said Lady Alden, faintly.

"So you see that it would be every way unfortunate if I were to meet Imbrie here, in your household."

"Yes, but you need not worry."

"I think I should return to Stanbury, but Emily says it will be better to face him and be done with it." Charlotte hung her head.

Surprisingly, Lady Alden agreed with Emily. Even more surprising, she was entirely sympathetic and said no word to censure her niece. "You cannot run away, Charlotte. For once Emily shows sense," she chuckled and patted Sharlie's hand. "You cannot avoid every man you reject, you know, or shortly you will never be able to appear anywhere in society! Lud, Waxe and Pelham, eh? Well, well, it appears my nieces have been sweeping the board in London, not that I'm astounded. You're a good pair of girls, and the men you choose will be lucky."

"Could you have *believed* it was Aunt Eliza?" Charlotte asked when they were dressing for dinner.

"Oh, yes," said Emily, fastening the clasps of her overdress. "I own she scares me to death sometimes, but mama says she is her nicest relative by marriage, and you know she would never entrust us to visit anyone else when we were young."

Sharlie grimaced, "*Not* an unmixed blessing, when I remember."

"But I do remember, and it can't have been easy when we developed the *measles,* but she was very kind, Sharlie. You're rather like her."

"Good God, *NO!*"

"Yes, you are," Emily insisted, stepping into her slippers. "You're prickly outside, but silky-satin whenever anything is really wrong. You have a—a *mind,* you see what's truly important and grow impatient with the rest. Aunt Eliza is the same. Like Eustace—you did it differently, but it ends the same way: she is keeping me busy, and you explained how I must do it."

Sharlie stared at her sister incredulously. "Well! You are certainly growing up. Such wisdom!"

"Not really," Emily colored, "but—when you give your heart, I fancy it does change things. You look at people and *think* about them . . . not that I've any great store in my cockloft, as Geoff would say, but I do see things I never saw before. Mama and Papa love each other, for instance, but Aunt Eliza is simply *married* to Uncle George. She does not dislike him, she considers always what will please him—but have you ever seen between them the sort of glance or chuckle we see with Mama and Papa?"

"No," Sharlie admitted, "but I do believe them to be sincerely attached, Emily. Uncle George is a much more *formal* man than Papa, I fancy he may show a different side in private."

"I do not think I would wish my husband to keep all his evidence of affection private," Emily said after a moment. "I think I should like him to escort me in public, and to dance with me, and sometimes stay home for a solitary evening—and do not tell me this is Gothick! It is what *I* should like." She looked at her sister, "Shall I do your hooks?"

Nothing more was said of Imbrie, but Sharlie could not put him out of her mind. She feared, yet longed, to see him again, and could not decide whether this would be easier in company or chance-met while riding, although she was careful to turn Moonshine in the opposite direction from Calydon. Her agitation might well be for nothing, since she had no idea whether Julian was at the castle and shrank from inquiry. Daily she wished she had not lost her way, never met his children or learned the proximity of Calydon. Ignorance would quite truly be bliss!

The children were darlings, though; Sharlie was more drawn to them than to her small cousins . . . and for all her dragon-appearance, the Calydon governess looked exactly right. The children obviously liked her. Sharlie could not but contemplate being a step-mamma, nor wonder how she should go on, whether she would be accepted or rejected by Imbrie's twins.

Lord Stanwood's arrival on the Monday posed another question. Sharlie did not doubt her mother had told him of Imbrie's proposal, but he had never mentioned it and *officially*—should he encounter the duke—her father knew nothing, for Imbrie had not offered to Lord Stanwood. Should she, or should she not, speak to him of it? As before, Charlotte consulted Emily.

"That depends on what you want to tell him," Emily said. "If you wish to avoid the duke at all costs, you had better warn Papa, for you know he liked Imbrie very well, and since there was no formal offer, Papa may pretend complete ignorance if he chooses—you know Papa's sociability."

"Yes," Sharlie said mournfully, "and I dislike to interrupt his easy relations, for if I bring it to his attention it must necessarily cause a stiffness between them, but . . ."

"Oh, stuff!" Emily remarked firmly. "Get it over with, Sharlie! I never knew you to be so—so wambly. There is no certainty that Imbrie will be here at all, for it is not the major hunt season. That is why Papa takes us, although I wish he would not," she shuddered. "I dread it, all that leaping over hedges and streams, ugh! But however, Papa calls it humbug country, suited to ladies, so it is most unlikely Imbrie will attend. I would say nothing to Papa."

However, it was not Imbrie, but Eustace who was at the opening hunt, and great was the astonishment on both sides! Even greater was Lord Stanwood's displeasure. "Good God, what's that curst puppy doing here? I thought he was in Spain."

"Obviously he isn't," Sharlie returned, "and he's

wearing the Hunt Club silks, which means he's a full member."

"Hmph!" Lord Stanwood snorted. "Probably invalided home as a half-pay officer. Well, I won't have him dangling after Emily, you understand?"

"Yes, but you cannot be impolite to him, Papa," Sharlie urged. "Remember, the only fault was writing secretly; you know there was not an improper word. In fact, I have wondered if, perhaps, he never realized it *was* illicit, but thought he was simply writing to all of us, for you know we made him almost a family member."

"Hmph," her father snorted again. "Damme, what a coil. Sharlie, stay beside your sister, and for God's sake, don't let her start *crying* again!"

"She won't," Sharlie promised, sidling Moonshine over to Emily. "Remember, do not allow papa to see any evidence of partiality!"

"No—but what can it mean, Sharlie? How comes Eustace *here?*"

That was quickly explained, as soon as Eustace had finished his courtesies in the club and gained their side. "Faith, it's glad I am to see ye, milord! I'd promised myself the pleasure of renewing acquaintance with you and Lady Stanwood did I ever complete the details," he said cheerfully, "for ye must know, my godfather has died, leaving all to me!"

"Hmph," said Lord Stanwood stiffly. "My congratulations."

"Aye, 'tis a rare bit of luck for me—not grand, but a very respectable property, and completely unexpected. I'd not thought he liked me above half, y'know, but he'd no relatives, so I suppose 'twas logical he'd think of me. The devil was in it, he'd die just as I'd got the majority and gone to Madrid, but when the news reached me, I made haste to sell out and return," Eustace beamed at them proudly, apparently unaware of Lord Stanwood's reserve. "And now I've the luck to encounter you at once. I'd not have known, but I've no great acquaintance in these parts. 'Tis why I asked to continue Mr. Cleghorne's membership, thinking it an easy way to introduce myself to my neighbors."

"I'm sure you'll have no difficulty," Emily said with her new assertiveness. "Uncle George," as Lord Alden nimbled up to them, "we have met a friend known to us in London, who has recently inherited the property of Mr. Cleghorne. This is Major Sir Eustace Gayle—our uncle, Lord Alden."

"Cleghorne, eh? Bit of a recluse, but a very sound manager, highly respected," Lord Alden observed austerely.

"I'll hope to continue his reputation," Eustace bowed. "Your servant, sir."

At that point, the Master sounded his horn and cried "Tally ho!" The hounds loped forward eagerly, the hunt was in motion, and Sharlie began to wonder if Eustace's fancy for Emily had altered. He made no effort to stay beside them. Together with Lord Stanwood and Lord Alden, Eustace was in the vanguard, leaving all but the most determined ladies far behind.

The pack found swiftly, the horn sounded View Halloo, and the horses advanced to a canter. Sharlie yearned to be in the thick, but loyally held back to encourage Emily, who was gallantly doing her best to keep up . . . and it seemed they had no sooner dispatched the fox than the pack gave tongue once more. This time Reynard had a good start, but at last there was View Halloo, and the hunt was streaming over the countryside in pursuit. Suddenly the fox doubled back, the Master blew Tantivy, and as the hunt swept around,

Sharlie and Emily found themselves leading. Sharlie could see her sister's face grim with determination, looking at the water jump ahead. "Come on, darling—throw your heart over. Firefly never refuses!"

Somehow Emily made it. They were in at the death, when she could not suppress a sick moan. "Look away," Sharlie muttered firmly. "I can't stand it, either, but you must NOT faint, even when you're blooded."

"No! Oh, Sharlie, I *cannot!*"

"Take a deep breath, hold up your head, and think of Eustace!"

Those were the magic words. Emily gulped, threw up her chin, and drew off her glove to accept the gory brush, while Lord Stanwood chuckled proudly and Eustace joined the general cheer—but with no more than a smiling wave as the hunt dispersed, he was trotting away beside the Master. Sharlie's heart misgave her; had Emily misinterpreted? Now that Eustace was a landowner had the change of fortune superseded his feeling for her? In London, he'd been at loose ends; she was beautiful, the Irish were noted for dramatic affections, easy in and easy out. With no future to it, had Eustace been enjoying a hopeless attachment? Today seemed evidence that he meant to establish himself firmly in the locality, hold his household and be respected. Might he not think it too soon for taking a wife, or even that he could do better for his altered circumstances than a London Incomparable?

She worried in silence; Emily was entirely calm. Beyond exclaiming happily at Mr. Cleghorne's generosity, "for one could not have dreamed of it. You recall he sounded the worst-natured old man in the world," Emily evinced no suspense. Indeed, she was following Sharlie's strategy all too well, and Lord Stanwood was delighted with her.

"Eh, puss, you've got bravely over your timidity. Good, good! It's pleasant for an old man to have two pretty daughters for company."

"Old?" Emily protested scornfully. "What fustian, Papa!"

"At least we know what to give him for Christmas, Emily: an ear trumpet and a cane," said Sharlie.

"I wish you will not mention age, Robert," Lord Alden observed, mildly. "I can give you a full five years, and have not yet finished setting up my nursery."

"Lud, it's a prolific lot on both sides," Lord Stanwood agreed, while his sister bridled and glared at the men.

Charlotte and Emily looked demurely at their plates, but later, "Could you have *believed* it of Uncle George?"

"No, but I expect it's very true, because Aunt Eliza was increasing two years ago, only she lost it almost at once," said Sharlie. "I overheard Papa telling Mama *her* work wasn't done yet, and he'd like another girl."

Emily's eyes widened. "You never told me."

"Two years ago you were too young."

"So were you!"

"Yes, but they didn't realize I was in the hall, and there is no reason to be *missish* about interesting events," said Sharlie. "Lud, Emily, between bulls and stallions and boars . . . even cockerels and drakes . . . one cannot avoid *knowing*."

Second Day dawned fair and crisp-cool. Descending the stairs in their riding habits, the girls encountered Lord Alden. "Good morning, good morning, . . . I'm for the stables, I'll send your mounts around shortly," he said. "Your father's engaged with Major Gayle, but I'll take you off to the hunt, if he's not finished."

"Eustace!" Emily breathed, as he vanished through the rear hall. "Oh, *Sharlie!*" She sped back to the study door, and softly eased it open a crack. "*Shhhhh!*" as Sharlie sought to pull her away.

"I'm aware 'tis not grand, 'tis no more than a competence of five thousand in the Funds with a hundred acres," Eustace's voice was impersonal, "but the house is sound, the stock is excellent, and I've the knowledge to manage. Mr. Cleghorne's reputation gains me all opportunity to prove myself. I've no fear I'll not advance for Emily's comfort."

"Phoo, nonsense, no more than five hundred a year? Good God, man are you daft?" Lord Stanwood demanded testily. "Emily's no heiress. She'll have what I settle on her, and I'll say now that the amount will depend on what her husband can put up for her jointure. On five thousand pounds you can't spare a penny. No, I'm sorry, but it's not good enough."

Before Sharlie could restrain her, Emily thrust back the door and tumbled into the study. "Yes, it *is,* and I don't want to be an heiress or—or sold to the highest bidder," she cried. "You needn't give me any dowry, if that's the way you feel, Papa . . . and I'll wait four years if you make me, but I won't marry anyone else, not even if Eustace gets tired of it. I'd rather be a spinster! Oh, Eustace!" Emily cast herself against him, whimpering with abandon.

"Oh, my *GOD!*" Lord Stanwood roared irascibly. "Is she back at *that* again?"

"Shhhh," said Eustace tenderly. "Sure, and ye'll be no spinster, me darlin', for I'll wait forever—but 'tis a shock-like for your father, when ye could do so much better."

"I'll never do any better," Emily declared fiercely, burrowing against him . . . but she stopped snivelling.

Lord Stanwood rumpled his hair wildly. "Well—well, we'll see what your mother decides. *I* don't know what she has in mind," he said feebly. "All *right,*" as Emily ran to hug him joyfully, "it's agreed she settles what's best for the girls—but you'll not make any display of particularity before her decision!" Lord Stanwood strove for vanished authority, but Emily only hugged him again.

"Yes, of course, Papa—but you'll see she agrees. Oh, Eustace!" She was back in his arms, smiling up at him adoringly.

"Me darlin'," he murmured fondly, "but your father's right, and we'll leave all to Lady Stanwood. If she says 'wait and see,' well—'tis not so long, and I'll use the time to develop our property." He patted her cheek lightly, "Now, we're delaying your father for the hunt. Come along, and no more tears. He'll come about, you'll see."

"If you say so," Emily allowed herself to be led docilely to the hall, while her father and sister stood transfixed.

"God bless my soul!" Lord Stanwood muttered.

"Yes," said Charlotte. "I'm sorry, Papa, but Emily doesn't give a tinker's curse for a peerage or lots of money. She enjoyed being an Incomparable, I'm sure Pelham wasn't the only rejection . . ."

"Good God, no; your mother had me turn down ten other offers," said Lord Stanwood, fussing bewilderedly with the desk blotter, "as well as three for yourself, Sharlie: Ogilvie, Beauchamp and Reston. She would have it you'd never consider them and should not be distressed."

Charlotte stared at him, wide-eyed. "Well! No more I *would* have considered any of them," she agreed, "but if you add Waxe, that means I actually had *four* offers . . . and God bless MY soul, Papa!" she chuckled. "Did you ever expect you'd have a choice of avenues to be rid of me?"

Her father grunted with amusement. "Lud, I've no fear for you, m'dear. You're one who needs time for the men to see your worth—like m'sister Eliza . . . but Emily," he shook his head and sighed. "I'll own I thought she'd end up with an earl or duke."

"Well, she won't—and you've no need of a rich son-in-law, Papa, for I know you're very well to pass," Sharlie said bluntly, "but you can give my dowry to Emily if necessary, for I've grandmother's fortune, after all."

"Phoo, nonsense," he roared. "I fancy I can care for the settling of all my children, miss."

"Then you'll not have the heart to deny Emily her share," she shrugged, "and if she chooses a younger son, at least Eustace is well-born, Papa."

While Lord Stanwood was stamping into his riding boots and arranging his stock, Sharlie flew to the writing desk for a letter to her mother. "I expect papa will write you—eventually—but why delay? Emily is all that is happy and comformable—Eustace also—but it must be an anxious time for them. Papa leaves the decision to you; pray send word as quickly as may be. Better yet, come in person . . . your loving daughter," but scanning her lines, Sharlie could not resist a postscript. "*Please,* Mama!"

Hastily she sought her aunt, "If this could be sent express?"

Lady Alden eyed both letter and niece. "I collect there is a development?"

Out of her new-found confidence in Aunt Eliza, Charlotte hastily put her in possession of the facts. "Eustace—Major Gayle—has come into Mr. Cleghorne's estate and offered for Emily, who declares she *will* have him, which completely oversets Papa, who says all must be decided by Mama . . ."

"How like a man," murmured Lady Alden.

"Yes—but the thing is that he will never trouble to write, and I think Mama should know, do not you?"

"I do, indeed," said Lady Alden, "and the sooner Nelly arrives to take charge of you, the better. I declare, I don't know what has happened to you and Emily. You were such *good* children!"

"You never said so when we *were* children," Sharlie remarked, irrepressibly, but her aunt merely sniffed and said, "No doubt I have forgotten. Go along with you, do."

The second day's hunt was not so glorious as the opener. Only one fox was found, and he was smart enough to lose his trail by swimming downstream until he could go to ground. By the time the pack had picked up his scent, the chase was hopeless; he would certainly have opened a rear tunnel and long since made his escape. "Oh, well," said Lord Stanwood, "tomorrow's another day."

That it was—and produced not merely the Duke of Imbrie but his cousin, Lord Arthur Voss.

"Oh, God," Charlotte murmured faintly, but Emily held firm.

"If I can do it, so can you," she said flatly, and grinned wickedly. "If you want him, go get him, darling." She nimbled Firefly forward demurely and said, "Your grace—Lord Arthur—how delightful to see you. We hadn't hoped you'd condescend to ladies' hunting —and did you know that Eustace has newly inherited a property in the neighborhood? Sharlie, where are you?"

Perforce Charlotte joined the group, although it was

not so bad as she'd feared. In the spate of conversation between Eustace, Lord Arthur, Emily . . . with Lord Stanwood jovially recognizing the duke . . . it was possible to bow and murmur politely before turning aside to chat animatedly to Mr. and Mrs. Ridgeway, who were manifestly surprised by so much recognition . . . but it was all Charlotte could manage to keep her countenance after meeting the glance of the duke's black eyes.

They widened, narrowed, flickered with determination—and she found herself totally unstrung. He couldn't still . . . or could he?

He could. At least, he could set Ajax beside Moonshine and pace her whether for canter or gallop, from the Tally-ho to the View Halloo that proved to be a hind, and required a Tantivy to sweep the hunt around for the death. The duke said nothing, he was simply—*there*: smiling at her as they soared over the water jump, and choosing the better path around a brush clump (where half the hunt came to grief, but Moonshine automatically followed Ajax), and they were still tantivy behind the Master and the pack, in at the death . . . when the duke said quietly, "I know it seems brutal, but remember a single deer can girdle enough trees to destroy a forest."

"Is a forest more important?"

"Yes, because it contributes. There is wood for firing, nuts and fruits, leaves for mulch, even acorns for hogs and branches for birds' nests. A deer does nothing but eat," he flicked that disturbing glance at her again, and said, "Your servant, Miss Stanwood. I'll hope to see you tomorrow." He trotted away leisurely, and was seen to be conversing with the MFH, moving on from one to another of the members until he fetched up beside Lord Stanwood, where he stayed for so long that Sharlie was trembling with nerves.

What could he be saying to Papa? Surely a hunting field was not the place to make a formal offer, but if he did? No, they were laughing heartily, turning to include Uncle George. It must be no more than casual gossip, but Sharlie could not withdraw her eyes from the group. Emily had been right that he would do nothing to distress her, nor had he, but only (she supposed) sought to put her at ease by ignoring the past.

So did everyone else, including Lady Stanwood who had arrived during their absence, much to her husband's astonishment. "Lud, Nelly, what do you here?"

"Oh, I had a sudden whim to join you," she returned airily. "It is a very long while since I have been hunting. I suppose you will not object to mount me? You have all your hunters here, and I have brought my saddle."

"No, of course you may have Countess. Well, well," he beamed, "it'll be like old times. We'll coax Eliza to make up our original quartet, eh? Remember that run over Haythorp, George?" He chuckled wickedly, drawing a guffaw from his brother-in-law and a helpless titter from Lady Alden, while Lady Stanwood said, "For shame, Robert!" At which they all laughed heartily and became lost in reminiscences that meant nothing to Charlotte or Emily . . . but in the privacy of the bedchamber he said, "Well, I am glad you are come, Nelly, because the devil's in it but Eustace Gayle has inherited a penny-farthing property hereabouts, and has offered for Emily on the strength of it . . . and here's Emily saying she *will* have him. *I* don't know what to do, *you'll* have to settle it."

"Oh?" said his wife innocently. "What sort of property?"

"A decentish small holding from what I learn," he shrugged, "and a grand come-up for *him,* of course—but what's a hundred acres and five hundred a year,

Nelly? Damme, Emily needs that much for her clothes alone, judging by the bills I've paid these past months."

"For a London season," she agreed thoughtfully, "but it would be far less when she is married and settled in a modest locality. Besides, she will have her dowry—or do you disapprove so strongly as to withhold it, Robert?"

"Good God, how can I tell?" he said violently. "No, of course she must have something, Nelly, but I'd allotted fifteen thousand for her and Louisa—ten for Sharlie, because she already has twenty from m'mother—but what's to do now, when Eustace has no more than five?"

"I fancy they'd go on very comfortably with twenty thousand pounds," she returned after a moment, "but much depends upon the exact circumstances of house and land, Robert. I believe we should see it for ourselves to determine the degree of comfort obtainable."

"He's asked George and myself to ride over for breakfast, or go back after the hunt and join him for dinner . . . but dash it, Nelly . . ."

"Yes, I'm disappointed too," she said obliquely. "I'd expected Emily to make a brilliant match, but she does not choose it. After all, Robert, our daughters are not to be married merely for the sake of *our* consequence. If she prefers to be Lady Eustace Gayle rather than Viscountess Pelham, why," she smiled demurely, "*I* took a lowly baron in preference to an earl."

"What?" Lord Stanwood stared at her incredulously. "Damme, Nelly, *what* earl? It's the first I've heard of it."

"Never mind which earl," she said serenely.

"I believe it's a hum!"

"No, it is not, and if papa were alive he would tell

you, for he was just as disappointed in you as you are in Eustace, but however, I had my way—and I think Emily must have hers, my dear."

"Damme, an earl, eh? God bless my soul!" Lord Stanwood was so much struck by his wife's revelation, and so occupied in casting his mind over the available earls during her season, that he readily (if absently) agreed to sanction Emily's betrothal as soon as Eustace's property had been approved by parental inspection. "Yes, very well, whatever you think best," he murmured, staring into space. "Was it Caterham?" he asked suddenly.

"No."

"Ampleforth?"

"No. Had you not better dress for dinner, my love?"

"Yes," he went off, still pondering, while Lady Stanwood made her own toilette with suppressed chuckles that baffled Miss Tinsdale. What could have so amused her ladyship? Nor was it clarified when his lordship cast open the door to announce triumphantly, "Richmond! That's who it was, and don't deny it, Nelly."

"Oh, dear, I hoped you'd forgot him," she sighed.

"Hah! *Richmond*, eh? By Jove!" and off he went, obviously in high twig, while her ladyship gave way to giggles. But she vouchsafed no word of explanation, and the dresser was dismissed to be tantalized by a mystery: why should the name Richmond cause hilarity?

CHAPTER XI

AT CALYDON TOWERS, Julian and Stepan were equally baffled. "Mees stays at Alden Manor, but that Maria is not with her," said Stepan glumly. "There is some mystery, milor', but I cannot discover it. The groom is polite, but he says *nothing* in a way that shows there is something to be said."

"Miss Stanwood says *nothing* in a way that shows she has no wish to say anything," the duke replied bitterly, "and I could wish my mother would follow her example."

Returned from Bath, Lady Imbrie had rapidly been apprised by Miss Clapham of Charlotte's presence in the neighborhood. Upon her son's arrival, the dowager had taken the earliest opportunity of informing him. "I wonder at it! What can she mean, to be coming *here?"*

"I suppose she means to visit her aunt and uncle."

"I wish her joy," Lady Imbrie sniffed, "for a more callous, *unfeeling* woman than Lady Alden I have never met. Luckily, they are not in our parish and we rarely encounter. I always speak when we do; I make it a point never to have bad blood in the environs, for that would reflect upon you, Imbrie."

"Very true. I thank you, madam."

Miss Clapham quailed at his sardonic tone, but

Lady Imbrie was oblivious as always, and continued to voice disapproval. "And now here is Arthur! You recall I always thought . . . but surely she could not have the effrontery!" The dowager's voice died away momentarily, then resumed, "I cannot understand it at all. He was never used to visit so constantly. One would think he *lived* here."

"At the moment I have need of him upon estate matters."

"Oh, in that case," she said grudgingly, "although you have a bailiff, after all, and ten to one that Arthur is calling at Alden Manor the moment your back is turned, Imbrie."

"Why, so shall I. There is a matter of an acre wanted by Ridgeway from Lord Alden in the section that abuts my land."

"Call at Alden Manor? But . . ."

"But *nothing*, madam. I have dealt with Alden these ten years, and his niece in no way affects our relations. I wish you will be a little less *busy* in what you fancy to be my behalf." Julian scowled impatiently, and strode from the room, leaving his mother open-mouthed.

He was as nervous as a green goose, setting forth for the hunt—and totally cast down on his return. "She was all that was polite," he told Arthur gloomily, "but she doesn't want me. That's clear to be seen, she'd scarcely a word to say to me, Arthur. I think I'll not go again, I can't distress her by attentions she obviously does not wish."

"If ever I heard a faint-heart!" Arthur exclaimed scornfully. "Good God, man—she let you stay beside her the entire course. What more could you want for encouragement?"

"What choice did she have?" Julian shrugged.

"If I know Miss Charlotte Stanwood's command of her horse, she had every choice to rein in, draw back, mingle with another group," his cousin remarked. "She did not. She rode with you—and what's more, her eyes were on you from the moment you'd parted. Oh, yes," as Julian's eyes swung to him hopefully, "she missed none of your conversation with this one and that . . . particularly her father and Lord Alden," Arthur chuckled. "She's wondering if you're still of the same mind, uncertain what she'd say to a formal application to her father. One thing's sure: the widgeon's bespoke."

"Where had you that?"

Arthur shrugged, "My dear Julian, it's not necessary! You said yourself the young'un wanted Gayle—and here he is: furnished with a bit of property. I don't say Stanwood'll care for it, but there's a set to Miss Emily's jaw . . . she'll have Gayle, or I'm a Dutchman." He laughed, "Damned if I ever thought to see such sport around Calydon! Here's Aunt Laura moaning plaintively about the humiliation, and her companion twinkle-eyed with excitement. The twins are wanting Miss Stanwood for a step-mamma, and Miss Tolliver agrees. Oh, did you not know? They met by chance, in the home woods."

"Good God!"

"Giles thinks she's too good for you," Arthur refilled his wine glass blandly, "and Cinda yearns for a step-mamma 'who will show me how to go on, because Tolly has never had a season and Grandmamma is too old.' " There was a long silence, while Julian stared into space, but finally his cousin said gently, "Try again, Coz. She'll have you, or I miss my guess."

Julian refilled his own glass, and said defenselessly, "What am I to do, Arthur? I would not distress her for the world, but if I wanted her before, I am twice of a mind on seeing her again."

"M'mother says you should speak privately to Lord Stanwood, telling him the whole and asking him to say nothing until you've had the chance for discovering Miss Stanwood's present sentiments," said Arthur, "but he'll tell milady, never fear, and she will handle all." He rubbed his nose reflectively, "I think *I* would also disclose the budget to Eustace, who will tell Emily, who will tell her sister—and you know I will do my possible."

"Good God, you make it sound like the plans for Agincourt."

"All's fair in love and war," Arthur returned, "and this sounds like a siege in which you will need reinforcement."

A mizzling intermittent rain halted the morrow's hunt, but was not sufficient to deter the duke from driving himself and his cousin over to the late Mr. Cleghorne's house, where they found not merely a warm welcome from Eustace, but both Lord Stanwood and Lord Alden.

"Faith, I'm honored by the topmost in the locality," he exclaimed delightedly. "I'll only hope my housekeeper can set out a nuncheon to suit ye, but if not, ye'll pardon me for the moment? I doubt she's accustomed to company. Mr. Cleghorne'd the gout, ye know, and what does a soldier know of ordering a household? I've my batman from Spain, but he's more used to stealing a chicken than saying how it'll be cooked."

"My man will tell him," Julian remarked, shaking hands heartily and looking about him. "I say, this is a very snug little residence."

"It is that," Eustace agreed, with a faint smile. "I think it'll suit Emily, do ye not?"

"Like that, is it? My dear fellow," Julian grasped his hand again, "my deepest congratulations."

"Faith, and I thought *you'd* be happy to learn it, though 'tis not settled in detail and ye'll not reveal it as yet—but however, his lordship agrees," Eustace eyed the duke blandly, "and I count your grace as—in a sense—one of the family."

Julian strove for composure, but Arthur's guffaw unmanned him. "Oh, Lord, is my heart so evident on my sleeve?" he laughed helplessly, clapping Eustace on the shoulder. "Well, if it prove so, I'll be glad of you for an in-law."

"Never doubt it," said Eustace, with a very direct look at Julian, "and if you are wanting a word with Lord Stanwood, the study is available." As Julian hesitated, he added, "Or have I misread you, Duke? If so, ye'll pardon the undue familiarity."

"No, no," Julian disclaimed hastily, "and I thank you for your consideration, Gayle."

"Lud, if I ever saw such a slow-top," Arthur remarked. "For God's sake, Julian, get it over with. Come on, Gayle—he'll never manage it for himself. Do get Lord Stanwood into the study with my cousin on some pretext, while I draw off Lord Alden."

Thus, the Duke of Imbrie found himself alone with Lord Stanwood, and exceedingly nervously he said, "Milord, I—uh—should like your permission to address your daughter Charlotte."

Lord Stanwood stared at him for a moment. "Hah! You mean you still want her?" he inquired incredulously.

"Yes—but not if it will distress her. I, uh, doubt not but you're aware I was—rather firmly refused," Julian examined his boots with deep interest. "My cousin and Gayle and, uh, various people think Miss Stanwood may have altered her mind, although I do not depend upon it. In asking your formal permission, I want merely to know that I would be acceptable to you and Lady Stanwood . . . but I do not wish any pressure upon your daughter."

"No, no, there'll be none," Lord Stanwood assured him. "God bless my soul! Of course you've our permission, we'd like nothing better than yourself allied to us—how can you doubt it, lad? But," he shook his head soberly, "there's no knowing how she'll take it, no knowing at all—although her mother declares she'll have you."

"Does Lady Stanwood indeed say so?"

"Oh, lud, yes, when she would have me give Waxe's offer to Sharlie . . . telling me 'she'll reject him, she wants Imbrie,'" Lord Stanwood looked suddenly as stricken as a schoolboy. "Good God, my tongue's too loose! You'll forget that, if you please."

"Never!" said Julian, his eyes dancing with satisfaction. "Not that I'll embarrass you by a mention, but *nothing* could hearten me more!"

"Ah?" Lord Stanwood raised his eyebrows. "In that case, I'll add that I've rejected three others I'll not name. It puts a man in prime fettle to know he was best in the field," he chuckled, and murmured to himself, "Richmond! Well, damme!"

"I beg your pardon?"

"Nothing, nothing," Lord Stanwood cleared his throat hastily. "So: you've my consent and my good will—but how you'll do it is another matter. D'you want me to tell her you've offered?"

Julian shook his head with a grin. "Tell Lady Stanwood, please."

"Now *that's* a clever idea! Aye, Nelly'll know what to do. Well, well," clapping Julian on the shoulder, "I'll be glad to welcome you, if so be you can contrive it—and if it fails, I trust there'll be no bad blood over it . . . for here's Emily settling on your doorstep, so to speak." He shook his head, bewildered. "What can she see in Gayle, I wish you will tell me—but however, she WILL have him, and her mother advises me to consent."

"I think you'll find it answers," Julian observed. "You and Lady Stanwood have reared your daughters to be women rather than pretty figure-heads, and—forgive me—Emily has not the mind for high political discussions or philosophical dinner conversations. I fancy she will become a leading figure in this smaller neighborhood, where less mentality and more compassion is expected."

"If you mean she's no brains, that's all too true," Lord Stanwood remarked, "but neither has Eustace, so perhaps he'll not notice."

Although nothing was said when Lord Stanwood and the duke rejoined the company, a single sharp glance from all of them was sufficient, and the party somehow became a family group. "I've naught but nags," Eustace apologized. "Mr. Cleghorne maintained his membership in the hunt, but with the gout and all, he'd let his stable go. We'd in mind to ride out for a glance at my land, but Imbrie and Lord Arthur—can ye put up with a pair of old joggers?"

"Oh, for riding the land, any mount will do," Julian declared. "We'll not be galloping, after all, or we'll not see the best features."

These, despite the heavy mist and drizzle, were heartily approved by the group, and from his authoritative comments, Eustace was revealed as a young man of considerable sense. By the time they'd returned to the house, it was tacitly accepted that he was Emily's future husband. Lord Stanwood was torn between disappointment that his pretty Emily had done no better than a younger son, and satisfaction that Eustace knew so much of management.

"You'll consult my bailiff or Arthur," said Julian. "Whatever seed or stock you need, or some special information on this country—it may be different in rainfall or frost from Ireland, which could lose your crops . . . but don't hesitate to ask."

"No, indeed," Lord Alden agreed, "although Cleghorne's man goes on very well—that's if you're retaining him? Oh, you are—well, then, you'll have no trouble, Gayle, but if you want any assistance, come over to me."

"Faith, and ye make me so welcome I feel at home already. We'll crack a bottle on it," Eustace declared. "Come away in and warm yourselves until the ladies arrive."

"Ladies?"

"Sure, ye'd not forbid me darling to see where she'll live? 'Tis arranged they'll drive over for tea and inspection."

"Oh, we're outstaying our welcome," said Julian. "Drink up, Arthur, and we'll be off."

"Good God, what IS the matter with you, Coz?" Arthur demanded. "It won't do itself, you know."

However, Julian couldn't do it, either, for Miss Stanwood was first pale, then pink, and finally attached herself so firmly to her mama that there was no getting near her. "I should call it a most promising situation," said Arthur.

"How so, when she'll not grant me a word beyond bare civility?"

"BUT, Julian, she is totally conscious of you at all moments," Arthur observed. "Her eyes follow your every movement about the room. She looks away when you turn, but she is listening for your voice."

"What of it? I can scarcely stand in a roomful of company and say 'Miss Stanwood, my sentiments remain constant—dare I hope yours may have softened'?"

"No," Arthur chuckled, "but do not be hasty. That's what undid you the last time. Now is the moment for strategy. Leave it alone, man! Let the yeast ferment. You've put the case to Lord Stanwood. In due course Miss Stanwood will learn of it. Allow her to consider her answer. I should make no effort to approach her for several days," Arthur said judicially. "Do not single her out in any way, whether in the field or in company. Say and do nothing that cannot be heard or seen by all the world, until she can feel comfortable again.

"Consider her emotions, Julian. Your mere presence must remind her of extreme awkwardness. Whether or not she regrets her refusal, she must certainly regret the manner of it. She cannot but feel there was undue humiliation of your pride," Arthur pointed out, "and under the circumstances—with Gayle newly betrothed to the sister she believed you to be wooing—it is every way uncomfortable. In plain words, she feels she has made a fool of herself and is the more uncertain."

"Nonsense! I always knew Emily wanted Gayle; now Sharlie knows it too," Julian returned. "If anything, all goes on more smoothly that the sisters would be situated for easy family intercourse."

"It is a compelling point in your favor, but not one she will recognize until she has conquered the past. *You* feel no humiliation, but Miss Stanwood does—both for herself and for you. I tell you again, Julian: let all rest for a space. Slow and easy does it; hold your horses, man."

Accordingly, under his cousin's firm guidance, the Duke of Imbrie adopted a pose of impersonal courtesy. He made no effort to ride again beside Charlotte in the hunt, was not even present the following day, and preferred whist to an impromptu dance gotten up the one evening they chanced to be in company with neighborhood friends of Lord Alden. Moving, twirling through the steps of a country dance, Sharlie put a bright smile on her face and chatted with animation to her partner. That he was the schoolboy son of the household pressed into service to even the couples in no way diminished Sharlie's appearance of enjoyment . . . and led to a disastrous misplay by Julian that cost him the rubber.

"Sorry, Arthur."

"Oh, think naught of it. We're aware your mind is not on the cards, but it might be easier if you take my seat and set your back to the dancing," Arthur suggested.

"It'd be easier still if we called it *finish,*" the duke said with a try for courtesy. "This is the rubber—do we ruin your evening to break it now? I'm not in good frame tonight."

"No, no, of course it ruins nothing," the host said heartily. "We'll have many evenings—or do you go roaming again, Julian?"

"I'm for Malta next month, hoping for passage from there to Greece—unless circumstances prevent," Julian shrugged. "Your servant, ma'am," to the hostess. In a spate of graceful good-nights, he was gone . . . when Sharlie discovered she did not really wish to dance but had the headache.

"A pity!" said her mother sympathetically. "Sit quietly beside me, my love, and we will shortly be leaving. Tomorrow you can rest, and by Monday you will be recovered for the second week."

"Yes, Mama."

Charlotte had no idea that her mother was playing a very cool hand. If, earlier, Lady Stanwood had been manoeuvring carefully to attach Imbrie for her daughter, now she was working even more cautiously to attach Charlotte to the duke. In a series of private conversations following her husband's revelation of Imbrie's formal offer, Lady Stanwood had straitly—vehemently—charged every member of the family to say *nothing* and leave it to HER!

"Do not think to assist, my love. Not a *word,*" she told her husband. "At the proper moment, I will tell Charlotte that Imbrie has spoken to you and the match has our approval . . . but for God's sake, do not try to help, Robert!"

"Lud, Nelly, there's no need to be so *fierce* with me," he protested, aggrieved. "I've said naught but that she's to choose for herself, and you'll handle all."

Lady Alden readily engaged for silence from herself and her husband, "although George thinks it would be a *very* good thing," she observed, "but however, he says so little upon all occasions that he would never overset Sharlie by a maladroit remark."

"Yes," her sister-in-law murmured slyly. "I have often wondered how on earth he managed to propose to you, Eliza."

"Very nicely, I assure you," Lady Alden lifted her chin—and spoilt the effect with an irrepressible giggle.

To Emily, Lady Stanwood was more open. "I wish you would discover as casually as you can, how Sharlie feels. I do not scruple to tell you, my love, that Imbrie has offered—but has Sharlie changed her mind?"

"I am certain she has—although between you and me, Mama, how *can* she?" Emily wrinkled her nose.

"There will be those who will say the same of you, for choosing an Irish baronet with no fortune but his face."

"It is not at all the same. Eustace is *young!*"

"You are neither of you dried behind the ears," Lady Stanwood agreed, "and Sharlie is not much farther advanced, but she has a different mind, Emily. I think them *ideally* suited. She had always a yearning for travel, foreign languages, country property—but it is exactly *that* which will give them a community of interest. You would find it boring, but you will see that Sharlie goes on very well."

"Well," said Emily after a moment, "if he is not precisely handsome, he is certainly very distinguished. Eustace thinks it would be a very good thing, for even if we will not move in quite the same circles, Sharlie would be near enough for frequent visiting. She would think nothing of riding over to see me any day, for it is no more than twenty miles."

"Oh, everyone thinks it would be a very good thing," Lady Stanwood remarked drily, "but how to accomplish it? She's as shy as an unbroken colt, a word will put her off. Guard your tongue, Emily. Say nothing of the offer, but only try to discover her feelings."

Two days later, "I'm sorry, Mama, but I cannot get a word from her," said Emily. "She will talk freely, enter into anything of my future—but at mention of Imbrie, she simply *agrees:* yes, it is good fortune that Imbrie is well-disposed to Eustace, she is certain he is an excellent landlord, all his tenants must find him so . . . and so forth—but it means nothing, Mama. Could we have been mistaken?"

"I am very sure we are not," but her ladyship decided on shock tactics. "My love," she said to Charlotte, "it has seemed to me that you are not wholly yourself. Are you quite happy?"

Sharlie protested that indeed she was enjoying the visit, but Lady Stanwood shook her head. "Does Imbrie's presence overset you, my dear? I would not have your father disclose it to you," she said artfully, "but Imbrie has spoken to him."

"Oh, Mama!" Sharlie said faintly.

"Your refusal was so firm that we feared to distress you. However, perhaps you should reconsider. *His* mind is unchanged; has yours? Papa must give some formal answer, you know. What shall it be?" Lady Stanwood patted her daughter's hand gently. "That is all I have to say."

She left Charlotte to her reflections, and by her thoughtful countenance was encouraged to hope . . . except that now Imbrie was nowhere to be seen. Hang the man, he was never around at the right moment! The club meeting was drawing to a close, the hunt ball would take place on Friday, after which Lady Stanwood and her daughters would return to Stanwood Hall, the most propitious setting would be lost.

Lady Stanwood was strongly inclined for the vapors!

As for Charlotte, she had been suppressing them from the moment her mother revealed Imbrie's formal offer. "That he should still want me, when I said *such* things," her cheeks grew hot, yet with his continued absence, she doubted. "Might he not have spoken merely to regularize the situation, for he should have done so before addressing me, and the offer is made in the certainty of my repeating my refusal?" By Friday, Charlotte had settled it that this was Julian's reasoning, "for aside from the first day, he has made not the least push to convince me he wishes an acceptance," she told herself unhappily.

Her deduction seemed confirmed by Lord Arthur, who turned up for the final hunt. "I've been escorting m'mother to her own home for the winter," he said cheerfully, "and Julian's been in London—or Portsmouth, perhaps. He's taken passage for Malta, but still hoping to find a ship going all the way to Greece."

"Oh? When does he sail?"

"Lud, *I* don't know—next month, I believe, if nothing arises to hold him in England." Lord Arthur's tone held meaning, but unluckily Sharlie missed it. The MFH set the hunt in motion just then, and conversation ended, but throughout the run her heart was despondent. Why, if Imbrie were serious, should he be arranging to travel? Even, she suspected he had relied on Lady Stanwood never to reveal his offer, and she wished her mother had *not*. In the period of thinking it a second chance, Sharlie had admitted Julian was exactly the man she could have loved. Had he been hunting every day, she knew she must have given him some sign of her altered affection, unladylike or not. Now all hope was ended, and for tuppence Sharlie would have pleaded thc headache to avoid the ball.

That was not possible. Lord Stanwood would announce Emily's engagement tonight, it would be Emily's evening, and Charlotte must forget her unhappiness in sharing Emily's bliss. Besides, Lord and Lady Alden were entertaining a dinner party of thirty covers; Lord Arthur was to take Sharlie in, and had already bespoke all the waltzes.

The company was nearly assembled by the time Sharlie descended the stairs beside her sister. Emily had never been in greater beauty! Standing beside Eustace, her three-quarter dress of white sarsnet over purest ivory satin was most elegantly displayed against the background of his long-tailed evening coat of bottle green. They were certainly a breath-taking couple, and Sharlie lingered deliberately to enjoy the harmony of guinea-gold curls *à la Méduse,* red-gold curls *à la Brutus,* and two pairs of brilliant blue eyes.

"Quite beautiful, are they not?" The Duke of Imbrie's deep voice said in her ear, and as she swung about, Charlotte once more met that dark determined flicker in his eyes. "Your servant, Miss Stanwood . . . I believe I am to take you in to dinner."

"No—no, it is Lord Arthur," she stammered, looking about wildly.

"Oh, he has resigned in my favor."

"But—but you cannot. It is to set you in quite the wrong seat."

"So long as it sets me beside you, Miss Stanwood, it matters not where it is." Julian calmly drew her hand within his elbow and led her forward. "Good evening, Lady Alden. It is kind of you to allow me to deputize for my cousin. Lord Alden, your servant, sir." The duke moved leisurely among the guests, exchanging greetings and pulling Sharlie along with him—perforce, for every time she sought to withdraw her hand, his elbow tightened. She felt ready to sink, could scarcely find her voice to say "Good evening," but it was impossible to free herself from that vise-like pressure, until at last they were at table.

For a few minutes they were occupied in choosing from the plentiful first course dishes, but when the soup plates had been succeeded by fillets of trout, *turbot soufflé*, vegetables, and great platters of meats and venison, Julian turned to look at her. "I am glad you are wearing that gown," he said conversationally. "It is the one you wore at Lady Abercrombie's on the night I first realized your beauty."

Sharlie choked uncontrollably and hastily set down her wine glass. "Oh, please do not . . . it is unkind in you to speak so to me in the midst of company, milord," she murmured.

"What alternative do I have—*Sharlie?*" he laughed softly. "When you try to look prim, you are only adorably confused, my love."

"*Please*—I wish you will not tease me," she whispered, agonized.

"I am not teasing," he said after a moment. "You *are* my love, Charlotte. Are you adamant, can I really never be yours?"

"Not," said Charlotte involuntarily, "if you are going to Malta."

Julian looked startled. "You have some objection to that island?"

"Not in the least, but it seems a poor start for a romance—unless you believe that absence makes the heart grow fonder."

"Why, upon the whole it does," he said thoughtfully. "I never love England so well as when I am in Calicut or Jamaica. Even Calydon Towers seems bearable—until I have spent a few days there . . . but for romance, Greece is the place! I felt sure you would enjoy it, but however, we will go where you choose."

"I?"

"You and no other," he said quietly. "Are you still opposed to being a duchess? Must I go to Malta alone, Charlotte?"

"Oh, damme," said Charlotte forcefully, "you do choose the most devilish moments for proposals!"

His hand dropped beneath the damask and found hers. "Don't I?" he murmured. "But I was ever impetuous, darling. I cannot wait for another two hours, until I can lure you into the conservatory behind the ballroom—which ten to one will already be occupied. Let me know my Fate at once, dear heart . . . and if you want me to kneel in proper form," he glanced behind him dubiously, "well, I believe there's sufficient space if the footmen move aside."

Unconsciously, Sharlie's fingers moved until their hands clasped gently. "I don't want you to kneel at all," she murmured severely. "You would certainly soil your knee-breeches, which would require you to return to Calydon for replacement before luring me into that conservatory, where I trust you mean to kiss me. Oh," she suppressed a gasp at the strength of his grasp, and went scarlet with sudden awareness of the interested gaze about the dinner table.

"It is yes?"

Beneath his dancing black eyes, Sharlie put up her chin. "How can I resist, milord? I had ever a longing for Greece—to say nothing of kisses."